***She turned and f* the man leaning against the house.**

It was Neil July.

"Evening." He touched his hat.

In an awe-filled voice she asked, "What are you doing here?"

"Came to see how you were faring."

Olivia had been secretly hoping for another encounter with him, but never in her wildest dreams did she imagine he'd appear this way, out of nowhere. The dark coffee skin, the vivid eyes, the lip-framing moustache; he was everything *good* women were supposed to run from. He was an outlaw, for heaven's sake, but the urge to know him better was strong. "You shouldn't have come."

He pushed away from the wall and inched closer. "Why not?"

Olivia's eyes brushed over his gun belt, his double-breasted shirt, and the way his denims hugged his hips and thighs. She forced her attention back to his face. "Sheriff Jefferson will jail you if he finds you here."

"Then we'll have to make sure he doesn't know." He raised her chin so their eyes could meet in the dark. "You owe me a kiss."

Special Markets Department, HarperCollins Publishers, Inc.
10 East 53rd Street, New York, N.Y. 10022-5299.
Telephone: (212) 207-7528.   Fax: (212) 207-7222.

Other **AVON ROMANCES**

Coming Soon

And Don't Miss These
ROMANTIC TREASURES
from Avon Books

BEVERLY JENKINS

Something Like Love

AVON BOOKS
An Imprint of HarperCollinsPublishers

AVON BOOKS
An Imprint of HarperCollins*Publishers*
195 Broadway
New York, NY 10007

Copyright © 2005 by Beverly Jenkins
ISBN: 0-06-057532-8
www.avonromance.com

First Avon Books paperback printing: May 2005

Avon Trademark Reg. U.S. Pat. Off. and in Other Countries, Marca Registrada, Hecho en U.S.A.
HarperCollins® is a registered trademark of HarperCollins Publishers Inc.

Printed in the U.S.A.

10 9 8 7 6

This book is dedicated to Mark A Jenkins.
1949–2003.
He was my outlaw, lover,
gentleman, and friend.
May he rest in peace.

Prologue

Chicago, Illinois
September 1888

Thirty-two-year-old Olivia Sterling was running away from home. Well, she would be just as soon as she took one last look around her dimly lit bedroom. It was the middle of the night, so she didn't dare turn up the lamp for fear of being discovered, but she couldn't afford to leave anything important behind; once she exited the house there would be no return.

Olivia didn't notice anything else that she needed to take with her, but for a few melancholy moments, her eyes lingered over her familiar bed and furnishings. This had been *her* room; a place of refuge, a place where she could spin her dreams and not have them snatched away by convention or society. After tonight she might never see it again, but she told herself it was the price to be paid for her decision.

1

With nothing left to delay her departure, Olivia doused the lone lamp, plunging the room into darkness. She grabbed up her black cloak, laid it over her arm, and carried her blue carpetbag to the door. The bag had been purchased specifically for her journey. Inside were a few changes of clean clothing, underwear, her toiletries, and her sketch pad and pens.

She very carefully opened the door. Except for the ticking of her mother's grandfather clock, the dark hall was silent.

She stepped out, then slowly eased her bedroom door closed again. She stood there for a long moment to make certain she hadn't been heard. Confident she hadn't, she moved quickly but soundlessly to the stairs that led down to the main floor of the house. On the way she passed the door to her father's bedroom. His snores were easy to hear even through the thick cherry wood. Her mother's door was closed too, as it always was. As long as Olivia could remember, she'd never known her parents to share a room—a fact no proper daughter should be concerned with, according to society, but Olivia did have concerns, and they were part and parcel of why she was running away.

Olivia made it down the stairs without being detected. As planned, her mother, Eunice, dressed in her night robe, stood waiting by the front door. They embraced. Basking in her mother's strong hug, Olivia felt tears sting her eyes. It was unclear whether she'd ever see her mother again, so Olivia held onto her for as long as she could.

Eventually, they had to part, and Olivia wiped at

her teary eyes with a gloved hand. Keeping her voice low, she said to her mother, "Papa's going to be very angry when he finds me gone. Are you sure you will be all right?"

"I'll be fine. James thinks me too dim-witted to have aided you. I won't be blamed."

There was a bitterness in Eunice's voice that Olivia knew stemmed from being in a marriage devoid of love.

Eunice touched her daughter's smooth cheek. "Godspeed, my dear Olivia, and may He keep you safe."

"You as well. I will write as soon and as often as I'm able." Olivia felt confident that any correspondence between them would go undiscovered, because her father never retrieved the mail himself. It would never cross his mind to go out to the box; that was Eunice's job, just like it was her job to present the mail to him every evening during his dinner.

It was time to leave. The hack Olivia had engaged for her escape would pick her up a few blocks away.

She and her mother shared one last good-bye embrace, then Olivia stepped out into the warm summer night. As befitting one of Chicago's best seamstresses, she was dressed in a fashionable dove gray traveling costume of her own design. To defeat pickpockets she'd sewn her life savings into the waistband and hems of her skirts. When she reached her destination, the funds would help start her new life.

Deep down inside she was terrified; she'd never done anything so bold before, but she had no choice but to keep going.

Two days later Olivia was seated on a train crossing the plains. She had no idea what her new life would hold, but she was convinced it would be better than the life she'd left behind in Chicago. That life would have cast her as the wife of one Horatio Butler, a man handpicked by her father but one she couldn't abide, let alone agree to love, honor, and obey until death do her part. Olivia owned a very successful modiste shop and hadn't spent the last ten years building her clientele and reputation just to turn the profits and property over to a man who thought women in the workplace should be guided by their husband's advice. This from a man who didn't know a seam from a hat pin.

Olivia could feel herself begin to boil up all over again just thinking about the greedy Mr. Butler and his plans to sell her building and invest the money in Lord knew what, because he wouldn't tell her. In response to her pointed questions on the matter, he'd told her not to worry her pretty little head; he would take care of everything.

So, Olivia had gone to her banker and had had a discussion. Unbeknownst to her father or Mr. Butler, she'd sold her business and the building housing it to the husband of one of her wealthier clients. The money Olivia received in exchange for the deed added up to a tidy sum; one tidy enough for her to be able to start life elsewhere. She'd decided on Kansas, where many all-Black settlements had been established during the Great Exodus of 1879. The newspapers called the movement Kansas Fever.

Thousands upon thousands of southern Blacks left the terror and bloodshed visited upon their lives by the Redemptionist Democrats and headed west to places like Kansas, Nebraska, and Colorado. Now, ten years later, many of the towns hadn't survived, but Henry Adams, Kansas, was supposedly thriving, and all thriving towns needed dressmakers.

So here she sat, looking out of the window at the passing plains. She was seated in the car's back row, hoping to be out of sight and out of mind. She'd seen the frowns on the faces of some of the passengers when she'd initially entered the car back at the Chicago station. Her presence was resented. With Jim Crow spreading across the country like a plague, it was becoming harder and harder for members of the race to escape its ugly edicts. Olivia hadn't boarded the train to stir the air; she was just trying to get to Kansas.

"Miss?"

Olivia looked up to see the conductor standing politely by her seat. "Yes?"

Out of the corner of her eye she could see a few scowling passengers looking on. She ignored them.

"I've been asked to remove you from the car."

Olivia steeled herself to keep her face emotionless.

"But I'm not going to."

Olivia hid her surprise.

"I rode with John Brown back in the sixties, and I ain't putting a pretty lady like you in the cattle car."

That last part was said loud enough for everyone within earshot to hear. The eavesdroppers spun back around in a huff.

Olivia let a smile peep out.

"If you need anything, just let me know." The conductor then touched his hat and left to continue his job.

Basking in goodwill and feeling much better about her fellow man, Olivia went back to watching the landscape.

Suddenly the emergency brake was pulled, and the car slowed so abruptly that everyone was pitched forward. Women screamed and men cursed as they were thrown from their seats. Unsure as to why the brake had been pulled, Olivia was righting herself and her fancy navy blue hat when a man's voice rang out. "Train robbers!"

Olivia's eyes flew to her window, but she didn't see anyone. She thought she heard guns firing but couldn't be sure. Having never experienced anything like this before, she watched the other passengers for a clue as to what to do. They were ripping off their jewelry and watches. Women stuffed their booty into their bosoms, while the men hid their valuables in the legs of their boots and inside their trousers. Concerned, Olivia touched her hand to her waistband and the hidden coins. Surely fate hadn't brought her this far just to be robbed and left penniless.

But a few moments later, the conductor was escorted roughly into the car by a mountain-sized man who appeared to be an Indian. He had flowing black hair, golden skin, and a gun as long as her arm stuck in the poor conductor's rib cage.

"Ladies and gentlemen," said the conductor in an angry clipped voice. "This man and his gang would like your valuables."

Alarmed cries greeted the announcement. A fearful Olivia drew back against the solid wood of her seat. This was her first trip west. Where were the authorities?

Another member of the gang boldly entered the car, and more than one of the women passengers gasped in reaction to his dark, heart-stopping handsomeness. He was tall, had dark eyes and equally dark skin. He was wearing a once white, long-sleeved shirt tucked into a pair of tight-fitting trousers that highlighted his muscular thighs and legs. Around his trim waist was a heavy gun belt. On his feet were some kind of knee-high hide boots with flat soles. The boots were covered with so much trail grime their true color was impossible to determine.

He looked out over the passengers and declared, "Folks, we just found out that the gold that was supposed to be on this train isn't. So you all are going to have to make up for it."

A man with a handlebar mustache stood up as if he were about to protest, but the outlaw shot a hole in the man's seat, then announced, "This isn't going to be a debate, sir."

The man turned beet red and didn't make another move.

"Now," the outlaw continued, "just so you'll know who's robbing you, the name's Neil July, and this is my twin brother, Two Shafts."

Two Shafts, still holding onto the conductor, gave them a friendly nod. "Afternoon, folks."

Olivia was so entranced by this bizarre event that she assumed she'd misheard July say, "twins" because the two men didn't favor each other one bit.

"Now," July said to the tense passengers, "the faster you cooperate, the sooner you'll be on your way."

While the Indian continued to guard the angry conductor, July opened a worn, dirty saddlebag and began moving through the passengers like a church deacon with the collection plate. Apparently, he was no novice at this. "Folks, I know you have your valuables hidden. Give them up freely and save yourself the embarrassment of me having to look for them. 'Specially you ladies."

Female gasps of outrage followed that remark, and the outlaw smiled, saying, "Glad you got my meaning."

Olivia fished out all of the coins in her purse, took her silver earbobs from her lobes, and undid the indigo ribbon from around her neck. On the ribbon hung a cameo with her mother's picture inside. It pained her knowing the cameo would wind up in the bottom of the outlaw's saddlebag along with the rest of the purloined loot, but she had no choice. She put all of the items in her hand and waited for July to reach the back of the car. Her pile of valuables was small, but she hoped it would be enough to pacify him, because she had no intentions of giving him the five hundred dollars hidden on her person.

Finally, Olivia's turn came. Upon seeing her, July's dark eyes glowed with surprise and delight. "Afternoon, lovely lady."

She nodded warily. Up close he was even more dazzling. Olivia had never been around a man who exuded such raw maleness. It radiated from his overpowering presence like heat shimmering on a sultry day. She shook herself, remembering that she was about to be robbed.

He asked in a soft tone, "What do you have for me?"

She showed him her offerings.

He eyed the slim pickings. "Is that all?"

"Yes, and I would think you'd have more honor than to rob a woman of the race, too."

"Why?"

"Because of your color."

He shrugged. "I'm Seminole and I rob trains. The only color I'm concerned with is gold, pretty lady."

"That's very disappointing."

Olivia could see he was amused by her. The thin mustache twitched, as if he were trying to suppress a chuckle.

"The last thing I'd want to do is disappoint a woman as lovely as you, but a fine-dressed woman like yourself has to have more than that."

Olivia was wearing a navy traveling costume whose bustled skirt and form-fitting jacket were at the height of fashion. "I'm a seamstress, Mr. July. I'm only finely dressed because I make my own clothing."

He looked her up and down approvingly. "I see."

Olivia met his gaze without a flinch, but in truth she was scared to death.

"I think you're lying to me," he said in a soft, low voice that seemed to play havoc with her insides.

Olivia didn't respond.

"I like tall, feisty women."

"I don't like thieves."

He cocked his head a bit. "I'm wounded, ma'am."

Olivia could feel herself becoming slightly woozy from being so near him, but she told herself it was due to the combined pungent smells of man and horse, not the knowing male look in his jet black eyes.

He must have seen her wrinkle her nose. "Train robbing doesn't leave a lot of time for scented baths, ma'am. Promise I'll smell better next time."

"I doubt there'll be a next time."

"Oh, there will be," he countered with eyes that teased her own, "and when we do, you owe me something."

"What?"

"A kiss," he told her softly.

Olivia tried to speak around her suddenly dry throat. "What on earth for?"

"For letting you keep the rest of your money."

She went stock still.

He waited, watching her silently.

Something passed between them that she couldn't name. Then she responded with the only thing she could think of. "Thank you."

He gave her a confident smile, then turned and walked back to the front of the car. Olivia touched her hand to her furiously beating heart, unsure about what had just transpired.

A few moments later, Neil July and Two Shafts departed, and the shaken-up passengers fell back against their seats with relief. As the train continued on its way, Olivia could see July and his five-member gang riding south. She doubted she'd meet him again, but parts of herself wondered what might happen if she did.

Chapter 1

◯◠◡◯

Henry Adams, Kansas
Great Solomon Valley
May 1889

The seamstress shop owned by Olivia Sterling operated out of a small Victorian house two blocks away from the town's main business district. Last fall, when she'd first purchased the building from the bank, she'd been concerned about not being located on Main Street, but she'd soon come to appreciate being off the beaten path. Being away from the center of town, with all its vehicles and people, made for a quieter existence; it was also cleaner. Olivia could open her windows and doors and not have to shake out her yard goods two and three times a day because of the dust generated by all the traffic.

Right now, Olivia wasn't much concerned with dust or traffic. Instead her attention was centered on customer Harriet Vinton. The middle-aged Harriet had just come out from behind the shop's wooden dressing screen, and all the large, bright yellow bows attached to the white satin ball gown made Olivia mentally shake her head in dismay. Mrs. Vinton's short, portly form was better served by a quieter, more mature design, but it was a dress she'd insisted Olivia design for her, and this was the result.

Mrs. Vinton twirled in front of the mirror and tittered, "Oh, Olivia. It's so beautiful."

Olivia genuinely hoped her responding smile didn't appear as false as it felt.

Harriet turned to get a side view of the big bow on the capped sleeve. "My Henry is going to be speechless."

Olivia didn't doubt that in the least.

"I'll be the envy of every woman in town."

The Elders Ball celebrating the founding of Henry Adams was going to be held later this month at the spanking-new town hall. All of the residents of the Great Solomon Valley would be attending, and Olivia had been sewing for the past six weeks to accommodate the ladies who'd wanted new gowns for the annual event. Many of the farm women couldn't afford to waste money on a gown they'd only wear once or twice in their life, but Olivia was thankful for the wives of the cattlemen and businessmen who could, because their orders kept Olivia in business.

"Olivia?" Mrs. Vinton asked, "are you going to the ball?"

Olivia shook her head. "No."

"Why not?"

Olivia countered confidently, "I'm going to spend

that evening resting and catching up on my correspondence. It's been weeks since I've written my mother. There are notes from the last Elders meeting that need to be reviewed and minutes of the Historical Society to place in the ledger."

"A young woman like you should be at the ball."

"Thirty-two is hardly young, Mrs. Vinton, but thank you. And yes, I would like to attend, but since I haven't been asked . . ." she shrugged. "I refuse to be one of the spinsters serving the punch and cake while everyone else is dancing. I volunteered my services last year, and frankly, it wasn't very enjoyable."

Harriet nodded. "I understand. Well, an evening of rest will probably do you good. With all you do it's a wonder you have time to sleep."

Olivia agreed. When she'd first settled in Henry Adams, Cara Lee Jefferson, the schoolteacher and wife of the sheriff suggested Olivia volunteer on some of the women's committees as a way of getting to know her new neighbors. Olivia had taken the advice to heart and now, after working with the church, the school, the Ladies League, and the Historical Society, she knew most, if not all, of the women around. There wasn't a day of the week that Olivia didn't have a meeting of one sort or another.

Mrs. Vinton surveyed herself in the mirror again. "I know you're devoted to your business, but my nephew in Philadelphia is looking for a wife, and I believe you'd be perfect."

Olivia knew from previous conversations that Harriet had a large number of nephews back east.

Every few months Harriet would come into Olivia's shop touting the latest one's virtues and marriageable attributes. "I don't wish to marry."

"You keep saying that only because the right man hasn't come along."

Amused, Olivia shook her head. "You need to go home and let Henry see you in your dress."

That shifted Harriet's attention back to her mirrored reflection and away from matchmaking. "I do look fine, don't I?"

All the bows made Harriet resemble a back-east Christmas tree, but if Harriet loved the dress, nothing else mattered. "I'm glad you're pleased with it," Olivia said genuinely.

"I'll take it off now so you can wrap it."

A few moments later, an elated Harriet Vinton left with her dress and Olivia put the payment into her cash box.

For the rest of the day, Olivia waited on customers in between working on dresses and hats. Reverend Whitfield's wife, Sybil, stopped in for the dress she'd had altered so that it didn't look so outdated. Sophie Reynolds, one of the town's pillars and owner of the Henry Adams Hotel, came in to get the final fitting on the pale gold ball gown she'd be wearing to the Elders Ball. Unlike Harriet Vinton, the middle-aged but still stunning Miss Sophie had chosen a design that flattered both her figure and age.

By the time dusk rolled in, Olivia had attended to half the women in the valley, or so it seemed. When she finally closed the doors at the end of the day, she was quite exhausted, but her cash box was smiling.

Olivia operated her shop out of the front of the house and lived in the rooms at the back, where there were two bedrooms and a small kitchen. Glad the day was over, she was on her way to the kitchen to prepare some supper when she heard the shop's bell ring and the door opening once again. Thinking one of her customers must have forgotten something, she hurried back out, only to see her nemesis, Armstead Malloy, standing there. He was a short, muscular, middle-aged man with thinning hair and a pug-ugly brown face, whose features were almost overshadowed by the elaborate waxed mustache above his lips. What he lacked in height and handsomeness, he made up for in greed. Back east had capitalists like Jay Gould; Henry Adams had Armstead Malloy.

Schooling her features, she said coolly, "Good evening, Mr. Malloy, may I help you?"

He flashed that smarmy smile. "Miss Olivia. Just stopped by to let you know my offer still stands."

Olivia sighed her frustration. "Nothing has changed since our last conversation, Mr. Malloy. I have no desire to sell."

His jaw tightened slightly and his eyes held hers, but she didn't back down. Malloy was a relative newcomer to Henry Adams, but in the year since his arrival he'd built the town's newest and biggest mercantile. He was also buying up businesses. Some folks, like the owners of the old Sutton mercantile, had sold out gladly; others, like blacksmith Handy Reed turned him down flat. A few weeks ago, Malloy approached Olivia with an offer. She'd declined, of course, but he seemed to think she didn't know her own mind and, as a consequence, kept coming around. So far, she'd been polite. Firm but polite.

He picked up a length of velveteen fabric, studied it critically, then asked, "And my other offer?"

Olivia did her best to hang onto her patience. "I'm not interested in marrying you, either."

"But you would grace my table so beautifully."

"I'm glad you think so, but I didn't come to Kansas to marry."

He rubbed his fingers over the fabric. "How much did you pay for this?"

"Why?"

"Just thinking I could get it cheaper. The ladies would probably appreciate buying their yard goods at a better price."

Olivia knew a threat when she heard one, and she now disliked Armstead Malloy even more. Because of the size of his store's orders, she was sure he could undercut her price. Women all over the valley patronized her, but if her customers began buying their goods from him, her shop's profits would be affected, and he knew that. "I'm sure the ladies will make up their own minds. Was there anything else?"

He looked around once more, taking in the dress forms, her Singer sewing machine, and the neatly stacked wooden boxes filled with threads, ribbons, and other items of her trade. "My next offer will be significantly less."

Olivia wasn't sure what type of reaction he expected that statement to garner, but she refused to be intimidated by a pompous little man six inches shorter than she. "The size of your offer is of no consequence. My shop is not for sale, and I would appreciate you not approaching me on the subject— or the subject of marriage—again."

Her response tightened his jaw again, but to Olivia, that was of no consequence either, so she added, "Now, if you'll excuse me, Mr. Malloy, I'm preparing supper."

He studied her for a moment before saying in displeased tones, "As you wish, madam. But I will be back. Good evening." He turned on his boot heel and left.

Olivia threw the bolts on the door.

Later, sitting in her kitchen, Olivia lingered over her bowl of soup and mused upon how life on her own terms was progressing. She continued to miss her mother dearly and wrote whenever she had the time, but outside of Armstead Malloy, she had no real complaints. Her shop was as successful as one could be stuck out in the middle of the Kansas plains. Realistically, she doubted she'd ever achieve the financial success she'd enjoyed back east, but she liked living in Kansas. Admittedly, on that first day when she'd stepped off the train and taken a good, long look around at where this adventure had taken her, she'd wanted to get back on the train and return to Chicago. She'd been surrounded by open land as far as her eye could see; everyone she'd met had been a stranger, and truthfully, Olivia had been under her parents' roof her entire life and hadn't known the first thing about living on her own. Yet she'd survived; flourished even, in this unlikely place.

Now if she could just convince Armstead Malloy to take his proposals elsewhere, then find a way to politely discourage folks like Harriet Vinton and the other well-meaning folks wanting to marry her off to their nephews, sons, and grandsons, life would be perfect. Smiling, she went back to her soup.

Monday morning, Olivia took the stage to Ellis, a small town thirty miles away. A widow friend of Sophie Reynolds had commissioned two dresses for herself and one for her daughter, and Olivia needed to take the necessary measurements before she could begin sewing. The process would be an all-day affair, so they'd graciously offered her a place to sleep for the night.

Tuesday morning, the work done, Olivia said good-bye to the widow and headed back to the depot for the ride home. She didn't want to be late. If she missed the stage, the next run to Henry Adams wouldn't be until Thursday.

She arrived at the ticket agent's table just in time to see Armstead Malloy standing there. As always, he was dressed in a cutaway suit that would have done a circus barker proud. This one had black-and-white checks. Her hopes for a nice quiet ride home plunged.

"Well, well, well," he voiced, pleased. "Are you following me around, Miss Sterling?"

She dearly wanted to ignore him, but she'd been raised better. "No. I had some business to attend to here."

"I see." He was looking her up and down with approval. "I came over to make arrangements to purchase the town's funeral parlor."

Olivia wasn't the least bit interested. "That's nice."

"You know," he said with a knowing tone, "I could rent us a coach and we could ride back to Henry Adams together."

"No, thank you. I prefer to wait for Mr. Gardner's stage."

"You sure? We could talk on the way. Come to agreement on some things."

Olivia turned to look him in the eye. She could well imagine what things he was referencing. "No."

Before he could reply the stage arrived, and a grateful Olivia walked away to meet it.

Once all the passengers were aboard, the driver, Old Man Gardner, and his rifle-toting aide got them underway.

Ten miles into the journey, Olivia mused upon why she hated traveling by stagecoach. The interiors were cramped, uncomfortable, and, at this time of year, so hot inside that one could hardly breathe. Thankfully the ticket agent hadn't oversold the conveyance, but Olivia still found herself squashed between a rather large jewelry salesman and his equally rotund wife. The woman smelled of cheap perfume, her husband, of liquor and cigars. Olivia got the impression the couple had had a spat sometime before boarding, because both looked put out, and they hadn't spoken a word to each other.

On the bench facing Olivia sat a young woman

with a baby that had been howling nonstop for the last two miles. Next to the mother sat her sour-faced aunt, and next to the aunt, Armstead Malloy, who apparently planned to spend the entire journey staring down Olivia's throat. It was July, it was hot, and she prayed the coach got to Henry Adams before her headache worsened.

The baby continued to scream. The poor mother was doing her best to comfort the infant, but the aunt, instead of being sympathetic, offered nothing but criticism on everything from the way the babe was being held to the color and cut of his bunting. Olivia knew the young mother had to be weary of the woman's smug sniping; Olivia certainly was.

Over the baby's din, Malloy tried to engage Olivia in conversation. "Where're you from originally, Miss Olivia?"

"Ohio," she lied.

Olivia kept her answers short. She didn't want her words to give him even the faintest hope that she had changed her mind on either of his proposals. Good women were in short supply in western Kansas; men were known to attach themselves to unmarried women like grasshoppers on crops in hopes of making them wives. She wondered how many times she'd have to tell him before he'd believe that she'd not come to Kansas to marry.

Malloy opened his mouth to say more when suddenly Old Man Gardner yelled down to the passengers, "Hang on, folks! Men riding down on us and I don't think they're wanting a cup of coffee."

The coach picked up speed. Malloy pushed aside

the window's leather shade and peered out. "I can see them on this side!" he yelled. "There's two of them, and they're riding hard!"

The aunt cried, "Oh Lord, what will we do?!"

Olivia had no idea, but she did her best to hang on. The increased speed was flinging the passengers up and down as the wheels hit the ruts and craters in the rough road. The jeweler hastily placed his case on his unsteady knees. He opened it and quickly began snatching out stones and bejeweled items, which he handed across Olivia to his wife. She shamelessly undid the top two buttons on her shirtwaist and stuffed the bounty into her ample bosom. Once the case was mostly empty, the blouse was once again done up, and they all held on.

Gunfire could be heard now, and Olivia prayed over the din. Malloy pulled out a small derringer. Leaning out the window, he added his lead to the fight, shouting, "They're gaining!"

The mother was holding her baby close to her body, and her eyes were closed as if in prayer. The old aunt was moaning with fright and clutching her niece's arm with a clawlike hand.

Suddenly the coach pitched to one side and they were all thrown from their seats. Olivia could hear the scream of the horses mingling with her own, then everything went black.

When she opened her eyes, she was still inside the overturned coach, with her back wedged against the door beneath her and the full weight of the passengers on top of her. The baby was screaming at the top of his lungs. Before Olivia could determine if she was injured, the door above their heads was snatched open and the dark, handsome face of outlaw Neil July stared down. Olivia's eyes went wide. He was wearing a dusty brown vest over his bare torso, boldly displaying the well-defined musculature of his arms and shoulders. His face, so memorable, was filled with concern as he assessed each occupant individually, but when his black eyes settled on Olivia, he gave her a smile softened with recognition. "Well, hello . . ."

Her heart began to pound. Speech seemed to be beyond her, so she offered an almost imperceptible nod.

He grinned. "Let's get you all out of there."

The furious baby was handed out first, and July expertly placed the howling infant against his shoulder as if he tended little ones all the time. Then the mountain-sized man Olivia remembered as July's fellow robber Two Shafts appeared in the doorway. "Anybody hurt?"

The aunt wailed, "Oh, please, just help us out of here!"

Olivia gave a silent "Amen." The hard wood of the door beneath her back was going to leave her bruised for weeks. That, coupled with the body weight piled on top of her, was making it difficult to breathe.

One by one the shaken passengers were assisted out, courtesy of Two Shafts's strong grip. Then it was Olivia's turn. She reached out to grasp his large hand only to see him hipped aside by July, who looked in at Olivia and said softly, "This honor is mine."

All kinds of strange feelings swam through Olivia in response. She expected him to assist her, but instead he reached in, scooped her up into his arms, and backed out with her before she could blink. Her startled eyes flew to his amused ones.

"Ever had a man carry you before?"

"No," she admitted, trying to maintain her dignity while shaking like a leaf. Her height generally discouraged this kind of thing.

"Relax, I won't drop you." His vivid gaze seemed to look inside her soul. "Do you remember me?"

Olivia toyed with lying but settled on the truth. "I do." The male heat rising from his body was so powerful that the feel of his arm beneath her thighs and the pressure of her hip against his chest made the July afternoon even hotter.

"Do you remember what you owe me?"

Her chin rose even as her eyes swept over the shape of his full lips. "Yes." She'd been praying he didn't.

"Do I smell better than last time?" The sly, soft voice was filled with mischief.

Olivia had always prided herself on being a level-headed woman, but this man made her dizzy. "Put me down, please." She wondered what the Creator had been thinking to make an outlaw so devilishly good-looking, because July was that and more.

"You sure you can stand?" he asked softly, teasingly.

Olivia could see the other passengers staring on curiously, especially Malloy. "Yes."

He eased her to her feet, and she nervously smoothed her blue traveling dress. "Thank you."

He was still standing too close. She took a step

backward. It didn't help. The effects of him could still be felt; teasing, touching, undermining her efforts to regain her composure. Something told her his dark eyes and mustached smile could dazzle a woman across a continent.

"If you're sure you're okay, I'll go and see how my brother is faring."

She adjusted her hat. "I'm fine," she assured him. Or at least she would be just as soon as he departed and took his overwhelming presence with him. He tossed her a grin and walked away.

The other passengers were still staring on, especially Malloy, but Olivia ignored them and reached into her handbag for her scented embroidered handkerchief. She dabbed delicately at the moisture forming on her neck above the white collar of her blouse and took in a deep, calming breath. In control again, she put the handkerchief away and walked over to join the others. Old Man Gardner and his second were looking at the axle. She hoped it wasn't broken, but she really wanted to know why the outlaws had ridden down on the coach in the first place.

The answer was apparently tied to a poker game, because when Olivia walked up, July was asking the tense-looking jeweler, "How much did you lose to my brother last night?"

"Fifteen dollars," the man croaked, his eyes moving furtively between July and Two Shafts.

"Did my brother cheat you during the game?"

"No."

"So the game was fair and square."

The jeweler nodded quickly. "Yes."

"And when you left the table last night you promised to do what?"

The jeweler answered guiltily, "Meet your brother in the morning and pay up."

"But what did you do instead?"

"I . . . caught the stage."

"You caught the stage."

July then looked to the jeweler's plump wife. "Are you his wife, ma'am?"

She nodded warily.

"Did you know any of this when you left town this morning?"

Her hard eyes flashed condemningly at her husband before she responded tersely, "No."

"I thought not," July replied, giving her that charming smile. "Beautiful woman like yourself would never be party to such uncouth behavior."

The woman giggled like a schoolgirl.

Olivia rolled her eyes. July was certainly an entertaining outlaw, if nothing else. He suddenly smacked the jeweler on the back of his head so hard that the man's bowler landed in the dust. "Do you know who we are?"

"No," the jeweler admitted, cringing.

"Ever heard of the Terrible Twins?"

The man nodded hastily, then, as if realizing that the question had not been a rhetorical one, his beady brown eyes widened with fright.

July nodded affirmatively. "Yep. That's who you tried to cheat this morning. I'm Neil July and this is my brother, Two Shafts. Although we may rob trains for a living, we don't like being robbed ourselves." He studied the jeweler for a moment before asking, "That make sense to you?"

The man nodded and hastily nodded again. Olivia, on the other hand, thought that to be a very self-serving statement, but she kept quiet. She already owed July a debt she didn't want to pay.

July held his hand out. "The money."

During July's interrogation of the jeweler, Two Shafts hadn't said a word—until now. "Pay up or we take everything you have, including your drawers."

The jeweler's eyes went wide as plates.

July added, "And I'm sure the ladies want to be spared that distressing sight."

Olivia looked to the young mother and the aunt and was quite certain they agreed with July's assessment.

"But I don't have the money."

"Then we'll start with your coat. Hand it over."

"You can't be serious."

July's gun magically appeared out of nowhere and came to rest between the jeweler's horrified eyes. "Your clothes or the money."

The shaking man shot his wife a hasty glance. "She has all my valuables."

July pulled the Colt back and stuck it into the heavy gun belt girdling his waist. "Now we're getting somewhere." Turning his attention to the wife, he purred, "Madame, if you would be so kind. . . ."

In response, the woman blushed, then turned her back and discreetly opened her blouse to retrieve the hidden cache. Once decent again, she handed the lot over to Two Shafts. He shifted the baubles and jewelry around on his outstretched palm. A gold bracelet caught his eye. He held it up for July to see. "Think Teresa would like this?"

July studied the piece and shrugged. "Don't see why not."

Two Shafts put the bracelet into the pocket of his faded blue army jacket. Olivia wondered who this Teresa might be. When she looked up, July was watching her, and all her wondering fled. Once again an unnamed something passed over and through her senses, and no matter how much she tried to ignore it, it wouldn't go away.

Two Shafts finished extracting his fifteen dollars' worth of restitution from the jeweler's stock and then told the man, "Thank you."

The jeweler scowled.

Two Shafts responded with a cold smile. "Be nice, my friend. I can still send you on your way as naked as Adam if I've a mind to."

The jeweler dropped his gaze.

Two Shafts turned away and went over to the men working on the wagon. Olivia was surprised to see him help the men right the coach. *Helpful outlaws?*

July was watching her again, and although Olivia was sure her reaction to him was experienced by every woman he encountered, maintaining her composure wasn't any easier.

Mr. Gardner, who'd been driving the route from Ellis to Henry Adams for over a decade, walked over and announced, "Folks, the axle is broken. I'm going to have to leave the coach here and take you all back to Ellis. We can take turns riding the horses. There's another stage coming through on Thursday."

No one was happy with the news. Thursday was two days away. A frustrated Olivia blamed the Terrible Twins and the jeweler for this mess. She certainly didn't want to ride all the way back to Ellis. She looked up at the sky. It was already mid-afternoon, the hottest part of the day. If she struck out now walking the remaining twenty miles across the treeless Kansas plains for home, she'd die of heatstroke. "Mr. Gardner, may I borrow one of the horses and go on to Henry Adams?"

The old driver shook his head. "Sorry, Miss Olivia. The stock belongs to the coach line. They all have to go back with me."

"My horse and I can escort you home."

July's voice startled her into turning around.

"That isn't necessary," she said, proud she hadn't stammered. His presence made her so warm that it was like standing next to a stove.

"My brother and I are heading up to Canada. Henry Adams is on the way." The seamstress Neil now knew as Miss Olivia was as beautiful today as she'd been the afternoon he'd robbed her and the other passengers on the train—still well-dressed, too. The navy suit framed a frilly, high-collared white blouse that looked as soft as a cloud, even though the clothing was too much for such a hot day. The hat, with all its flowers and netting, was more for fashion than for protection from the sun.

Olivia knew that if she returned to town under his escort the resulting scandal would follow her to her grave. "Thank you, but no."

"I insist," he countered softly. "After all, were it

not for our jeweler friend, you wouldn't be in this situation."

"Were it not for *you,* I wouldn't be in this situation." Olivia decided he had the longest lashes she'd ever seen on a man. She also wondered how long it would be before she could look into his face and not be burned to a cinder.

Neil chuckled. "I was wondering when the sassing would start." She'd sassed him a bit during that first encounter, and that had pleased him, just as it did now. He enjoyed spirited, statuesque women. "You don't really want to go all the way back to Ellis."

"True, but I'm not traveling alone with you, either." Olivia dearly wished he'd turn his considerable handsomeness on someone else. She could see the displeasure on Malloy's face; not that it mattered, but she didn't want any gossip linking her and the outlaw in any way.

"I assure you, I can be a gentleman," he replied, refocusing her attention on his provocative presence.

"I'm sure you can."

Neil turned to the driver and said, "I'm escorting Miss Olivia back to Henry Adams."

Her reply was firm. "No, he is not. I appreciate your offer, Mr. July, but no thank you."

The young mother with the baby said into the breach, "Then take me and the baby."

Her aunt looked appalled, but the mother didn't seem to care. "Please. I will pay you. I've traveled all the way from Boston to join my husband, and I can't wait for the next stage. My husband's never even seen the baby."

The baby was finally asleep, but the aunt snapped, "We're going back to Ellis, Mary Ann."

Mary Ann ignored her. "Please, Mr. July. Please."

Neil looked to the young mother and then to his brother, who nodded almost imperceptibly. Neil responded, "Well, little lady, seeing as how this is partially our fault—sure. Shafts and I will take you to your husband, and it won't cost you a cent."

Tears of gratitude filled the woman's eyes. She then turned to Olivia and said, smiling, "Now you can go, too. With me and the baby along, you won't have to worry about what folks might say. That is what you were worrying over, wasn't it?"

The woman was correct, but Olivia was still wary of traveling with July for myriad reasons, the least being the debt she owed him.

Neil waited to see what Olivia would do. Before the young mother had spoken up, he'd toyed with the idea of just tossing the seamstress over his horse's back and riding off, he found her that fascinating. He was an outlaw after all, but the mother had given him a way to spend more time with the lovely Olivia and not be charged with kidnapping. That was a good thing, because there were more than enough Wanted posters with his name on them already. "So, you coming along?"

Olivia studied him for a moment. Was she seriously reconsidering the idea, knowing she didn't know a thing about him other than the fact that he robbed trains?

He added softly, "You have my word that you won't be harmed in any way."

There was an honesty in his voice and gaze that made her believe he was telling the truth, but then again, that was probably part of his charm.

Malloy puffed himself up to his full height, threw out his chest like a rooster, and declared, "For propriety's sake I insist on going along, too."

Neil assessed him emotionlessly, then turned away.

Although Olivia could barely tolerate the self-important Malloy, his presence would hopefully quell any gossip that might arise. Neil July's pledge to keep her from harm notwithstanding, Olivia felt better having a non-outlaw male along. Apparently Mary Ann's aunt did too and decided to go along as well.

While the passengers went with Gardner to retrieve their bags and trunks from the boot, Neil and Two Shafts went to retrieve their mounts. Two Shafts looked at his brother and said amusedly, "Canada? I thought we were on our way to Kansas City to relieve the army of that gold."

An embarrassed Neil shrugged. "It's all I could come up with at the time." His eyes strayed over to the Junoesque Olivia talking to the coach driver. "I think I'm in love."

"You're always in love. You don't even know her."

"Ah, but I do." Neil knew her to be the most feminine woman he'd met in quite some time. Her perfume was vivid in his memory, as was the feel of her nervous trembles when he'd had her up in his arms. The need to learn more about the seamstress was strong enough to make him delay leaving for Kansas City. Escorting her and the others back would add another day or two to the journey, but gold trains were plentiful; women as bewitching as the lovely Miss Olivia were rare in his world.

Shafts shook his head. "You know women like her don't mix with men like us."

"Sure they do. Remember the territorial governor's daughter a few years back?"

Shafts laughed. "You made your point. I wonder where she learned all those *tricks*?"

"I'm not sure, but I certainly enjoyed the ones her mother showed me, and besides, doing this will give us an excuse to drop in on Jeff." Jeff was Chase Jefferson—an old friend and the sheriff of Henry Adams.

"Let's hope he doesn't celebrate our showing up by putting us in jail."

Both men laughed, then grabbed the reins of their mounts and led the horses back to the folks standing by the coach.

Olivia watched Neil July approach and told herself she was not going to let his maleness overwhelm her. She'd lost herself back there, but she attributed that to the surprise of seeing him again. Now she'd regained control of her faculties and was ready to meet him head on.

Neil took the carpetbag from her gloved hand and tied it to the saddlebags on the horse. She met his gaze with her chin raised and her back ramrod straight. It made him wonder if she'd ever had a man stroke that iron spine into softness; if she'd ever purred for a man. He doubted she had, and that drew Neil too. "Ready, ma'am?"

Olivia watched Two Shafts helping the mother and her aunt onto the back of his big brown gelding. Once the women were settled across the saddle, he handed the baby up to its mother. Only then did Olivia turn her attention to July. His dark, fathomless eyes were waiting. Over the increased pace of her heartbeat, she wondered if it was normal for a woman to be so affected by a man she barely knew. "Yes."

Olivia didn't need his help mounting. Sticking her booted foot into the stirrup, she grabbed the horn and swung herself up with as much grace as she could in all the skirts and petticoats. She settled astride the saddle. In response to July's widened, impressed eyes, she adjusted her skirts and kept her smile hidden.

A few moments later the small band of travelers waved good-bye to Old Man Gardner and his aide. They and the still angry jeweler and his wife struck out for Ellis, while Olivia and the others began the twenty-mile ride to Henry Adams. Under the glaring heat, the men walked and the women rode.

Malloy, in his checkered suit and back east bowler, had taken up a position on one side of July's horse, while July walked on the opposite side. Neil would have preferred that the man walk elsewhere, but he kept it to himself. He didn't want to antagonize Miss Olivia.

Malloy said to July, "Name's Armstead Malloy. I own many of the businesses in Henry Adams, don't I, Miss Olivia?"

Olivia replied emotionlessly, "Yes, you do."

Malloy smiled, then asked, "You own anything, July?"

Neil had encountered smug little men like him before. "Just my horse. Man like me doesn't need much more."

"Oh, that's right. You steal for a living, don't you?"

Olivia was taken aback by the unwarranted attack. She didn't believe such sneering was warranted or necessary. They were traveling under the outlaws' protection, after all.

Malloy added, "I'm also trying to convince Miss Olivia to marry me."

Neil couldn't hide his surprise.

Olivia's lips tightened. "And I've repeatedly told Mr. Malloy, no."

Neil smiled inside. *The woman was beautiful and smart.*

"Some women like to be chased," Malloy countered tightly.

"Then maybe you should turn your attention there," she answered. "I'll not be changing my mind. I didn't come to Kansas to marry."

"Right man would change all that," Malloy argued evenly.

"I don't want my life *changed*, Mr. Malloy. I'm pleased with it the way it is."

"A woman needs a man. 'Specially out here. Wouldn't you agree, July?"

Neil didn't know why Malloy was suddenly seeking his opinion. "Depends on the woman. If you tell my sister, Teresa, that she needs a man to take care of her, she's liable to draw her Colt and shoot you."

Malloy stared. "What kind of woman is she?"

"Outlaw woman."

Olivia was surprised. "Your sister is an outlaw?"

"Yep. Rides with the old Dick Glass gang down in Indian Territory. Got almost as many Wanted posters as me and Shafts. Pretty proud of her."

The stunned Olivia wondered what kind of family this man came from, where women were applauded for having their own Wanted posters. He had to be pulling her leg.

Neil called to his brother. "Hey, Shafts, what do you think Tee would say to a man that says she needs him to take care of her?"

"Before or after she shoots him?" Two Shafts replied with a straight face.

Neil grinned.

Olivia smiled inwardly. Their sister sounded like a formidable woman. A question she'd been mulling over for awhile came to mind. "Mr. July, why do you call Two Shafts your twin?"

"Because he is."

Olivia studied Two Shafts's dark, golden skin and handsome features, but for the life of her, she couldn't see any resemblance strong enough to declare him July's twin.

July offered an explanation. "Shafts and I have the same daddy but different mothers. His mother is Comanche."

She was confused. "But how does that make you twins?"

"We were born on the same day."

Olivia had never heard of such a thing. In an odd

sort of way she supposed they were twins. *What a peculiar family.*

Malloy asked in haughty tones, "What made you take up train robbing?"

"Poverty."

Olivia went still and studied him. She'd never heard such a succinct and moving one-word response in all her life. Olivia realized there was more to Neil July than met the eye. Apparently the answer affected Malloy as well, because he kept his questions to himself after that.

Chapter 2

They'd been on the road about an hour when they spotted an abandoned homestead standing like a tired sentinel on the open plains. As they rode closer, Olivia scanned the tumbledown place and experienced a bit of melancholy. Most of the valley's original settlers had come to Kansas as part of the Great Exodus of 1879. The newspapers had dubbed the migration Kansas Fever. The participants, forty thousand men, women, and children of the race had dubbed it *survival* as they'd fled the terror and killings that had followed the withdrawal of the last Union troops from the South. However, many of the families who'd made the long, arduous trek to Kansas, Nebraska, and the western territories in search of the freedom denied them by the South's Redemptionist Democrats had arrived woefully unprepared for the hardships of carving out a life where none had existed before. Some had come with no tools, others too little money. Still others had quit their farms because of debt, loneliness, and despair. This small house with its broken-down windmill had once stood as a proud testament to someone's dreams; now it was overgrown with grasses and wildflowers. Eventually the land would reclaim the structure, and the testament would be no more.

The sight of the pump beside the house made the band halt. Shafts walked over to see if the implement worked. It did. All of the travelers were equipped with canteens, but fresh water meant they wouldn't have to ration their supply.

Malloy came around to lend his assistance to Olivia's dismount, but he was brought up short by the scowling face of Neil July, who told him, "You go see about your canteen. I'll help the lady."

For a moment, Olivia thought Malloy would challenge the outlaw, but apparently he had more sense than that. Instead he shot July a hostile look, then did as he was told.

July turned his attention to Olivia. Shafts had already helped the other women to the ground, and with the baby in tow they were following him to the pump.

July placed his hands on Olivia's waist, and she felt the heat of them penetrating the many layers of her clothing to her skin. She had no time to deal with that because she was being lifted down, and his eyes and the intensity reflected in them were all she could see. Having been five feet eight inches tall since the age of fourteen, she was unaccustomed to being around a man she had to look up at in order to make eye contact with. That fact added even more ingredients to her uncharacteristically flustered state. He towered over her by a good six inches.

It took Olivia a moment to realize that his hands were no longer on her waist and that she was standing on solid ground, but for the life of her she couldn't move.

Scanning her lovely face, Neil was again tempted by an overpowering urge to ride off with her, but he fought it down. He'd promised to be a gentleman, and he was trying his best to keep the vow. It was difficult, though. *Dios, she was lovely.* "Let's get that water."

His words broke the spell and brought Olivia back to reality. Nervously mumbling her thanks for his help, she hurried off to catch up with the others. Neil watched her retreat with appreciative eyes.

Determined to put Neil July out of her mind but failing miserably, Olivia filled her canteen, then used some of the pump's water to wet her handkerchief. She could still feel the warmth of his hands. His dark, mischief-filled eyes seemed to be permanently burned in her mind. She couldn't ever remember being rendered speechless. *Men like him had no business showing up out of nowhere and putting innocent women in flux.* Removing her hat, she used the dampened cotton to mop at her hairline and the heat beneath the collar of her blouse. Her dearest wish was to get home and strip herself of the hot, confining clothing so she could cool off, but there were still miles to cover before they reached town. Until then, she was forced to endure the unrelenting sun and its sibling, the blistering heat. She looked toward July and found him watching her. *Had he really taken up the outlaw life because of poverty?* He impressed her as being intelligent, so why, she wondered, hadn't he chosen an honest profession? Why train robbing? She doubted she'd ever know the truth, but she was, admittedly, curious. Not that she should be. The man was a wanted criminal after all, and no self-respecting woman had any business pondering him, even if he could melt females with his smile.

Neil was pondering her too, every magnificent, God-built inch of her. This was no skinny back east woman. The tall, dark-eyed Olivia was as shapely as a female Mexican deity. He already knew that her copper skin would be like silk to his touch, and her mouth . . . she had a mouth a man would rob a thousand trains for just to kiss. Her lips would be sweet; yielding. Arousal warmed his blood. He forced himself to concentrate on less volatile matters. The seamstress was probably as virgin as she was tall, and he had to remember that.

Once everyone filled their canteens, the horses were watered and the group started up the rutted road. They were moving as slowly as before. The oppressive heat and the unrelenting July sun made Olivia feel like a hen on a spit. Were she not in mixed company, she would have already taken off her suit jacket, but with the men present such a move was frowned upon by polite society, so she suffered in the tight corset, the camisole atop it, and the blouse and cotton jacket that were on top of them. Beneath her skirt were thigh-length drawers, a cotton slip, and two petticoats. Throw in the long black stockings on her legs, and one had a properly dressed woman who was wilting.

From her seat atop the saddle, Olivia glanced down at July, who was keeping a slow pace at the horse's side. He didn't appear at all bothered by the heat. The brown, flat-crowned hat shaded his head and face from the harsh sun, and the brown leather vest covering his torso left his well-developed, dark arms bare. His attire was hardly proper, but he appeared far more comfortable than she. Maybe in the future women would be allowed the freedom to go about in public with their arms and shoulders bare, but for the present, she roasted.

The farther they traveled, the hotter she became. Olivia had never done well in the heat. When she was younger, no summer Sunday service at Chicago's Pleasant Valley African Methodist Episcopal Church had been complete without her being assisted from the church because of her reaction to the stifling temperatures. Although the doctors had assured her parents that folks fainted from heatstroke all the time, Olivia had hated the reaction because she'd always equated fainting with simpleminded, empty-headed females attempting to draw attention to themselves. Now that she was older, the number of incidents had decreased dramatically, but every now and then, when the temperatures were high—like today—she'd get light-headed, then woozy. To her dismay, that feeling was creeping up on her now. She drew in a deep breath to keep it at bay, then attempted to stay focused on the road.

A half mile later, perspiration was coursing down her spine like a river. She discreetly wiped at the small streams rolling from her hairline.

"How are you doing up there, Miss Olivia?" Neil asked.

"I'm a bit warm," she allowed, "but well. And you?"

"Not doing too bad, but I'm used to the heat." He viewed her for a moment, taking in the sheen of moisture on her brow. "You should take off that fancy jacket. Might make you cooler."

Olivia would like nothing better, but she shook her head. "Not in mixed company. It isn't proper."

"What's proper about heatstroke?"

She managed to keep her smile hidden. "Nothing, but society dictates I broil."

He shook his head. "Sometimes society needs to be ignored."

"I'm fine, Mr. July. Truly." It was a lie; she wasn't *fine*. If she didn't find some shade soon, she was going to faint. Only sheer will was keeping her from tumbling from the saddle.

Neil didn't think she looked *fine*—she looked like she was about to keel over. "Well, I'm going to keep an eye on you. Don't want you falling off with no one to catch you."

Olivia could see the tight-lipped Malloy looking on. "I appreciate your concern, but I was raised on a timber farm and rode horses before I could walk. I doubt I'll fall off."

Neil now knew the reason why she sat the horse so confidently. "Good to hear, but begging your pardon, you don't look like a farm girl."

"How am I supposed to look?"

"Less elegant."

Another succinct response that caught her off guard. One seldom heard of outlaws using the word *elegant*. He truly didn't fit the mold of what she'd always assumed a train robber would be.

Malloy asked with a cynical edge to his voice, "When did you rob your first train, July?"

Neil had been enjoying Olivia's company, and he wasn't pleased by the starched collar's interruption. "Why?"

"Thinking of starting a newspaper in Henry Adams. Thought you might make a good story."

Olivia frowned. "You're going to open a newspaper?"

"Yep. Been thinking about it for awhile. Town needs one, don't you think?"

On the surface she agreed. The *Nicodemus Cyclone* was the closest Henry Adams had to a local paper, but she certainly didn't see Armstead Malloy being the owner. He'd never impressed her as being overly literate. Greedy, yes; literate and well-read, no.

Malloy asked, "Where are you from, Mr. July?"

"Florida, Indian Territory, Mexico. My people have lived everywhere, it seems."

"Why?"

"Broken treaties mostly. Everywhere we've been, we were promised one thing and given nothing."

Olivia could hear the bitterness in his tone. "Where is your family now?" she asked.

"Town called Brackettville on the Texas Mexican border." Neil thought about the young men at home who were descending into alcohol and crime because the country was in no mood to honor its promises and because their way of life was fading like the winter moon. He pushed the thoughts away. "And your family?"

"I'm an only child. My parents are both living and in good health."

"And what do they think of your coming all this way to live?"

Olivia kept the truth to herself. "I'm sure they're concerned, but I'm doing well." She watched a bird fly overhead and wished for a human set of wings so she could soar home and get away from the heat. As it stood, they had a good ten miles to go, and it would be dusk, if not dark, by the time of their arrival. Right now, the sun was at its zenith and the heat continued to bear down. Malloy said something but she didn't respond. Her vision began to blur, her surroundings shimmer. She heard Neil July's voice, but he sounded as if he were inside of a tunnel and she couldn't make out the words. Tiny black spots swam across her eyes. She began to sway atop her mount, but she could not summon the will to stop it. Feeling herself melting like candle wax, she pitched forward.

When she began to tumble from Black's back,

Neil was there to catch her. He'd been watching her since their departure from the old homestead because he could see the distress in her face and her attempts to keep it hidden. Concern etching his face, he hollered at Shafts to stop, then eased Olivia to the grass-covered ground. Seconds later, Mary Ann and her aunt hurried to his side.

Mary Ann gave the baby to Neil, then instructed the men to stand over Olivia to give her a bit of shade. Out of respect they then turned their backs. Mary Ann quickly opened Olivia's blouse and loosened the corset beneath to help her breathe better. A water-soaked handkerchief was applied to Olivia's forehead and neck in hopes it would revive her. It did. A few moments later, she opened her eyes and tried to sit up, but she was gently eased back down.

"Just lie still for a moment, Miss Olivia," she heard Mary Ann say, then a cool cloth was bathing her face. "Looks like you got a touch of heatstroke."

Olivia fought to make her eyes focus and saw the men standing with their backs to her. Hazy, she noted that July and Two Shafts were large enough to pose as buildings. She also noted the pricks and sticks of the parched grass she was lying in, and she struggled to a seated position.

Neil wanted to turn around so badly he could taste it. He assumed she'd come around, but he wanted to see for himself. Watching her fall from the horse had scared him. Of course a gentleman didn't turn around when a lady was half dressed, but Neil was worried about her.

For a moment Olivia could do nothing more than sit and try to get her bearings. Her headache had increased tenfold, and her stomach was queasy. She lowered her head and took in a few deep and what she hoped would be calming breaths. It seemed to help. After a few moments, the uneasiness settled down. She redid her buttons. The corset beneath she left undone. Although society frowned on such action, she thought the impropriety was warranted.

She stood then, slowly and shakily, and the men turned, their faces a study in concern.

"You need to see a doc," Neil declared.

"I'm fine." Or at least she would be once she got home. "Thank you all for your assistance." Olivia was embarrassed down to her toes.

Neil wondered if she knew how pale she looked. He doubted it—otherwise she wouldn't be insisting on how fine she was. Rather than argue with her, he took matters into his own hands. Not giving her time to say yea or nay, he scooped her up and began walking to his horse.

"What are you doing?"

"Taking you to town so you can see the doc."

"That's not necessary."

He didn't slow.

"Mr. July, I insist—"

"You can insist all you want once we get you home."

He put her up on Black's back, then swung up behind her.

For the second time a surprised and scandalized Olivia asked, "What are you doing?"

"Riding you home."

"But—"

"You can tell me off on the way."

That said, he swung the horse around and said to his twin, "I'll meet you there."

Shafts nodded.

Armstead Malloy yelled, "Hey! You can't just ride off with her like this. For propriety's sake, I should go, too."

Neil shrugged. "Suit yourself. Keep up if you can." He urged the horse forward and left the angry Malloy standing in the dust.

As the horse increased the distance between its riders and Shafts's party, Olivia tried to make July see reason. "This is entirely unnecessary."

"So you keep saying."

"I'm perfectly able to assess my own health, Mr. July." In reality, though, she still didn't feel all that good. If his arms hadn't been around her, she doubted she would have been able to stay upright.

"I'm sure you are, but humor me."

On the one hand, Olivia was glad to be traveling home at a speedier pace, but on the other hand, she would be riding into town with an outlaw. All she could think about was the gossip ahead. She put it out of her mind; pondering the future only sharpened her headache.

In spite of the two humans on its back, the horse didn't seem bothered. His long strides were powerful and sure, and it made Olivia feel as if she were on the back of Pegasus himself. Too bad her malaise prevented her from enjoying it. She was a good rider.

She loved letting her mount have its head and feeling the rush of excitement as she and the animal became one. Not today. Today she was perfectly willing to let July handle the reins.

Neil decided maybe this ride hadn't been such a good idea after all. She looked pale and wan, and the desire to have her examined fueled his intentions. But she was lying against his chest like a lover. Although her eyes were closed, every inch of his body was as awake as a dawn-crowing rooster. He knew he had no business letting her soft curves distract him from this mission of mercy, but because the good Lord had seen fit to make Neil July a male, he was very much aroused. Once again he forced himself to think of calmer things, and he directed his attention to the ride and away from the woman cuddled against him like a courtesan.

The sun had gone down and dusk was claiming the plains when Neil saw Henry Adams on the horizon. He pulled back on the reins to halt the horse.

Olivia opened her eyes and looked up at him before asking sluggishly, "Why are we stopping?"

"Do you think you can ride on your own?"

"Yes," she replied, though in reality she wasn't sure. "Why?"

"Want to spare your reputation. It'll look better if I'm walking when we get there."

For a moment, Olivia didn't know what to make of an outlaw who showed such understanding. "Thank you, Mr. July." Were she feeling up to snuff, she might have asked him where he'd learned to be so chivalrous, but the lingering effects of the heatstroke had her at such sixes and sevens that she simply wanted to get home and lie down.

"You were worried about the gossips."

"I was."

"Well, this way, you won't have to be."

Their eyes held. Unable to resist, Neil ran a knuckle down her brown cheek. The feel of her satin-soft skin hit him like the kick of a mule. "Let's get you home."

His touch made Olivia's insides reel; not even sunstroke could shield her from the riot of sensations brought on by his charged presence. When he'd dismounted, the brief moments of contact between his powerful body and hers had set off sparks against her skin.

On his feet now, Neil took hold of Black's bridle, and she took up the reins.

Although they were again underway, Olivia struggled to stay upright in the saddle. The motion of the horse and the waves of distress washing over her joined forces to undermine her determination. She kept telling herself, *Just a bit more and you'll be home*, but she wasn't sure how much longer she could hold on.

Neil hadn't been to Henry Adams in years, and he looked forward to seeing Chase Jefferson again. They'd met initially as military men. Chase had been a sergeant with the famous Tenth Cavalry, and Neil had been a member of the celebrated Seminole Negro scouts. Now, Neil robbed trains, and Chase wore a star. Neil and Shafts didn't commit crimes in this portion of the state out of respect for Chase—and because they knew he'd toss them in jail if they did. Chase Jefferson took his job seriously, just as seriously as he'd taken being a Union soldier, and later, after the war, a Buffalo Soldier.

Neil was surprised to see how much Henry Adams had grown since his last visit. It was his business to stay abreast of the ways of the railroads, and he knew about the rumors that claimed the railroad was coming to serve the Black residents of the valley. Everything he'd heard said Henry Adams would be the town chosen, as opposed to the better-known Nicodemus. Many businesses were also placing their bets on Henry Adams and were deserting the other colonies in Barton and Rice Counties to resettle here.

Leading the horse down Main Street, he kept one eye on Olivia and the other on the new businesses. He saw a bank, a barbershop, and a hotel on land that he remembered being open and unplowed. He contrasted this thriving township with his poverty-stricken hometown, where there were no stores, hotels, or newspapers—just old people and children trying to survive on whatever their able-bodied family members could provide. Thinking about home made the old anger rise. He pushed away the festering bitterness and looked for the doctor's office.

Because it was the end of the day, there were only a few citizens on the plank walks that connected the string of shops and businesses. The sight of a distressed-looking Miss Olivia seated on the back of a big black horse being led by a big, muscular Black man made them stop and stare curiously.

Sheriff Chase Jefferson was on his way to the telegraph office when he saw them. He too stopped. *What in the hell is Olivia Sterling doing with Neil July?!* Stepping off the walk and down into the street, he went to find out.

Neil noted that the doctor's office was no longer where it had been on his last visit. He looked up at Olivia, intending to ask her where it was, only to see her weaving slowly back and forth, as if she'd lost the battle to ride into town under her own steam. Alarmed, he said, *To hell with the gossips*, and eased her from the saddle and into his arms. "I have you," he said softly. "Don't worry."

Looking around at the shocked, frozen faces of the townspeople, Neil shouted, "Somebody get the doc!"

Seeing Chase running toward him filled him with relief. "She needs a doc!"

Chase could see the staring citizens. Feeling the need to guard Olivia's reputation until this could be sorted out, he said to Neil, "Doc Johnson's up the street. I'll carry her."

"No. Just show me!"

The serious set of Neil's features told all, so Chase didn't argue and led the way.

When Olivia came around this time, she noted the darkness and a small light glowing somewhere, lifting the gloom. She was in a bed, and she recognized the surroundings as her bedroom. The chair beside the bed was occupied by her good friend, Cara Lee Jefferson. Cara was reading a newspaper by the dim light of the lamp on Olivia's nightstand.

"Hello," Olivia croaked from her dry-as-a-desert throat.

The paper was immediately lowered and set aside. "Hello, yourself. You had us all worried."

Olivia offered a shaky smile in reply. "Sorry for all the bother. It was the heat. Lord, I'm so thirsty, I could drink the Great Solomon."

"How about we start with a *cup* of the Solomon first?" Cara Lee picked up a pitcher and poured water into a cup.

Olivia struggled to sit up and took the cup with shaking hands. To aid her, Cara placed her own hands on top of Olivia's and helped guide the vessel so Olivia could drink.

"Slowly," Cara warned. "Not too much at first."

Obeying, Olivia satisfied her thirst, then the cup was placed back on the nightstand.

Cara asked, "Now, how do you feel?"

"Like I was dragged behind a horse."

"Doc says you might have eaten some tainted food. He wants you to drink plenty of water for the next few days."

Olivia thought back on her visit to Ellis, but her mind was too foggy to remember what she'd eaten. "What time is it?"

"Almost midnight."

"Did Mary Ann and the baby make it?"

Cara nodded. "She and the others rode in a few hours ago. Her husband had tears in his eyes when he held the baby."

Olivia was glad to hear they'd arrived safely. "She said he'd never seen the child."

"They had a very happy reunion."

"The aunt was a crow, though. Mary Ann's going to have to lock her in the storm cellar."

Cara laughed. "You must be on the mend—that legendary wit has returned."

"The woman was awful on the ride in the coach."

Silence stretched between the two friends, then Cara said, "Neil July was very concerned about you."

The memory of him was sharp, even if nothing else was. "Are he and his brother still in town?"

"Yes. Last I saw they were on their way to Sophie's poker game."

"I'll always be grateful for his assistance."

"He wants to see you before he rides out in the morning. Think you're up to it?"

"If not, I'll pretend. I'd like to thank him personally for his help."

Cara nodded. "I'll have Chase let him know. In the meantime, Dr. Johnson doesn't want you to be alone tonight, so the ladies and I volunteered to take shifts. Mine ends at midnight."

"Who takes over then?"

"Sophie."

"Isn't she playing poker?"

"That she is, but she's promised to have the

men's wallets cleaned out by the time she's due to relieve me."

Olivia quipped, "If the twins had any gold on them when they came to town, they won't when she's done fleecing them."

At that moment, the bell on Olivia's front door tolled, signaling a visitor. "That must be her now," Cara said.

Sophie Reynolds's pale gold complexion glowed as it caught the flickering light of the dimmed lamps. "How are you, Olivia?"

"Mending."

"Good to hear. You gave us all a fright."

The owner of Henry Adams's two hotels turned to Cara and said, "You can go on home now, Cara Lee. I left your husband enough money to buy you something pretty, but not much else."

Cara's head shook with amusement. "Thanks, Soph." She then squeezed Olivia's hand in parting. "I'll see you later today."

Olivia held onto Cara's hand for a moment and said genuinely, "Thank you."

Cara waved off the words. "I'd be a poor friend if I hadn't come to see about you."

Cara showed both women a smile, then quietly departed.

Sophie took the chair vacated by the schoolteacher, and Olivia drifted back to sleep on thoughts of Neil July.

The next morning, Olivia awakened to the smells of coffee and the familiar female voices of her neighbors Daisy Miller and Rachel Eddings drifting in from the kitchen; both made her smile. The two elderly women were members of the original colonists who'd founded Henry Adams, and they were known around town as the Two Spinsters. Originally there'd been Three Spinsters, but Lucretia Potter had died of pneumonia the winter before Olivia's arrival.

Rachel, dressed in her usual attire of men's trousers and shirt, stuck her gray head around the doorjamb. Upon seeing Olivia awake, she removed her pipe from her mouth and called to Daisy. "She's up."

Without further word, Rachel walked over and placed a motherly palm on Olivia's forehead. "Skin's cooler," she declared. "How about your other parts?"

Olivia's head was clear and no longer pounding. "I feel much better." The queasiness in her stomach was gone as well. She still felt weak as linen, though.

Rachel sat in the chair by the bed. "That's good news. Delbert says we're to keep an eye on you. No activities until the end of the week."

Delbert was Dr. Johnson's given name, and Olivia had no intentions of lolling around until week's end. "The Elders meeting is tonight."

Wearing a faded brown dress, Daisy Miller entered the bedroom carrying a tray that held a cup of coffee and a plate holding two hot brown biscuits. "Yes it is, but *you* won't be attending. I'll take your place as secretary until you're back on your feet."

Daisy was the town telegraph clerk and the past recording secretary for the Elders, so Olivia knew not to worry about the job being done well. She also knew from experience that arguing with the Two Spinsters about anything only made them dig in their seventy-year-old heels, so she sat up and accepted the tray from Daisy's hand.

Daisy then added, "Reverend Whitfield says he'll conduct the junior choir rehearsal tomorrow night for you, and of course all surveying will be suspended until you're really better."

Olivia heard the inflection on the word *really* and smiled to herself. They'd been mothering her since she'd come to town and purchased the late Lucretia Potter's millinery store. They'd also become her friends, and she appreciated them as much as she did their concern for her welfare. The surveying had to do with the Henry Adams Ladies Historical Society and their project to redo the maps of the original homesteads. The old maps had been discovered in a trunk back in '82, but they'd been so damaged by mildew and mold many were undecipherable. Olivia and a few volunteers were combing the countryside searching for the homes and farms established by the original colonists so the maps could be restored. "Can I attend the Literary Club meeting tomorrow evening?"

"We'll see how you're faring," Rachel replied. "For now, Daisy and I will tidy up your kitchen. You. Rest."

Rachel handed her a copy of *The Colored Patriot*, a newspaper published in Topeka. The date on the banner read April 20, but people in the west were accustomed to reading old news.

The Two Spinsters went back to the kitchen and Olivia opened the paper. She scanned an article on the newly appointed minister to Liberia, a North Carolina educator named Ezekiel Ezra Smith, then turned her attention to the editorial. It voiced disgust at Jim Crow's increasing stranglehold on the race but urged its readers to continue to strive with the hopes that one day "Every man shall be free and equal—equal under the law, equal in every condition, equal in every avenue and walk."

At noon, Cara Lee Jefferson arrived to relieve the Two Spinsters. Accompanying her was Neil July. Olivia would have preferred to receive him fully dressed and standing, but being in bed in her night rail was all she had. He was dressed as he had been yesterday, and he had his flat crowned hat in his hand. If it were possible, he seemed even more handsome than she remembered; an ebony god with a gun belt girdling his loins.

"Afternoon, Miss Olivia. Came to see how you were doing."

"Much better, thanks to you."

When he smiled in reply, Olivia decided it was the smile that was most devastating. The accenting mustache added to the potency.

"So I passed the gentleman test?"

She amended her earlier assessment; his eyes were equally powerful. And yes, he had passed the test. He'd been kind and concerned, unexpected qualities in a man wanted by the law. "You passed with flying colors, Mr. July. I couldn't have asked for a more gracious escort."

Neil was pleased by her words. He also liked the way her smile made him feel inside. "Then I expect you to be up and around when I come back to visit the sheriff. He and I are old friends."

Olivia was surprised by that news; she didn't know the two were acquainted. However, the underlying directness in July's gaze gave her the impression that Sheriff Jefferson wasn't the only person he would be coming to see, and that made her heart pound with an uncharacteristic anticipation beneath her white cotton nightgown. Chastising herself for having thoughts and reactions more suitable for a silly young girl, she grabbed hold of herself. "I will be, and I'll be expecting the return of my cameo next time we meet."

"I'll have it."

Their eyes held, and Olivia found herself responding to a silent call she'd never heard before this particular man had entered her life.

Neil didn't want to leave her, but Shafts was waiting, and so was that Kansas City gold train.

Olivia didn't want him to leave either. Even though the thought was highly improper considering who he was and how he made his living, she knew there was more to Neil July than his penchant for robbing trains. "Hopefully, you'll be gainfully employed when we meet again."

He gave her a grin she felt down to her toes, then said, "I think you already know my answer to that." Neil studied her beautiful face and once again wished he didn't have to leave. "The doc said I'm not to tire you out, so I guess I should be going."

Olivia fought to hide her disappointment.

"*Adios*, Miss Olivia."

Resonating in response to his soft words of parting, she said, "Good-bye, Mr. July. Thank you again."

He nodded to her, then to Cara, and departed, his boots sounding loud on the plank wood floor.

When the women were alone, Cara surveyed Olivia for a long moment, then asked, "Is it just me, or did the temperature rise in here a bit?"

An embarrassed Olivia dropped her eyes to the crocheted white coverlet covering her body.

Cara said, "He's an outlaw, Olivia."

"I know, but—"

"But what?"

"Let's just say, I wish he weren't, because he's a very interesting man."

"Yet you're talking about meeting him again?"

"Just so I can get back my mother's cameo."

Cara studied her skeptically.

Olivia explained the circumstances surrounding her first encounter with Neil July but left out the part about the kiss she still owed.

At the end of the tale, Cara searched Olivia's features and said sagely, "I get the sense that there's more to this than you're letting on, Miss Olivia Sterling, but I won't press. He is a handsome devil, though."

"That he is, but he's also a wanted man. It's a shame, really."

Cara Lee said, "Can you imagine the gossip if you took up with an outlaw?"

"I'd be run out of town on a rail."

"Sybil Whitfield once told me a man that handsome could make a woman break every code she's ever lived by."

"I don't doubt that. He probably has a string of brokenhearted women from here to Mexico." Olivia then asked, "Was Mrs. Whitfield talking about anyone in particular when she said that to you?"

Cara didn't respond.

Olivia searched her face. "Cara? Was she?"

Cara finally replied, "Yes."

"Who?"

"Chase."

Olivia's eyes widened.

Cara gave her an embarrassed grin. "I'll tell you the story one day when you feel better."

"I'm better *now*," Olivia countered with a laugh. "So, did you?"

"Did I what?"

"Break every code?"

Cara smiled as if thinking back, then confessed in a satisfied voice, "Oh, yes."

Their eyes met, and their combined peals of laughter filled the house.

Chapter 3

The Two Spinsters were correct; Doc Johnson didn't let Olivia resume her activities for the remainder of the week, but by church on Sunday she was rested and feeling like herself again. Monday morning she walked over to the Malloy Mercantile to see if a new batch of the scented soaps she was partial to had come in. Armstead Malloy's edifice to commerce was two stories high and three lots wide. On the shelves inside were the latest firearms from Smith and Wesson, magazines like *Life* and the *Ladies' Home Journal*, farm implements, and postage stamps and saddles. He sold ready-made suits and dresses, modern stoves, washer machines, and perfume he claimed came all the way from France. He stocked such a variety of goods that the sign over the door stated, IF MALLOY'S DON'T SELL IT—YOU DON'T NEED IT.

There were quite a few customers inside when she entered, and many greeted her with smiles, which she returned in kind. To her delight, the soap had indeed arrived. There was also a new shipment of ladies' hairbrushes. One with a tortoiseshell handle caught her eye, so she took it and her two bars of soap to the counter. There were three people in line ahead of her, so she waited her turn. The jars of penny candy on the counter reminded her that she needed to replenish the candy jar she kept in her shop for the children who accompanied her customers. On the opposite end of the counter was a short wooden crock filled with pickles in brine. The pickles, like the cracker barrel standing by the front door, were standard fare at most stores on the plains. Olivia liked crackers but wasn't particularly fond of pickles.

Malloy was behind the counter. Olivia hadn't seen him since their ill-fated journey from Ellis last week, and she hoped he was through pestering her with his unwanted proposals. When he glanced up from the register and saw her, his eyes turned cold and he looked away. He waited on the folks in front of her, and when it was Olivia's turn, she stepped up to the counter and placed her purchases on it.

"Well, if it isn't the outlaw lover," Malloy said harshly.

Olivia was caught off guard. "Excuse me?"

"I said, if it isn't the outlaw lover," he repeated. "Did you let him kiss you?"

Confused, Olivia studied him as if he'd grown two heads.

"Did you let that filthy killer kiss you?"

Now she understood, but before she could respond, he snarled, "Don't play the innocent. I saw the eyes you were making at him, and the way he was making them back. Heard he carried you through town."

Olivia looked around at the faces of the other customers. Every eye in the place was focused on her. Gossip would follow this incident for sure. She said coolly, "Yes, he carried me through town—to Dr. Johnson's office."

"Same way he carried you around when he took you out of the coach?"

Now that he had everyone's undivided attention, he called out, "I tried to save her reputation, but July put her on his horse, snuggled up real close, and rode off. Left me standing in the dust."

Olivia didn't believe he was twisting the truth this way. "I was ill, Mr. Malloy, and there was no room for three people on the back of the horse."

"Bet that vermin took all kinds of liberties."

Olivia's eyes widened, and anger began to build. "There were no liberties taken. July was a perfect gentleman."

Malloy scoffed, "Do you deny that you spent more time talking with him than you did to me?"

"Is that what this attack is about—your pride?"

"My pride and your reputation."

Olivia had no intentions of enduring any more of his verbal nonsense. "Keep the soap and the brush. I'll be shopping elsewhere from now on. Good day, Mr. Malloy."

"That's fine. You go ahead and run off. No telling what you two were engaged in on the ride back to town."

She wanted to throttle him. "I demand an apology!"

"Demand all you want. I'm the one needing an apology for thinking you were a *lady!*"

Gasps came from the female customers.

Malloy gave her a nasty little grin. "First story I print in my newspaper is going to be about you and that outlaw seed you're probably carrying."

The scandalous implication made Olivia want to shake him until his teeth rattled loose. The need to retaliate in some form or fashion surged through her frame with such force that she thought she might explode. Had there been a weapon on the counter she might have shot him. Instead, spying the pickle barrel, she picked it up and pointedly dumped the contents over his head. While he sputtered and cursed, she tossed the barrel aside and snapped, "Print *that* in your newspaper, little man!"

As she pushed her way through the doors, applause broke out behind her, but she didn't stop.

Sure that steam was pouring out of her ears, Olivia returned to her shop. As a Christian woman, she regretted her loss of control. Pouring a pickle barrel over Malloy's head had not been the most charitable thing she could have done, or the most ladylike, but he'd deserved the dousing. Olivia had always harbored a temper, but because society demanded women suppress those parts of their personalities, she'd worked hard all of her life to keep it hidden. Not today. Today she'd had no control. This was the same lack of control that had fueled her decision to sell her shop and leave for Kansas. Her father had encouraged her to ride, read, go to Oberlin, run her own shop, and take pride in all of those accomplishments, yet he'd expected her to go meekly into the marriage he'd arranged because that is what females were supposed to do. Underneath it all she loved her father, but apparently it had never occurred to him that the unconventional way in which he'd raised her might butt horns with his desire to make her a traditional wife. *Maybe temper in a woman is good thing*, she decided. It certainly let men like Malloy and her father know that she was not to be taken lightly. In the end, Olivia wasn't sorry about what happened with Malloy at all; her only regret was that the pickle barrel hadn't been larger.

Later that afternoon, the sheriff stopped by her shop. "Heard you had a run-in with Armstead Malloy."

Olivia set aside the fabric she was pinning onto a dress form. "Yes, I did."

"He's filed an assault complaint."

"He should be glad I didn't take a bullwhip to him after what he accused me of."

"So I heard, but next time can you come to me first, please, and I'll handle it."

"It was my reputation he smeared, Sheriff. Not yours."

"I understand that, but I can't have you pouring pickles on somebody every time you get mad."

She turned and faced him. "Have I ever done anything like that before?"

"Well, no, and frankly, the people in the store were real surprised. Miss Olivia, town committee member and Sunday school teacher, waking snakes—we've never seen this side of you."

Olivia chuckled at his reference to waking snakes. The phrase meant causing a ruckus, and it had become one of her favorite plains sayings. "That's probably because I've not lived here long enough, nor have I ever been publicly slandered before. Had I been a man, I would have called him out."

"Had you been a man he couldn't have made the accusation." He smiled. "So, now that you've shown your true colors, I'll be adding your name to my list of unruly females."

Eyes sparkling, Olivia asked, "Who else is on it?"

He thought about the question for a moment, then said, "Let's see. There's my wife. Sophie. Sybil Whitfield. The Two Spinsters. Did I already mention my wife?"

Olivia thought Chase Jefferson was the best sheriff a town could have. "I'd be honored to be in such august company."

"Don't doubt you would," he replied, chuckling, then added, "but no more pickle fits. I'll speak to Malloy about his mouth and about dropping the charges."

"Thank you, Sheriff, because pigs will fly before I give him an apology."

"Duly noted." Chase headed toward the door, then stopped, as if he'd remembered something else he wanted to say. "Oh, the Terrible Twins and their friends stuck up a gold train a few days ago."

Olivia found the news disappointing. "They didn't hurt anyone, did they?"

"Just the pride of the army and the railroad. Even with Pinkertons posing as passengers, the Twins got away with the strongboxes. Warrants for their arrest came over the wire late last night. The railroad's offering a king's ransom for their capture."

"How much?"

"Thousand dollars. Dead or alive."

Olivia's heart sank. "That means bounty hunters, doesn't it?"

"Yep, but they've been after the Twins for years. So far only one has ever brought them in. Man called the Preacher."

"Were they sent to prison?"

"Nope. Busted out of the jail the night before the judge arrived. Trial was never held."

Olivia shook her head in disbelief.

Chase added, "So, if Neil and his brother come back this way, the marshal in Topeka will be expecting me to arrest him."

Olivia met his eye without guilt. "Of course, but I doubt Mr. July would be that reckless."

Chase was silent for a moment, then said, "Beautiful woman will make a man do all sorts of crazy things."

Olivia stared. *Surely he isn't implying. . . .*

He touched his hat and with a smile, was gone.

For the next few moments, Olivia stood in the silence, thinking about the sheriff's departing words. Would Neil July really come back here—to see her? Deep down inside she found the prospect thrilling, but common sense said no. He'd been robbing banks a long time, and she assumed he and his brother would find a safe place to hide until the smoke cleared rather than risk returning to Henry Adams and maybe be arrested.

Apparently Sheriff Jefferson thought otherwise. Had July said something about her to the sheriff to make Jefferson say what he had? July had promised to return her mother's cameo and *you still owe him a kiss,* a voice in her head offered as a reminder. Olivia pushed the voice aside. Neil July was a man with a price on his head; she'd probably never see him or her mother's cameo again, and for reasons she couldn't explain, the knowledge saddened her.

Over the weeks that followed Olivia spent all of her days and many of her nights sewing for her customers and helping spruce up the town in preparation for the Elders Ball. Centerpieces had to be made for the tables, dishes for the potluck had to be coordinated, musicians had to be found and auditioned, decorations for the new town hall had to be fashioned, and because Olivia was on the ball's organizing committee, much of the overseeing fell on her shoulders. She didn't mind—not really—but she was looking forward to the night of the ball and the end of her involvement so she could keel over from exhaustion.

The night of the ball finally arrived. Olivia was seated on her back porch, which faced the open plains, listening to the lively music and the happy voices of the celebrants over at the spanking-new town hall floating on the air. Granted, she would have preferred to have been there in person as opposed to sitting home alone, but she'd made up her mind not to be one of the unmarried women relegated to serving the attendees punch and cake; all the pitying looks she'd received last year had left her depressed.

So this evening she was in the old rocker on her back porch. She had a cold tumbler of lemonade sitting on the upside-down barrel she used as the porch's table, and in her pocket was the letter she'd just written to her mother. Now, with the day's chores behind her, she just wanted to relax and listen to the sounds of the celebrating.

Last year's ball had been held on a Saturday night and had gone on until the wee hours of the morning. As a result, folks were so tuckered out from the good time, very few had shown up for church. Out of respect for Reverend Whitfield—and because no one wanted to hear another fire-and-brimstone sermon on the Responsibilities of Church Attendance, this year's ball had been moved to a Friday night in the hopes of everyone recovering in time to say their amens come Sunday morning.

Olivia had been in Henry Adams less than a year now, but even she could recognize the sounds of Handy's expert fiddling. No one in the valley could match his skill on the instrument. The lively tune he was sawing at now made Olivia tap her feet. The music captured her, and before she knew it she was up and dancing in the darkness. Claimed by the spirited music, she was soon waving the hems of her skirts and thoroughly enjoying her play. All around the porch she went, twirling past her barrel table and the old overstuffed rocker. She stepped in time to the fast-paced jig and was soon laughing aloud. She turned her back and sidestepped across the porch. She turned again and froze at the sight of the man leaning against the house. It was Neil July, and Olivia could neither speak nor move.

He touched his hat. "Evenin'. Mighty fine dancing."

In an awe-filled voice she asked, "What are you doing here?"

"Came to see how you were faring."

"I—I'm fine."

"I'm fine, too."

Olivia admitted that she'd been secretly hoping for another encounter with him, but never in her wildest dreams had she imagined he'd appear this way, seemingly out of nowhere. The dark coffee skin, the vivid eyes, the lip-framing mustache; he was everything that *good* women were supposed to run for the hills from. He was an outlaw, for heaven's sake, but the urge to know him better was strong. "You shouldn't have come."

He pushed away from the wall, and his shadowy form came closer. "Why not?"

Olivia's eyes brushed over his gun belt, his double-breasted leather shirt, and the way the leather trousers hugged his hips and thighs. She forced her attention back to his face. "Sheriff Jefferson says the marshal down in Topeka wants you arrested."

"Then we'll have to make sure he doesn't know I'm here."

Olivia's heart was beating so fast.

Neil feasted his eyes on the tall, beautiful Olivia. He had no idea why he'd come. Shafts had declared him loco for wanting to ride to Henry Adams instead of directly to Indian Territory to lay low and visit with their sister Teresa while the Pinkertons chased their tails looking for the stolen gold. In the end, Shafts had opted for the territory and Neil had ridden on alone, still not sure why, but driven by an unknown force to see the seamstress. And here he stood, bewitched by a woman he barely knew and he'd found her dancing. "Usually after a job I head for a hole in the wall, but for some reason, I had to see you first. . . ."

The soft, sweet power in his voice and words closed her eyes. "You should go, Mr. July. . . ." Those were the words she was supposed to say, even if she didn't mean them.

"I will, in a minute."

The sounds of the celebration could still be heard, but to Olivia they seemed miles and miles away.

"Brought you something." He slipped his hand into his shirt and withdrew her mother's cameo.

On shaking legs she walked over to the edge of the porch, then stepped down into the moonlit grass. She held out her hand to take the broach, but he shook his head and smiled. "Turn around," he said.

She did, and he gently draped the indigo ribbon around her neck and tied a tiny knot in the two ends. The cameo had been given to Olivia by her mother on Olivia's eighteenth birthday, and she was pleased by its return. She faced him again, and all she could see and feel was him.

The slow ballad now rising from Handy's fiddle replaced the lively tune she'd danced to earlier, and the pure, flawless melody rode on the night's gentle breeze.

"Dance with me . . . and I'll go." Neil wanted so much more, and not all of it had to do with physical attraction. He wanted to sit with her, talk with her; hear about her childhood, listen to her dreams. In reality they were strangers, but deep down inside, hidden parts of himself were surfacing to let him know that he *knew* her. In many ways he wanted to jump on his horse and ride away as fast as he could. Olivia was a life-changing woman; a woman capable of making a man lay down his guns just to please her, and that scared him to death. On the other hand, the smell of her lavender perfume was as vivid in his memory as the softness of her brown skin the one time he'd stroked her cheek. *Life-changing*—but he held out his arms to her anyway.

Olivia hesitated. Would she be a changed woman when the dance was done? She was no child; she knew the answer and went to him willingly.

When she placed her hand into his, every inch of her was shaking. His hand was large, the fingers long. The gentle hand resting against her blouse-covered back unleashed a warmth that snaked up her spine and slowly fanned out across her shoulders and down her arms.

They began to waltz. His steps were flawless, and once again she was surprised by the outlaw Neil July. He danced with the skill of a Haitian prince. "Where did you learn to waltz?"

"Indian school. They thought teaching us to waltz would make us forget our culture."

"How long were you in school?"

"Long enough to know that many of the teachers hated us even more than we hated them."

Soon they were moving all over the yard, and she matched him step for step. Olivia loved to dance and knew she'd remember this particular moonlit night forever. She smiled up into his sparkling eyes, and in response he grinned and began to twirl her, faster and then faster, until finally he slowed and they were no longer moving. The world seemed to have slowed as well. When he raised her hand to his lips, then gently kissed the tips of her fingers, Olivia's knees went weak.

He raised her chin so their eyes could meet in the dark. "You owe me a kiss. . . ."

She couldn't speak.

He leaned down and kissed her, no warning, no chance to say no, and she let it happen; let the warmth of his mouth settle onto hers, showing her what it meant to be kissed by a man. Heated, feather-light brushes of his mouth over her bottom lip and the trembling corners of her mouth made them part. Passion swept through her for the very first time in her life. He slid his hand around her waist and eased her close enough to feel his hard frame singe her through her clothing. After a few more passion-filled moments, the sensations became too much for a woman who had no experience with men. Olivia dragged her mouth from his and backed away dazzled, dizzied, and breathless.

The moonlight caught the glitter in his eyes, and she didn't know what to do or say. She now understood what Cara and Mrs. Whitfield meant about certain men making a woman break every code; Neil July was one of those men. For the sake of herself and her reputation, she couldn't see him again.

The kiss left Neil just as moved. Every male inch of his body wanted more; now. He wanted to ride with her across the moonlit plains and kiss her until the rising of tomorrow's sun. It was not to be, however; she was a good woman and he was a wanted man. By all rights he should go. He'd returned her mother's cameo, and the memory of her kiss would resonate for a lifetime, but he didn't want to go. "Will you sit with me a while, Olivia? . . ."

With his kiss still echoing within her, Lord knew she wanted to say yes, but what if they were seen? She'd already been subjected to Armstead Malloy's vicious tongue; she didn't want to be gossiped about again. But being with him out here in the dark made her feel like Eve in the garden standing before the tree of forbidden fruit. Instead of denying his request, she asked, "Will you promise to be a gentleman?"

Amused by the question from this good woman, Neil replied, "Seeing as how I want to kiss you again . . . all I will promise is that I will try. How's that?"

Olivia was certain that Neil July was dangerous in ways she was too naive to recognize. She knew nothing about the heat between a man and a woman because it was not something she and her mother had ever discussed. From her limited experience, it was apparently something no women ever discussed. She suddenly needed a cold drink. "Would you like some lemonade?"

"Yes, ma'am, I would. Thank you."

"Take a seat and I'll be back shortly."

Olivia went into the house and poured him some from the pitcher in her icebox. As she poured a fresh tumbler for herself, the voice of reason in her head asked if her brain was addled. In a way, she believed it was. No self-respecting woman would be entertaining a wanted criminal on her back porch, let alone offering him lemonade.

Neil took the cold metal cup from her hand and took a sip. The beverage was tart but sweet—just the way he liked it. He noted that she'd taken a seat in the rocker instead of sitting on the porch by his side, but he didn't mind; the kiss they'd shared would breach any distance. "Why'd you come to Kansas?"

"To escape an arranged marriage."

Neil turned and studied her in the dark. It was not the answer he'd been expecting. "Why didn't you want to marry?"

"The man didn't value me, and I doubted he ever would."

Neil said, "My da once told me that a woman who knows her own mind is worth more than gold."

Olivia thought his da was very wise. "The man set on marrying me would probably disagree."

"Did your parents approve of you coming out here?"

"My mother did—does, she and I correspond regularly. My father—he doesn't know where I am."

Neil went still. "Why not?"

"Because I ran away from home. Can you imagine, at my age."

He thanked the ancestors for the full moon. It helped him see her face. She was smiling. "You must have been very upset to come all this way."

"I wanted to be far enough away that my father couldn't find me."

He laughed softly.

"What's so funny?"

"You're one of those rebellious females."

She grinned and shrugged. "I suppose I am, but I refuse to be treated like a potted plant. It isn't how I was raised."

"How were you raised?"

"To read the weekly papers, to go to school and then to Oberlin."

"You went to Oberlin?"

"Yes. Finished the woman's program and found that my graduating certificate qualified me to do very little besides marry, so I returned to the dress shop I had been working in since adolescence. When the owner died, she willed the place to me, and suddenly I was a businesswoman."

Neil was impressed. She was not only beautiful and articulate but also intelligent and smart enough to know her own worth. "So now you are in Kansas."

"Yes, and enjoying living my life on my own terms."

"So am I."

Olivia had to ask, "Did you really start robbing trains to feed your family?"

He nodded.

"Are your people that destitute?"

"At the time, more destitute than the old chiefs could ever have imagined. Our children, our elders; were it not for the gold they would not have survived."

"Did the authorities know this?"

"That my people were starving? Yes."

"No. I mean do they know why you do what you do?"

"No, and if you told them they'd never believe it anyway. In this country the native tribes are supposed to starve."

She now understood the root of his bitterness. According to the newspapers, the Indians' problems stemmed from their own refusal to accept assimilation. As a member of a race of people newly freed, Olivia knew that the issues surrounding the tribes had to be more complex than that. "So what are you going to do about the bounty hunters? The sheriff says you have almost a thousand dollars on your head."

"Do what we've always done—ignore them."

"But what if they find you?"

"They won't, so how about we talk about something else," he offered in a quiet voice.

Considering the dangerous men he might be facing, Olivia thought he was being very cocky, but he was the outlaw; she was just a seamstress. "Such as?"

"Such as, why aren't you over at the hall dancing with some fella instead of here in the dark with me?"

The rush of the kiss came back on the heels of his words, and she unconsciously touched her fingers to her lips and the memories they held. Gathering herself, she told the truth. "No one asked me."

"That's hard to believe."

"Not really. A woman living life on her own terms is not what men want out here. They want meekness, compliance, and for me to give up my business and all I've learned so that I may sit at their table and nod yes to everything they say."

Neil scanned her dark form. Outside of his sister and a few old cathouse queens, he knew very few women who didn't want to rope some poor dope into hitching his wagon to hers and supporting the children she planned to have. "Well, stick to your guns."

"I intend to."

He wanted to take her in his arms again and see if her lips were as sweet as they'd been a few moments ago, but he drained the remainder of his lemonade instead. "I better get going."

Olivia stood. More than anything she wished he were a clerk or a cooper, or even a sheriff so that what had begun here might continue, but he wasn't. "Thank you again for the cameo."

He stepped up on the porch, and her senses began to shimmer.

"Here's your cup back," he said, drinking her in with his eyes.

She took the vessel from his hand. "Thank you."

"And thank you for the kiss," he whispered. He leaned down and gently brushed his lips over hers, then slowly repeated the caress. "Good-bye, Olivia . . ." he murmured.

The kiss, the voice; she was melting like ice on a stove. He backed away and touched his fingers to her lips in farewell. A moment later he was gone.

Olivia stood in the darkness a long time.

The Henry Adams Ladies Historical Society met once a month at the home of Cara Lee Jefferson. The house, one of the largest in the area, was situated on the plains outside of town. When Olivia arrived for the meeting, she wasn't surprised that the only other buggy parked outside belonged to the Two Spinsters. More than likely everyone else was home sleeping off last night's festivities.

Cara and the spinsters were on the porch enjoying the cool morning breeze and metal tumblers of lemonade. Branch Jefferson, Cara and Chase's five-year-old son, was seated on the steps with a cup of his own. He was the spitting image of his father, but he had his mama's smile.

Cara Lee called out, "Morning, Olivia. You're not carrying pickles, are you?"

Olivia laughed, and Rachel Eddings pulled her pipe out of her mouth and cracked, "Too bad there wasn't enough brine in the barrel to drown him."

Olivia replied, "I agree. Nasty little man."

Cara Lee said, "Well, that nasty little man may be the next mayor."

Olivia patted Branch lovingly on the head as she passed him on the steps and asked, "What do you mean, the next mayor?" She took a seat, and Daisy poured Olivia some lemonade.

"Martin Stuckey died last night."

"What? When?" Martin Stuckey had been the mayor for many years. He was in his eighties but still spry enough to have sent away for a mail order bride last year who was to everyone's surprise five decades his junior.

"Died dancing one of Handy's jigs."

Olivia couldn't believe her ears. "Last night at the ball?"

"Yep. Keeled over and was gone before anyone could get to him," Daisy explained.

The news saddened Olivia. Mayor Stuckey had always been a nice man.

Rachel said, "We all knew that young woman would kill him. Never thought it would be on the dance floor, though."

Cara looked to her son and said, "Branch, honey. Go and see if the hens have any eggs."

"Yes, Mama." He took off at a run for the coops behind the house.

Cara said, "Now that little ears are gone, we can talk."

Olivia said, "I'm sorry to hear about his passing, but where does Malloy fit into the picture?"

"As the men were carrying Martin's body out, Malloy announced his intentions to run for mayor."

Olivia's mouth dropped.

Cara said, "My sentiments exactly. Can you imagine how he'll be strutting around if he gets the post?"

Daisy said, "He'll have to be elected first."

Like women in some of the other Black townships on the plains, the women of Henry Adams were allowed to vote on local issues. The ladies took full advantage of the privilege and came out in force on election day to ensure that their voices be heard on township matters.

"Is anyone else going to throw their hat into the ring?" Olivia asked hopefully.

Cara Lee shook her head. "Far as I know, Malloy is it for now."

Olivia didn't like the sound of that at all. "There has to be someone interested."

Rachel said, "Harvest is coming—folks are too busy to play politician. The Elders have called for an emergency town meeting tomorrow evening to sort it all out. Let's pray someone challenges Malloy for the nomination. Otherwise . . ."

Olivia sighed. Contemplating Malloy as mayor did not make for a happy rest of the day.

Chapter 4

On Sundays, Henry Adams rested. In keeping with the Sabbath, stores were closed, farmers set aside their tools, and everyone went to church. After church, families usually gathered over supper. However, on this particular Sunday, instead of spending the remainder of the day resting, visiting, or reading their Bibles, the citizens headed to the new town hall to see who wanted to be mayor. The late Mayor Stuckey had been laid to rest at this morning's church service.

Olivia was seated at a table in her shop leafing through the latest editions of Godey's Lady's Book in search of new pattern ideas when she glanced up at the clock on the wall. Seeing it was half past seven, she hastily set aside the magazines and prepared to leave. The town meeting called by the

85

Board of Elders would begin in less than thirty minutes, and it wouldn't be good for the recording secretary of the board to be late.

Taking a quick look around to make sure no lamps were burning, she grabbed up her ledger and handbag, and headed outside to her buggy. The hall, situated on the outskirts of Henry Adams, was only a short ten-minute drive away. Normally, she would have walked, but she really didn't want to be late.

When Olivia arrived, the low-slung building, with its fresh white paint and red roof, was surrounded by all manner of carriages, buggies, wagons, and buckboards. She recognized many of them as belonging to neighbors from all over the valley. It pleased her to see so many citizens interested in the future of their township—she just wished they'd left her a place to park.

The field behind the building offered a few open spaces, so she tied the reins of her horse to the hitching post and hurried to the door. On her way she passed many of her neighbors. They waved and Olivia waved back but didn't tarry.

Once inside she was met by a sea of Black folks, talking, laughing, sitting. A meeting like this not only functioned as a forum for decision making but also had social benefits. It offered everyone an opportunity to come together to catch up on gossip, political issues, and small-town goings-on, and all talk today centered on the candidates for mayor.

Since it didn't appear to Olivia as if Asa Landis, the president of the town's Elder Board, had arrived yet, she made her way through the crush to the front of the room where Cara Lee Jefferson stood talking with her sheriff husband.

"Oh, there you are," Cara said with a smile. "Trouble finding a place to leave the buggy?"

Olivia nodded. "They may have to start stacking vehicles on top of each other out there pretty soon." She couldn't believe the number of people in attendance. "My goodness, there are a lot of folks here."

Chase said, "Real impressive, don't you think?"

Olivia agreed. She'd thought she knew everyone in the valley, so she was surprised to see more than a few faces that she didn't recognize.

The room was loud with the buzz of dozens of conversations, but when Asa Landis finally stepped up to the table where the Elders were sitting, the noise faded to silence. Asa was as tall as an oak, and his dark skin bore the kiss of Mother Africa. "Let's get started."

People moved to the long, pewlike benches and took seats, but there were more people than seats, so the folks left standing took up positions along the four walls.

Behind Asa sat the six other male and female members of the elected Elder Board, which served as the town council. Behind them sat Olivia. Her job as recording secretary was to chronicle the proceedings. Pulling out her pens and ink, she opened the ledger and waited for the meeting to begin.

"First of all, I know we had the service for Mayor Stuckey this morning at the church, but let's take a moment of silence in his memory."

Everyone bowed their heads and closed their eyes.

After a few long minutes, Asa said, "Thanks. Now, we're here this evening because we need a new mayor. I'd like all the candidates to stand."

Armstead Malloy stood at once, then walked to the front of the room, smiling widely at the people he passed. As always, he was dressed in a fancy cutaway suit. This one was patterned with small black and green checks that made him stand out like a carnival barker against the plain flannel work shirts and cotton trousers worn by the other men in attendance.

Asa asked the assemblage, "Is there anyone else?"

When no one else came forward, the low buzz started up again as neighbor whispered to neighbor and husbands to wives over the lone nominee.

Then Sophie Reynolds stood and called out, "I nominate Miss Olivia Sterling."

A shocked Olivia looked up to see everyone in the room staring at her. Sophie continued, "Since her arrival almost a year ago, she's served on committees at the church, the school, and with me on the Ladies League. As secretary to the Elders she's been at every meeting without fail. She's smart, resourceful, and a businesswoman. I believe she would make a good mayor."

Before Sophie could sit down Malloy told the crowd, "Henry Adams doesn't need a *good* mayor, we need an *effective* mayor. Besides, a woman can't be mayor."

Daisy Miller rose to her feet and tossed back, "If you knew anything about the history of this place, Mr. Malloy, you'd know that the first mayor of

Henry Adams was female." And she sat down to applause.

Malloy's eyes flashed angrily, but he gathered himself and turned to Olivia. "I'm sure Miss Olivia is flattered by Miss Sophie's kind words, but what would a woman like *her* know about overseeing a town?"

Olivia assumed he was still angry over her interactions with Neil July, and she was tired of his sneering. Keeping her temper in check, she put down her ledger and stood. Looking Malloy straight in the eye, she said, "I accept Miss Sophie's nomination."

Shouts of joy erupted from the crowd. Olivia smiled. She doubted she would win the post, but letting Malloy run unopposed was unacceptable.

Malloy shot her a very false looking smile before facing the crowd and declaring in a loud voice over the din, "A vote for me will be a vote for progress. I intend to take Henry Adams into the future—bring in the railroad, make Henry Adams the county seat, and start a campaign to bring in more citizens. What about you, Miss Olivia?"

Olivia raised an eyebrow and replied, "I prefer to concentrate on bettering the schools and services for the residents already here." Applause rang out, and Olivia was buoyed by the support. "Our school is wholly inadequate in terms of size and space, and since I'm a firm believer in education as a means to uplift the race, I want to raise funds to correct the situation."

Malloy scoffed. "Education? See. Women don't

have the mental capacity to run a town as well as a man."

The slur made Olivia and most of the women in the room quite furious. Malloy considered himself very intelligent. If you didn't agree with him, he'd offer a pitying smile, then explain why your position was wrong and his was right. Now he must have seen the blood in the eyes of the women in the room, because he immediately raised his hands and proclaimed, "Now ladies, don't get me wrong. I'm sure Miss Olivia is as smart as any woman here, but I don't believe that qualifies her to be mayor."

A few men applauded. Chase Jefferson, who didn't applaud, asked pointedly, "Tell us about your qualifications."

Malloy nodded. "Well, many of you know that I ran a successful dry goods store back in Richmond and am always looking for ways to be even more successful. Unlike Miss Olivia, I don't have an Oberlin education, but how many of us here in this room do? I made myself what I am today with hard work and a sharp mind. It's all anyone needs."

There was a smattering of applause.

Asa asked, "Are there any more nominations?"

Silence.

"Then the election will be held here on Saturday. May the best candidate win."

After the meeting, Olivia was overwhelmed by supporters who pledged their votes and promised that their husbands and neighbors would do the same. Olivia thanked them profusely, but she didn't think she stood a chance.

That evening, as she prepared for bed, a knock sounded on the door. Glad she hadn't undressed yet, she hurried out to the front, then peered out the window before opening the door. It was Armstead Malloy. She sighed heavily and opened the door.

His face was tight. "Good evening, Miss Olivia."

"Mr. Malloy."

"I've come to ask you to withdraw so as to save yourself the embarrassment of losing hands down."

Olivia really did not care for this man. "Your concerns are noted. Good evening, Mr. Malloy."

"All right then, but don't say you weren't warned."

"I won't." And she closed the door.

Olivia changed into her nightclothes and went to sit on the back porch. She was sure Armstead Malloy would have plenty to say were he to learn she was out here in her night rail, but it was hot inside the house. Out here, a light breeze stirred the humid air, and for the first time since the meeting she could feel herself relax. The clouds were hiding the stars tonight, but she didn't mind. She sat and listened to the sounds of the insects playing against the otherwise quiet darkness.

She was actually running for mayor. Would wonders never cease. Again she doubted she'd win the election. Many men would rather have their teeth pulled out by a pig than vote for a woman for anything, but she felt better giving the women a choice. Malloy running unopposed would be a travesty of the democracy that townships like Henry Adams stood for, and besides, it felt good to be the fly in his ointment. *Nasty little man.* In her mind, he didn't deserve to be mayor, but the people would eventually decide.

She put both the election and Malloy out of her mind and concentrated on just enjoying the night. Unlike the last time she'd sat out here, there was no music, nor was there Neil July. Her thoughts slowed at the memory of him, so dark and dangerous. Where was he? she wondered. Was he safe, or in the clutches of bounty hunters? She'd never danced with a man under the stars before, and even now she could feel the light weight of his hand against her back as they'd waltzed, could vividly remember how that touch had sent sensations spreading over her skin like a slow-moving flood. Olivia knew mathematics, and how to lay out a pattern, and could even speak a smattering of French, but she knew absolutely nothing about the raw male power of a man like Neil. She'd never even been kissed before, yet she'd stood with him in the shadows and let him kiss her until she'd been breathless. Had he been disappointed by her inexperience? Had he laughed at her when he'd ridden away? Did he think her loose? The questions didn't matter really, especially considering his occupation and how she, as a properly raised woman, was supposed to conduct herself when confronted with such rough company, but she wondered anyway, just as she wondered if she would ever see him again.

The next morning, Olivia was just getting ready to open the shop for the day when she heard Daisy Miller at her back door call out, "Olivia, are you ready to go?"

Confused, Olivia went to see what her neighbor wanted. She opened the door and let her in. "Morning, Daisy. Am I ready to go where?"

"Campaigning."

Olivia saw that Daisy had on one of her best dresses and her straw church hat with the big silk rose on the band. "Campaigning?"

"Yes. Armstead Malloy thinks this is going to be a coronation, but we have news for him. Put your Closed sign back in the window and let's go."

"Daisy, I hadn't planned on campaigning today." Truthfully, she hadn't had time to even formulate a campaign.

"Plans change. Rachel has the buggy waiting out back. We're due at Cara Lee's in twenty minutes."

Olivia didn't know what to say. As always, she knew it was better to go along with Daisy on something like this, so she set the sign in the window, picked up her handbag, and followed Daisy outside. Sure enough, there was Rachel behind the reins, a situation Olivia planned to change.

"I'll drive," Olivia said, walking around to Rachel's side of the buggy.

Her chin thrust out, Rachel frowned. "You will not."

"If I don't drive, I don't go."

Rachel dismissed that. "We're going to be late."

"And that's why I want the reins."

Olivia loved Rachel to pieces, but driving with her was akin to taking one's life in one's hand; she drove like a madwoman, over hills, through trees. And she drove fast, so fast she often had spills. Although she always escaped unscathed, her passengers emerged from the wrecks with bumps, bruises, and, in Olivia's case, a broken wrist. The only person in town willing to ride with Rachel was her housemate, Daisy, who always rose to Rachel's defense by declaring, "You should have driven with her when we were young. She's much more careful now."

Olivia begged to disagree. Olivia's introduction to Rachel and her driving had come only three days after Olivia's arrival in Henry Adams. She made the mistake of riding with Rachel out to the Jeffersons' home. The ride had been a terrifying dash across the countryside that made Olivia fear for her life—and rightly so, because a few seconds later, the wheels hit a large rock hidden in the tall grass, the buggy careened out of control, and Olivia had been thrown free. Dr. Johnson declared her lucky to have escaped with only a broken wrist.

Everyone knew that Rachel had the best racing horseflesh in the county and that she loved letting the animals run all out. Olivia loved a fast horse as much as the next woman, and maybe the younger Rachel had the skill to control such wild riding. But she'd celebrated her seventy-fifth birthday a few months ago, and everyone in town, including Olivia, was terrified she'd kill herself or her passengers during one of her tears across the plains. "Move over, Rachel."

Rachel opened her mouth to argue but then closed it. Sullen, she moved over and declared tightly, "The only reason I'm conceding is because I want that nasty little man to lose, and you're our only shot."

Olivia picked up the reins. Smiling, she said, "And I love you too, Miss Rachel." She slapped down the reins and headed the two-horse team toward the outskirts of town.

Olivia was surprised to see all the buggies and buckboards parked in the Jeffersons' front yard. She turned to the Two Spinsters. "What am I supposed to do when we get inside? Am I giving a speech?"

Rachel, who was now speaking to her again, offered, "We're going to discuss some strategies. You'll be speaking this afternoon, though."

Amused by the fire and determination of the Spinsters, all Olivia could do was shake her head. She assumed she'd find out soon enough what these two had in store, but for now, Olivia parked the buggy and followed them up to the house.

The Jefferson parlor was filled with dozens of valley women—women Olivia did committee work with, women with children in her Sunday school class and in the junior choir. There were ladies who were regular customers at her shop, and some women Olivia didn't even know, but when she entered the room, they all began to applaud enthusiastically.

The wave of support flowed over and through Olivia with such force that she was standing in Cara Lee's parlor with tears glistening in her eyes. She didn't know what to say or do in the face of their welcome. "Thank you," finally came out in a whisper.

The applause continued until Rachel said sharply, "All right. That's enough sentiment, let's get to work."

Everyone laughed, and the first meeting of the Committee to Elect Olivia for Mayor began.

They spent the balance of the morning making ribbon roses. They were little more than twists of fabric, neither fancy nor elaborate, but they would serve as her campaign's medalets, usually coin-sized pieces of metal that bore the face of the candidate upon it and were used in both national and local elections. Olivia's supporters had no money for proper medalets, and even if funds had been available, the election was a short six days away. So the roses, Cara Lee's suggestion, would be used instead. The plan was for Olivia's supporters to wear them on their dresses and to give out the fabric roses to others planning to vote for her. Olivia thought the idea a very clever one and promised to donate all the leftover ribbon in her shop to the cause.

Olivia and the Spinsters left the Jefferson home around noon and spent the rest of the day going to as many homes as the day could hold asking for votes. She had no idea how or when the Spinsters had had the time to arrange the many stops on the schedule, but Olivia went along without complaint, glad they were on her side.

By the time Olivia and the Spinsters returned home it was evening, and Olivia was as tired as she was hoarse. She'd talked to farm families and families that raised cattle. She'd talked to the wives whose husbands worked in town and women raising children alone. Early evening found her at Sophie's hotel, where the Henry Adams Ladies Historical Society hosted a small supper for her and the members.

Everyone in attendance had on an Olivia Rose, as they were being called, and at the sight of the support, Olivia beamed both inside and out.

So now, after giving Daisy and Rachel a kiss on the cheek for their help and a wave good-bye, Olivia walked into her quiet house and wanted nothing more than to bathe, then sit on her back porch for a few moments before heading to bed.

She was too tired to pump enough water to fill her old claw-footed tub, so she settled for filling the small hip tub instead. The white tin tub was only large enough to stand in, and the bather washed and rinsed by stooping down to access the water. After she was done in the tub, Olivia dried herself and slipped into a clean cotton gown. She poured herself a tumbler of lemonade, stepped outside onto the dark porch, and sat in the old rocker.

It was another hot, sticky night. Although bathing had refreshed her, the humidity was still oppressive. The weather had been drought dry for weeks, and the local farmers were praying for rain. Olivia prayed, too, hoping a good storm would usher in cooler temperatures and drier air.

She took a sip of her lemonade and wondered if the weather was this warm back home in Chicago, prompting thoughts of her mother. Olivia missed her mother dearly. The letter Olivia had written to her on Saturday had been posted today. As mothers were prone to do, Eunice Sterling often wrote Olivia, telling her how worried she was about her only child. Olivia hoped that her own weekly correspondence helped allay some of Eunice's parental fears. Ten months had passed since her midnight flight from home. She assumed that Horatio Butler, her father's hand-picked husband, had moved on and was preying on some other woman's wallet by now. Her heart went out to the woman, whoever she might be.

Olivia sat for a few moments longer, then stood to go back in the house. When Neil July walked out of the night like a gun-wearing specter, she closed her eyes against the furious rush of her blood. *I can't allow this to happen again*, she voiced inwardly; no matter his breathtaking presence and fiery kisses, she hadn't been raised to tryst with an outlaw in the dark. "Mr. July."

Neil caught the cool tone in her voice, but he didn't let it deter him. "Evenin', ma'am."

"You can't come around here anymore."

Neil studied her for a moment. "Why? I mean besides my being an outlaw and you a beautiful woman?"

Olivia told herself she wasn't affected by his low tone, but it was a lie. "Truthfully?"

"Yes."

"I've no experience . . . at this."

He wondered how she'd react if he carried her away. Everything about her drew him so strongly that he could hardly stand still. "I know you don't."

She continued in a voice she wished were firmer in tone, "And, I'm sure you're more accustomed to women who are."

He didn't lie. "I am."

Her words came out a whisper. "I'm not a loose woman, Mr. July."

Neil felt the sincerity in her words. "Never thought you were," he replied quietly.

"Then you understand why this can't go any farther."

"I do," he acknowledged, "but you're a fascinating woman, Olivia, and I enjoy talking to you as much as I do kissing you. So if that's the problem—I promise not to kiss you again unless you ask me to."

The richness of his voice set Olivia's heart pounding. Why did he sound as if he were challenging her? Did he know how his kisses still echoed within her? "That was not the response I was seeking."

"No?" he asked softly.

Olivia imagined that very few women sent him on his way. "No. I expected you to say you'd bow to my wishes."

"I am bowing. I haven't attempted to kiss you yet, have I?"

In spite of her determination not to be moved, the question awakened her senses, and the heat in her blood began rising again. "This isn't a game we're playing, Mr. July."

"Sure it is, darlin'. Men and women have been playing at this since the Creator placed us on earth."

"Well I prefer not to."

"That's not what your kiss said the other night."

Olivia had to look away. She didn't need to be reminded how overwhelming those moments had been, or that deep inside herself lay a woman who wanted more; more than the sensible side of Olivia would ever admit. "I thought you'd be in Indian Territory by now."

Neil noted that she'd changed the subject, but he didn't call her on it. "Decided to stick around. Enjoying the scenery."

Olivia had no trouble interpreting the true meaning of the words or feeling the intensity of his gaze. "You should go before you're seen. You don't want Sheriff Jefferson to know you're here."

"No, I don't, so how about I sit on the porch and we talk awhile? I've already promised not to kiss you."

"Do you really keep the promises you make to women?"

"Depends on the woman." He then added, "You, I would never lie to."

Olivia decided he was the most seductive man she'd ever met. Add to that dashing, charming, with an air of danger around him, and it summed up a man she had no business being around. In truth, she wouldn't mind sitting and talking; Neil July undoubtedly lived an exciting life, and she admitted to being curious about it and him as well, but good women weren't supposed to entertain men whose line of work resulted in Wanted posters. "Mr. July—"

"Name's Neil. It's real easy to say. Only one syllable. Try it."

She smiled before she could snatch it back. Exasperated and amused, she said, "Neil."

"Very good. Wasn't hard at all, was it?"

"No."

"Now, you were saying?"

"I was saying, I'm running for mayor, and if anyone sees us out here, I won't get any votes?"

He walked closer to the porch. "Did you say mayor?"

She nodded. "Yes."

He scanned her in her nightgown. "I'm impressed."

She backed up a step, hoping the shadows would hide her nightgown and act as a buffer between her and the power flowing around him like a lightning rod. "I doubt I'll win."

"Why not?" Neil fought down the urge to step up onto the porch and pull her into his arms so he could reacquaint himself with her scents and the taste of her lips.

"My opponent's purse is much heavier than mine, and he won't hesitate to spend it to promote himself and his views."

"I can get you some gold."

She laughed. "No thank you. The last thing I need is to have Armstead Malloy find out I'm campaigning with stolen gold."

"Armstead Malloy, the man from the coach?"

"Yes."

"He still after you to marry him?"

Olivia thought back on the pickle encounter. "No. Not anymore. In fact, I am now the lowest of the low in his eyes."

"What changed his mind?"

"You, and a barrel of pickles."

She sensed Neil's puzzlement, so she took a moment to explain to him all that had occurred the day in the store.

Neil was stunned. "He really said that to you? To your face? And you didn't shoot him?"

She chuckled. "It did cross my mind, but unlike you, seamstresses don't carry firearms on their persons."

"Maybe you should." Neil thought back on her story and said, "That little toad. Think I'll pay him a visit. Where's he live?"

"Behind the store, but that isn't necessary. The pickles satisfied me."

"Doesn't satisfy me, though."

"Please, let it be. I don't want anyone hurt."

"I'm not going to hurt him, I promise."

"It will only cause more talk."

"Don't worry. I have a fine imagination, Olivia. I'll think of something that won't point to you or to me as the culprit."

"But—"

"It's okay. I haven't had fun in weeks."

Olivia couldn't imagine what kind of *fun* he had in mind and decided she might be better off not knowing.

Neil knew it was time for him to leave her, and he sighed inwardly because of it. "Guess I should get going, Lady Mayor."

Olivia was amused by the title, but she was just as relieved by his imminent departure as she was disappointed by it. "I'm not the mayor yet."

"You will be. Only a horse's ass would vote for a toad like Malloy."

She liked his wit. His quick mind was yet another quality that didn't fit the mold of what an outlaw was supposed to be. "Are you off to your hole in the wall now?"

"No. Plan to stick around a while. Town's got a seamstress I'm hoping to see again."

"You're going to wind up in the town jail."

"Not real partial to jails, so I do my best to avoid them."

"Then you should avoid walking on the wrong side of the law."

He smiled. "Well, she's preaching at me again. Guess it's time to go."

Olivia smiled, then said softly, "Keep yourself safe."

Neil wanted to kiss her and slide a finger over the soft brown skin of her cheek, but he'd made her a promise. "I will."

"Goodnight, Neil."

He was thrilled to hear his name on her lips. "Night, Miss Olivia."

And then he was gone.

Neil was glad Henry Adams was such a small town, because at this late hour most of the good citizens were asleep and unaware that he was skulking around. As he got to the main street, he peered around the corner of the undertaker's place to make sure Jefferson or his deputies weren't making their rounds; not that such vigilance was needed in a town that lacked saloons and any other place that fed vice, but with Chase around, Neil wasn't taking any chances on being seen.

Staying in the shadows as much as he could, Neil made his way past the darkened shops. When he spotted Malloy's mercantile, he quickly crossed the street and slipped around back. There was a small house behind the store. He assumed it to be the place Olivia had spoken of. Malloy had accused her of allowing Neil to take liberties—well, Neil planned on taking some liberties of his own; liberties Malloy would not soon forget.

Picking the lock on the store's back door took Neil only a few moments. He then slipped inside. It was as dark as Hades and he really needed a light, but he decided it would be safer to let his eyes adjust to the darkness. It wasn't easy, though. His unlit journey through the store resulted in his bumping into items, including a barrel of something that would have fallen over and probably wakened half the town had he not righted it in the nick of time. His hand said the contents were potatoes. He was glad they hadn't hit the floor, because more than likely he would have turned his ankle stepping on them in the dark.

Deciding he did need a light after all, he pulled a match out of his shirt pocket, struck it on his belt buckle, and held it high. He took a quick look around. Seeing what he needed, he smiled. He shook out the match and silently thanked Malloy for stocking the items so close to where Neil now stood.

Neil left the store carrying a flour sack, two bandanas, and a length of rope. Senses alert, he crossed the short, dark distance to Malloy's house. Getting inside Malloy's house was a snap. For all of Malloy's money, he, like most of the people in the area, had windows that had no screening, so Neil simply hoisted himself in and looked around.

He didn't need a match to find his way to Malloy's bedroom. The man was snoring like a buffalo, so Neil followed his ears. The Lakota called confronting your enemy in this manner *counting coup*. Neil planned on counting big coup. As he'd told Olivia, he hadn't had any fun in a while and he was looking forward to this.

Malloy had on a union suit. Because of the heat, he had no covers over him. He was lying on his side and snoring loud enough to be heard in Topeka. Neil didn't waste any time. He used one bandana to blindfold Malloy, who didn't awaken until the knot was tightened. By then the second bandana was in his mouth. Gagged and blindfolded, Malloy was roughly tossed onto his stomach; Neil stuck a knee in his back to keep him down and quickly tied his hands and then his feet. Malloy was tied like a Texas steer and squealing like a scared pig. A pleased Neil backed up and savored his work. It had taken him less than ten seconds to get the job done. He wished he'd had Shafts with him so they could have timed it all. Neil swore he'd broken the time record with this one.

Through it all, Neil hadn't made a sound. Malloy

had no idea what was going on, and Neil planned to keep it that way, for now. Malloy was struggling mightily and yelling behind the gag, but Neil wasn't real concerned. Still smiling, he picked up the tied-up toad and carried him outside.

Chapter 5

〇〇◇〇〇

Olivia awakened the next morning just as dawn was pinkening the sky. The house was cool, and as she lay in bed listening to the quietness surrounding her, her mind replayed last night's encounter with Neil July. The logical parts of herself were proud of her decision—sending him away had been proper; nothing but scandal would result from encouraging further visits. However, other parts of herself were disappointed by the thought of never seeing him again. She supposed every good woman had a man in her life when society deemed unsuitable, a man who offered temptation, excitement, and the opportunity to taste things forbidden. Hers was named Neil July, and forgetting him and his kisses was going to take a long time.

Putting him out of her mind as best she could,

Olivia left the bed to take care of her needs. Because she'd spent most of yesterday campaigning with the spinsters, her shop had been closed to customers. Today she planned to be open; there were bills to pay and dresses to make. Keeping her business afloat was far more important than running for mayor.

To that end, after a breakfast of a boiled egg and some toast, she dressed and grabbed her handbag for the walk over to Main Street. She'd noticed that her shears were becoming dull, and although she'd been searching for the last few days, she hadn't been able to find the file she usually used to sharpen them. So a trip to the store to purchase another was the morning's first order of business.

Olivia loved mornings; she always had. They signaled new beginnings and the chance to start again. The quietness and the freshness of the air filling her lungs as she walked made her believe that anything in life was possible, even for a woman like her living in a land where her contributions as a citizen were rarely appreciated; where Redemptionists could ride roughshod over dearly won rights; and where the number of men of color still serving in the halls of Congress could be counted on one hand. The race was resilient, however, and so was she. Olivia was convinced that one day hurdles like Jim Crow and bigotry would no longer be the law of the land, and that a man of the race might one day govern this same country as president. Until then, she planned to keep placing one foot in front of the other and thanking the good Lord for every morning, come rain or shine.

Since Olivia had vowed never to spend another cent in Malloy's mercantile, she headed up the street to the much smaller establishment owned and operated by Harriet Vinton's husband, Henry.

There were very few people about at this time of morning; most of the stores and shops were still shuttered. However, the folk she did see were all rushing somewhere. Many of them, both men and women, passed her at a run. Confused, she saw a farmer she knew from church and shouted, "Mr. Joyce, why's everyone running?"

He grinned and hollered, "Just come on. You'll see."

Olivia hurried to catch up. A small crowd stood in front of Malloy's mercantile. What she saw stopped her dead in her tracks. Malloy had the biggest flagpole in town. It measured at least seven feet high. Usually the flag of the United States flew from it. Today, a man in his union suit was hanging there by his hands and feet, and it appeared to be Malloy! Olivia's hand went to her mouth in surprise, and her eyes were wide. His arms were trussed behind him, as were his feet. Somehow he'd been slipped onto the pole like a stitch on a knitting needle and was up there, positioned belly down. He had a flour sack, of all things, on his head, and he was flailing and squirming like a caught beetle. Olivia could see a stern-faced Sheriff Jefferson and Asa looking up at him and talking as if they were discussing what to do. In the meantime, a curious Olivia moved through the crowd to get a better look. Who would do such? . . . Instantly she knew the answer, and as unchristian as it was to gloat, she thanked Neil July for the early morning treat. It was a prank that would be talked about until Christmas, but how had he gotten Malloy up there, and how would the men get him down?

As word of the sight spread, the crowd began to grow. Some folks took one look at Malloy and rolled in the street laughing. Olivia had to admit he did look quite comical mounted up there like a masthead on a ship, and as more and more people arrived, more and more giggles could be heard.

The sheriff hollered up, "Hold on, Malloy. The only ladder tall enough to get you down belongs to Handy and he can't find it. Could be the folks that hung you up there used it and then hid it."

Olivia prayed Neil hadn't hidden the ladder anywhere on her property, but then she remembered him promising not to leave a trail that pointed to either him or herself. She relaxed. She looked up at Malloy and shook her head at the inventiveness and lunacy of the stunt. July was a wicked genius. Olivia would never have conceived a revenge so harmless yet so publicly humiliating as this. If July ever showed up on her doorstep again, she'd give him a big kiss. He'd earned one.

The flour sack on Malloy's head made it impossible for the crowd to tell if he could see them, but Olivia was sure he could hear the laughter. Folks were pointing and laughing behind their hands, while others made wisecracks about him not being in red, white, and blue long drawers. Malloy was twisting and turning, and mumbling furiously from within the sack. She wondered why his speech sounded so muffled; was he gagged? Whatever the reason, it was plain to all the onlookers that Armstead was mad as a wet hen.

By now half the town was staring on; people brought their children, dogs were barking and chasing, and everyone waited on Handy to find the ladder. Finally he arrived, and the crowd cheered boisterously. The big blacksmith carried the heavy ladder with ease and planted it against the lip of the mercantile's overhanging roof. He climbed up. Using a large bladed knife, he began sawing at the rope binding Malloy's ankles. The sheriff climbed up too and took up a position a few rungs below Handy. When the rope parted, Chase caught Malloy's legs and eased them down. No one knew how long Malloy had been mounted on the pole, but it was plain to see his legs wouldn't hold him, so everyone guessed he'd been posing as a flag for quite some time. The wrist ropes were cut next, and Malloy's arms dropped uselessly to his sides. The men carried him down and sat him on the edge of the walk. The sheriff took off the hood and undid the blindfold and the gag to reveal Malloy's furious face.

Someone handed the sheriff a canteen. He passed it to Malloy, who took a long swallow, then handed it back. When Malloy looked into the smiling crowd and saw Olivia, his eyes blazed at her before he snarled, "Sheriff, I want the people responsible for this found, then jailed, and hung. Hung!"

Jefferson nodded, adding, "Okay, Mr. Malloy, but let's get you to the doc—"

"I don't need a doctor. I need those people found. Aren't you responsible for the safety of this town's citizens? Where were *you* last night when those hooligans attacked me?"

Olivia thought the tirade was uncalled for, and, from the grumblings she could hear around her, others thought so as well.

Jefferson seemed determined to take the high road. "I'll come by after you've rested up and you can tell me what happened. In the meantime, I really think you should have Doc Johnson give you a look—"

The furious Malloy jumped up to give the sheriff holy hell, but as soon as Malloy stood on his feet, his eyes rolled back in his head, his legs and hips wobbled unsteadily, and he fainted right there in the street.

The crowd howled.

The tight-lipped Sheriff Jefferson shook his head and said to Handy, "Go get the doc."

Flagpole Malloy, as he'd been christened after the event, became the town's main topic of conversation. Every customer who came into Olivia's shop wanted to talk about it. At noontime, Olivia placed the Closed sign in the window and walked down to Sophie's hotel for lunch. As she took her seat at a small table in the large dining room, she could hear, all around her, snippets of conversations humorously recounting the sight of Malloy hanging from the pole and the fainting aftermath. Seeing Olivia, a few diners came over and asked if she thought Malloy might withdraw from the mayor's race. Olivia declined to speculate and referred the questioners to Malloy.

Cara Lee Jefferson stopped by Olivia's place later that afternoon. Once again, Malloy was the topic of conversation.

Cara said, "I hate that I missed it."

Olivia couldn't stop her chuckle. "It was quite a sight. I have never seen anything remotely like it in my life."

"Chase is still trying to figure out who put him up there."

Olivia kept her thoughts on the culprit to herself. "Did your husband tell you that Malloy accused him of being negligent in his duties as sheriff?"

"Yes, he did, and I'm glad I wasn't there to hear it. Were it up to me, Malloy would still be posing as a flag. Nasty little man."

Olivia smiled. "Folks have been asking if he's going to quit the race for mayor. Have you heard anything?"

"No, but I'd bet Chase's badge he won't. He'd be more of a laughingstock than ever. Maybe he'll just leave town."

Olivia deadpanned. "We should be that lucky."

And they weren't.

The next morning, Asa Landis delivered a message to Olivia from Malloy, who wanted to debate her. Olivia blinked. "A debate?"

"Yep."

"When?"

"Tomorrow evening at the hall."

Olivia had done mock debates at Oberlin and she was sure she could hold her own, but this was very unexpected. "Please tell Mr. Malloy I will be there."

"Will do," he replied before asking, "wasn't that something this morning?"

Olivia nodded. "It was indeed."

"Wish I knew who did it. Between you and me, I'd like to give the person a medal. We haven't had this much excitement since the Liberian Lady burned down back when Chase was courting Cara Lee."

Olivia knew from the historical society that the Liberian Lady was a saloon that once operated on the outskirts of town. It had burned down back in '82. "I keep hearing about those times."

"That was a year I'll never forget, let me tell you." Then, changing the subject, he said, "Debate starts at seven, so get yourself ready. Lots of folks pulling for you."

He then moved to the door. "Good luck, Miss Olivia."

"Thanks, Asa."

That night, Neil skinned the two rabbits he'd caught in his snares and readied them for the makeshift spit hung over the crude fire pit he'd dug. Once they were positioned and roasting, he sat back against his bedroll and gazed at the flames. He wondered what Olivia was doing. Was she sitting on her porch and wondering about him? Her face floated across his mind's eye, and he could see her as clearly as if she were seated across the fire; the heart-shaped, copper-colored face, the dark eyes, the wide, full mouth. She had a good head of hair, which she wore pulled back in a spinsterish knot, and that tall, full body could make a man never want to leave her side. He guessed they'd found Malloy and cut him down by now, but were it up to Neil, Malloy would have stayed on that pole until the geese flew south. Putting his ugly mouth on Olivia had earned the store owner a much worse fate, but out of respect for Olivia's wishes Neil had only played with Malloy a little bit.

He hoped she'd had the chance to see Malloy before he was cut down. Neil was pretty sure she'd know the prankster's identity, but he was equally sure she wouldn't tell anyone. Neil wanted to see her, bad. She'd asked that he not come back and he wanted to respect that wish too, but he didn't know if he could. She was not for him, he knew that, but he couldn't make himself ride away—thus this camp he'd set up behind an abandoned homestead about ten miles outside of town. In truth he knew next to nothing about her, but by the ancestors he wanted to know more. Much more. The need to learn everything there was to learn about one Olivia Sterling pulsed through him with a strength he'd never felt before with any other woman, and Neil had had many women. He was experienced enough and honest enough to admit that inside that statuesque body could beat the heart of a shrew who'd make his life hell once he got to truly know her, but Neil didn't think so. She impressed him as being a strong, good woman, but one who'd never known a man. The inexperience in her kiss had been expected, but he hadn't expected to taste passion as well. The memory of her being in his arms wouldn't leave him alone.

He moved over to the fire and turned the rabbits. They were scrawny little things and it wouldn't take them long to cook, but they weren't done yet. He was as hungry as the proverbial bear, and not just for food. Forcing his mind away from the tempting seamstress, he wondered if Shafts had reached Indian Territory safely and if he'd been able to find Teresa. Was she on the road with her gang or cooling her heels in some local's hooscow? That was a legitimate question. The net was closing on the west. In ten years' time, outlaws were going to be as extinct as the tribes. In truth, being an outlaw these days was almost more trouble than it was worth. The trains were getting bigger and faster, making them harder to ride down on and board, and the increase in the number of passengers meant gangs needed more men to control all of those good citizens during a robbery. Added to that were the Pinkertons, now posing as paying customers; most stood out like white buffaloes and were easy to spot, but when they weren't spotted they played havoc with a gang's carefully worked out plans. A younger Neil had found train robbing exciting; the danger alone had been worth every job he and Shafts had undertaken. Now . . . Now, one of their best train robbing partners, Griffin Blake, was married and a sheriff in Texas, and when men like Griff left the business, it was time for everyone he knew to take stock of themselves and their place in a world that had little future. Towns were passing laws; good women were building churches; and farmers were putting up fences on the High Plains. Ten years ago, there'd been no Nicodemus or Henry Adams; this area had been as wild and free as any land on this side of the Mississippi. Not anymore. Towns brought civilization, and civilization was destroying the west he knew and loved.

The debate on Wednesday drew as large a crowd to the town hall as there'd been at the nomination meeting on Sunday evening. If anything, there were more people, Olivia realized as she watched them all file in. She would have been foolish to deny the butterflies in her stomach; she was very nervous, but she was looking forward to stating her positions on the issues facing the town she now called home. It pleased her to see the spinsters and Cara Lee and the rest of her supporters sporting their Olivia Roses. None of the men in the hall were wearing any, but she supposed that was to be expected.

Olivia and Malloy drew straws from Asa's closed fist to see who would go first. Malloy got the short straw. Obviously angry, he stood up to begin. In the silence that prevailed as he pulled himself together, a few snickers were heard, apparently in response to yesterday's flag pole incident. He glared in an attempt to silence them, then began to speak. "I come before you today to ask for your vote. Henry Adams has a bright and glorious future, but only if we elect a person with the vision to see and shape that future. My opponent is a fine woman, but there's the rub—she's a woman."

Hissing and catcalls filled the air on the heels of that remark, but he smiled smugly and continued, "God took woman out of the rib of *man*, not the other way around. If women were meant to run a town, they would have been given the vote, but they weren't because we all know that a woman might do well in her own sphere of committee work, church work, or running a *seamstress shop*," he pronounced pointedly, turning around to look back at Olivia, "but politics is *men's* work."

The supporting applause was loud, strong, and prolonged. Many women in attendance looked up at their clapping husbands with surprise. Some men sheepishly sat down, but others ignored their women and added their hands to the din. Olivia noted that many of the men applauding the loudest were the unmarried men, the field hands, and small farmers.

"So in closing, let me say this. On election day you can vote like your wife wants you to vote"—laughter rang out—"or you can be *men* and vote your conscience. Henry Adams needs a man's hands on the reins. Thank you."

He was given a cheering ovation. Looking pleased, Malloy bowed. When he took his seat, he shot Olivia a nasty little smile, then folded his arms contentedly.

Olivia walked before the crowd and said, "Well. I guess we women know where we stand with Mr. Malloy."

Applause and amens came from the women.

"But I'm not here to pit husbands against wives, or brothers against sisters. We presently live in a nation that is already dividing its citizens by race, and I refuse to promote such ignorance."

Shouts of female yells filled the hall.

"But I do wish to set the record straight over who has done what here in Henry Adams. I'm admittedly a newcomer and was surprised to learn that not only was the first mayor a female but a female laid out this town. Miss Rachel, stand up, please."

Rachel Eddings stood.

"This, ladies and gentlemen, was the surveyor for the original Kentucky dusters who founded Henry Adams in '78. *She* decided where Main Street would be. *She* plotted the town's boundaries. *She* oversaw the drawings of the first maps."

Apparently many of those present hadn't had any idea Rachel had played such a prominent role, and they were staring her way in amazement.

Olivia added, "Miss Rachel was owned by a surveyor before emancipation and as a result was the only founder with the skills necessary to do what needed to be done."

While Rachel took her seat again, Olivia looked back at Malloy. He stared at her with cold eyes. She turned away. "So, let's not debate which gender did this, or which is more valuable than that. Henry Adams was built so that *all of us*, men and women, could exercise the freedoms promised us by the Constitution."

She then looked out over the crowd and said seriously, "If there are those here who wish to vote for Mr. Malloy because of his qualifications, then by all means do so, but don't vote for him simply because of his gender. That is not why this town was founded. Thank you."

Applause erupted; both men and women jumped to their feet. It was louder and longer and stronger than the support shown Malloy. Olivia was once again so moved that tears sprang to her eyes.

When the room quieted again, Asa stood up and asked Malloy, "Anything else you want to say?"

Malloy waved him off. "No."

Olivia was surprised by his response. Hadn't this been billed as a debate? Was he that confident of winning, or had he been shamed by Olivia's rebuttal? She had no way of knowing.

Asa turned to Olivia. "Anything else?"

She shrugged. "No."

Asa faced the crowd and said, "All right, the candidates will take questions. Who's first?"

Doc Johnson stood. "Mr. Malloy, how do you plan to bring in all these new citizens you've been talking about?"

The doctor sat and Malloy stood. "By bringing in attractions that will be unique to Henry Adams. Folks coming west these days are looking for amusements, something to take their minds off plowing and planting. We could build an opera house or a world-class saloon."

Olivia stared. "But the last thing this town needs is a saloon."

The women applauded.

Malloy countered in a patronizing voice. "Spoken like a true woman."

The men applauded.

Malloy went on, "Men need a place to relax after a long day in the fields or at their businesses. In a saloon they can talk freely without worrying about offending tender feminine ears. And what is so wrong about playing a little poker and smoking a few cigars?"

Male voices chimed in approvingly.

Olivia had to admit, he was smooth. "How will a saloon benefit our families or our children?"

"It won't. That's why you ladies build churches, to look after those sorts of things."

Olivia shook her head in disbelief.

Asa asked, "Anybody have another question?"

Cara Lee Jefferson stood and asked, "Mr. Malloy, what are your plans for the school? It's too small, the roof leaks, and we lack basic supplies, like books."

Malloy frowned. "Personally, I don't believe formal schooling is for everyone. Our children should be encouraged to explore ways to lift themselves that don't involve sitting in a classroom for hours a day. Where is the emphasis on learning a trade? Earning a living by the sweat of your brow should be just as valued."

More applause.

Cara Lee pressed him. "You didn't answer my question."

"My answer to your question is that when I'm elected mayor we'll discuss the matter."

An obviously angry Cara sat down.

For the next half hour the candidates expressed their views on everything from taxes, to the impending arrival of the railroads, to what should be done about the desertion of the race by the Lily White Republicans, as the party of Lincoln was now called.

Points were made by both sides, and each received rounds of applause. When the last question was asked, Asa closed the proceedings, then said, "Voting starts here Saturday morning, nine o'clock sharp. May the best candidate win." He gave the gavel a bang, and the debate was over.

Olivia spent a few minutes being greeted and congratulated by her supporters. Cara Lee gave her a kiss on the cheek, then left to get Branch home to bed—there was school in the morning. The Two Spinsters waited for Olivia to finish up, then walked her home.

Daisy said, "I do hope that nasty little man doesn't win. Can you imagine him representing Henry Adams at conventions and such? They'll think we're all a bunch of bombastic fools."

Olivia agreed. "Did you see the faces of the folks who didn't know Miss Rachel surveyed the town? A few literally dropped their teeth."

Rachel said with a chuckle, "And one of them was Malloy. His eyes looked ready to bulge right out of the sockets."

Olivia grinned. "Good."

Rachel and Daisy's house was about five hundred yards from Olivia's, and the two homes were the only ones on Third Street. As Rachel and Daisy stepped up onto their back porch, Daisy said, "I think we should have a torchlight parade on Friday night." Olivia thought that a great idea. Torchlight parades were a popular and dramatic preelection event all over the country. Supporters of sponsoring politicians marched through the night with lit torches. The parades back east were usually conducted the night before the vote. During presidential campaigns, participants numbered in the thousands.

Of course there wouldn't be that many marchers at a Henry Adams parade, but Olivia thought the idea might go over well.

Daisy said, "We should start spreading the word tomorrow."

Rachel added, "I believe we should all wear white and pin on our Olivia Roses."

Daisy turned to her old friend. "And if someone doesn't have a white garment?"

"They can wear a white bonnet or a scarf or gloves."

Olivia was pleased she hadn't been volunteered to sew up white dresses for the supporters. She didn't have time for such a project.

The three women spent a few more moments discussing preliminary details for the march, then Daisy and Rachel offered Olivia their good-byes and went into the house still talking plans for Friday night's march. Always amazed by their energy, Olivia walked the remainder of the way home.

As she lay in bed that night, she thought back on the day, but when she turned over to go to sleep, her last thoughts were of Neil July.

* * *

Cara Lee came charging into Olivia's shop Friday afternoon, seething. "Do you know what that nasty little man has planned for this evening?"

"Getting back up on his flagpole?"

Cara chuckled for a moment, letting her anger dissolve, then she said, "No. Fireworks."

Olivia, in the process of inventorying her threads, looked over at her friend. "Fireworks?"

"Yes, and they start thirty minutes *before* the march."

Olivia's lips tightened. "You have to give him credit. He's going all out."

"And he's lower than a snake's belly. No one is going to come to the march when they can see fireworks instead."

"True." Olivia was very disappointed by this turn of events.

"The children were so excited in school this morning, I had to almost tie them down to make them stay in their seats. Malloy's fireworks were all they could talk about."

"You have to admit it does sound exciting. I haven't seen fireworks since I left Chicago."

"Which is why I didn't argue when Chase said he was taking Branch."

Olivia didn't fault Cara's decision; she understood. "So, shall we cancel the march?"

Cara shrugged. "What do you think?"

"I say no. Malloy's head would swell even larger if we call it off. I'll march alone if I have to."

"Then there will be two of us."

Olivia was glad to have Cara Jefferson as her friend.

Cara said, "Then I'll spread the word that we are going to march."

"And I'll do the same."

Friday evening at dusk, eight women wearing white gathered in front of Sophie's hotel for the torchlight parade.

"Are we ready?" Olivia asked. The ladies were lined up, torches lit. However, not one person had shown up to view the march. No one. The street was as empty as a ghost town, and the lack of supporters was as hard to overlook as the bursts of colorful lights in the sky.

"Ready," Sophie called back.

So they began the walk to the other end of Main Street. They marched slowly, past shuttered stores and windows with signs saying CLOSED. They could hear the *ohh*ing and *ahh*ing from the crowd on the outskirts of town, and it only added to their glum mood. They'd planned to sing, but no one felt like singing.

So they marched on.

It didn't take them long to reach Handy's livery, the last business on the street. Upon reaching it, they doused their torches, said their good-byes to each other, then silently dispersed.

A disappointed Olivia walked home with the spinsters. No one had anything to say; there was nothing to say. When they reached Daisy and Rachel's home, the two gave her a strong hug, then silently went inside.

Olivia continued on to her own home, taking the worn path through the high grass. She had so hoped for a large turnout tonight. She'd even been silly enough to fantasize about the streets being filled with cheering and waving supporters as she and her ladies marched by. Eight people—that's all that had shown up, and they'd been marchers. Humiliated didn't begin to describe how she felt, but it came real close.

On Saturday morning, Olivia took down the navy walking suit she'd been saving for a special occasion and put it on. She'd based its design on one she'd seen in a Bloomingdale's Brothers catalog. The skirt's front was plain, but it had wooden buttons bordering a series of pleats on one side and a bustled back. The jacket, high-necked and long-sleeved, was simple, but the small wooden buttons that ran diagonally across the bodice made it very stylish. Her pulled-back hair was oiled and glossy and twisted in a fashionable chignon low on her neck. Her bangs were curled and split down the front, according to the fashion. She topped off the ensemble with a frothy little bonnet decorated with small blue flowers, then tied the satin strings beneath her chin. If she was going to go down in defeat, at least she would be well dressed.

The line to go inside the town hall was long. The process involved making a mark on a ballot, then dropping the ballot into a box overseen by a member of the Elders. As she waited, she spotted Armstead Malloy strolling out of the hall. Apparently, he'd just voted and was looking very smug and bark-erlike in a black-and-white checkered cutaway suit. Seeing Olivia, he and a few of his cronies strolled over to where she stood waiting.

"Ah, my worthy opponent. How are you this fine morning, Miss Sterling?"

"I'm fine, Mr. Malloy."

"I heard your march wasn't as successful as you hoped."

"No, it wasn't. I'm sure everyone enjoyed your fireworks."

"The whole town was there."

Olivia didn't respond.

Malloy contemplated her for a moment, then said, "Had you hitched your wagon to mine, we could have gone far."

"I'm sure you'll find someone much worthier."

"I'm sure I will," he tossed back, then said, "Good day, Miss Sterling. If you have to take to your bed after being trounced, I'm sure everyone will understand."

As he walked away, he and his cronies laughed. Olivia sneered. Too bad she couldn't take Neil July out of her pocket and sic him on Malloy again. Suddenly Neil's dark, mustached face shimmered before her mind's eye, and she forgot all about Malloy. *Where is he?* she wondered again. Out of her life, she presumed. Pushing aside thoughts of her kissing bandit, she focused on the line of people stretched out in front of her. She waited for her turn to enter the hall. After voting, she spent a few hours shaking hands and encouraging those in line to consider her candidacy, then she went back to her shop to await the results.

It was almost five o'clock in the afternoon when Cara burst into the shop shouting, "You won!"

A stunned Olivia looked up from her seat at the sewing machine.

"All the votes are in," Cara exclaimed excitedly, "and you are officially the newly elected lady mayor of Henry Adams, Kansas!"

Olivia's mouth dropped with astonishment. She'd won! Jumping up, she and Cara shared a happy hug in spite of the great differences in their heights. Olivia certainly hadn't expected her reluctant candidacy to bear fruit, especially after last night's disappointing march, but it had, and she was elated. Before she could ask Cara for more details, the small shop was filled with well-wishers all bearing congratulations and smiles. Sophie Reynolds rushed in, accompanied by a beaming Asa Landis. Sophie gave Olivia a strong hug, saying emotionally, "You won. Isn't that something?"

"It certainly is."

Asa told her, "Your opponent wanted a recount, so we gave him one, but the best woman still won."

"How's he taking it?"

"Badly of course, but that's why he lost to begin with. No character."

Sophie added, laughing, "He was giving away cigars and his best whiskey to the people voting for him, but he forgot to inform the clerk he'd left in charge at the store to make certain his supporters voted *before* they began imbibing. Some of the field hands got so drunk they couldn't even make it to their tied-up horses, let alone the hall to vote."

Chuckling, Olivia shook her head.

That evening, after a celebratory dinner at Sophie's, Olivia went home feeling as if she were walking on air. Never in her wildest imagination had she thought she'd win, but she had.

Because of all the excitement, she was too wound up to sleep, so she plopped down onto the rocker on the back porch. She smiled. *Take that, Armstead Malloy!* People were wondering now if he'd leave town, but Olivia didn't think so. She figured he'd stay around if only to bedevil her. Right now, she didn't care one Confederate dollar about Flagpole Malloy. She, Olivia Jean Sterling, was mayor. Mayor! Her mother was going to pop her buttons when Olivia wrote to tell her the news, and she made a mental note to do so immediately after she returned from church tomorrow. *Mayor Olivia Sterling.* She certainly liked the sound of that. She was so full of restless energy that she felt as if she could walk to Chicago to tell her mother the news and then turn around and walk right back to Kansas. She wanted to dance, jump up and down, run across the plains, howl at the moon, and let the world know how happy she was.

She heard the horse before she saw it; it sounded like it was moving slowly, easily. Instinctively she knew who the rider would be. A heartbeat later, Neil July rode out of the darkness.

Chapter 6

Olivia had been hoping he'd show up tonight, but she'd pushed the thoughts aside, chalking them up to silly schoolgirl yearnings that had no place in the sedate and proper life of a newly elected lady mayor. Yet there he sat, astride his large, seventeen-hand stallion looking for all the world like a dark-skinned centaur. Every cell in her body felt his presence. The day had already been remarkable, and now fate seemed determined to make it even more so. "Good evening, Mr. July."

He touched his hat. "Evening, ma'am. Thought I'd come by to make sure Malloy wasn't bothering you. How'd the election go?"

Her elation returned. "I won," she said with sparkling eyes. "I am the new mayor of Henry Adams, Kansas."

"Well, hot damn," he replied with a laugh. "Congratulations."

"Thank you."

"Are you celebrating?"

Amused, she shook her head. "No."

"Why not? You've done something no other woman I know has. A man would be drunk by now."

"I'm not a man."

"No, you're not."

His voice was so knowing that Olivia felt heat creep into her cheeks.

Sensing he'd touched her, Neil asked, "So, how do seamstresses celebrate? Do you count threads, knit, purl—what?"

"No. We really don't do anything."

"Then how about a quail hunt?"

"A quail hunt?" Her voice sounded dubious.

"Sure, that's how I celebrate—go out at night, find some quail, build a fire."

"A quail hunt? At night? I believe you're pulling my leg, Mr. July."

"What happened to 'Neil'?"

The caress in his voice made Olivia drop her gaze for a moment. When she raised her eyes to his, she said softly, "Neil. I think you're pulling my leg."

His answering chuckle ruffled the darkness. "I am. No such thing as a quail hunt. Just fishing for a way to get you to go riding with me."

Olivia's excitement over the election was replaced by emotions far more complex. A night ride with him was the most tempting proposition any man had ever proposed, and as giddy as the day had been, she really didn't want it to end. She did need to celebrate, *so why not?* "We won't go far?"

"We'll only go as far as you want, darlin'."

That low, drawling voice sent a wave of anticipation over her senses. Even a woman as inexperienced as she knew he wasn't necessarily talking about the ride. She forced herself to breathe slowly. "Is there anything we'll need on this quail hunt?"

He shrugged his wide shoulders. "Person can get pretty thirsty quail hunting. If you have any of that lemonade around, it might come in handy."

Spellbound by all that he was, she finally tore herself away and went into the house. The first thing her conscience screamed was, *Have you lost your mind? You're the mayor now.* Olivia admitted that maybe she had, but she took the ade out of the icebox and filled up a canteen anyway.

Back outside, she handed him the canteen. He laced the rope over the saddle, then reached down a hand for her to grab. Olivia found the heat of his hand even more potent than she remembered. As the effects of him spread through her like smoke, his strong arm pulled her up behind him. A nervous Olivia adjusted her skirts. They hadn't been this close to each other since the time he'd kissed her, and she again questioned her sanity, even as the memory of those kisses filled her mind.

"You should hold on, Madam Mayor. Don't want you falling off."

Olivia realized the only thing to hold onto was him, and the boldness of such an action made her hesitate for a moment. Casting aside her rising trembles, she eased an arm around his waist, feeling the warmth of his skin and the leather belt around his waist. She was careful to establish a respectable distance between their bodies; not that it mattered—his nearness filled the space like steam.

Neil was convinced he'd died and gone to heaven. Having her close enough behind him to feel the heat of her body and smell her perfume thrilled him like a boy courting his first girl. He turned so he could see her face. "Ready?"

Olivia nodded at the man whom destiny had sent to alter her life and said, softly, "Yes."

He signaled with the reins, and the horse galloped away from the house.

Olivia would have loved for their ride to have been under the moonlight, but in reality she was far more thankful for the clouds. This had to be the most reckless act she'd ever agreed to, and she didn't wish to be seen by anyone.

Once the town was behind them, Neil slowed the horse and asked, "Where to?"

Olivia had no idea. "This is your quail hunt, you decide."

"If I pick, we'll be heading for the Texas border."

He swiveled around and gave her a smile.

She met that powerful gaze, and even though being with him made her question her sanity, she wondered what it might be like to run away with him. "Since I can't be mayor if I'm in Texas, there's an old homestead about a mile from here. We can go there."

Neil would have preferred Texas. All the sweet, passionate things he wanted to do to and with her on the way flared over him and tightened his groin, but he had no business fantasizing about such an encounter, so he headed the horse west.

The horse's stride was long and sure, and although Olivia had planned on maintaining a proper distance between her body and his, she wound up having to lean closer in order to hold on. As a result, every movement of the horse made her breasts brush against his back, and the sensations hardened her nipples like sun-dried grapes. Hoping to turn her mind away from her body's scandalous reactions, Olivia wondered what her mother would think were she able to witness this? Would Eunice be appalled and scandalized, or secretly applaud her daughter's headlong plunge into brash behavior? Olivia was certain her mother had never done anything remotely similar; women of good standing rarely ventured off society's set path of decorum. Had Olivia followed that path, she'd be Horatio Butler's lawfully wedded wife now instead of riding through the Kansas night on the back of Neil July's horse.

Neil was having thoughts of his own. Even though the seamstress had on the layers of clothing that proper women encased their bodies in, the pressure of her curves against his back was enough to make a man sweat. He turned his mind from speculating on how it might feel to slowly remove all those layers and slide his hands over the velvety skin beneath, or at least he tried to.

Olivia was surprised when they reached the

homestead she'd referred to, because she'd been so
deep in thought she hadn't given him directions.
They were here, however, and since she didn't believe he was that magical, she said, "You knew about
this place."

He halted the horse and turned in the saddle to
face her. "Yep. Have a camp set up around back."

Now she understood. "I wondered how close by
you were."

"Not as close as I wanted to be. . . ."

His meaning was easy to read, and she had to look
away or be turned to a cinder.

He dismounted, then reached up and helped her
down.

Once again, the warmth of his hands on her waist
penetrated to her flesh. He set her on her feet less
than a breath away, then reached out and gently
raised her chin so their eyes would meet. For a moment he studied her silently, then he said in a hushed
voice, "Never met a woman like you. . . ."

Feeling all the new emotions rising up inside herself, she whispered back truthfully, "Never met a
man like you, either. . . ."

His finger beneath her chin traveled gently over
her lips, slowly learning the shape of them, making
her breathing stick in her throat.

"I'm about to break my promise not to kiss you,
Olivia."

Olivia couldn't speak; she was shaking so badly
no words came to mind. Then she remembered that
she owed him a kiss for getting back at Armstead
Malloy, but July was brushing his lips across her

cheek, her jaw, and she couldn't even think, let alone speak. Finally, her mind returned and she whispered, "I owe you a kiss. . . ."

The words were music to Neil's ears, even though he hadn't a clue as to what she meant. "What did I do?" He traced a mesmerized finger over the ripe lines of her mouth once more.

Shimmering, Olivia tried to stay focused long enough to respond, but it was difficult. "You put Armstead Malloy on the flagpole."

"Did you enjoy that?" he asked, while placing faint yet stirring kisses on her parted lips.

"Immensely," she breathed.

His lips against her ear, he murmured, "You'll enjoy this more. . . ."

He lowered his mouth to hers, and Olivia began to understand just how much she didn't know. She didn't know that with the right man a kiss could melt the fiber of your being, or that the right man could make a woman moan in response to the fire-tipped seekings of his tongue. The last time they'd kissed had been the appetizer, but this—this feverish, wonderful moment was the main course. His magnificent kisses fueled her blood and made her slide her hand behind his neck so she could draw him closer. He eased an arm around her waist and drew her closer as well. Following his lead, Olivia touched the tip of her tongue to the corners of his mouth and thrilled at the low groan of satisfaction he gave in response.

Neil wanted to touch her, taste her, but he settled on nibbling gently on the tempting curve of her bottom lip. The virginal passion he'd tasted the last time they'd done this was stronger tonight, and the sweet force made his desire surge. Fueled by that, he kissed her fully; deeply, coaxing, and inviting her to come play. His hands were moving too, up the sides of her waist and over the back of her fancy ladies' jacket. The caresses let his fingers savor the strength in her spine and the way it flared into her waist and hips.

Olivia felt his hand on her waist and placed her hand on his to keep it from traveling lower. Even though parts of herself were drowning in sensations that demanded more, it was all too much, too fast. She drew away to catch her breath.

Neil watched her and smiled. She was a lot more passionate than even she knew he sensed, and that pleased him. He had no plans to rush her, however. "How about I start a fire?"

As far as Olivia was concerned, a blaze had already been set. "Okay."

He placed a soft, short kiss on her lips, then took her by one hand, took the reins in the other, and walked her and the horse through the dark and tall grass to the back of the house.

Olivia no longer felt like herself. The no-nonsense seamstress mayor had been replaced by someone more daring and bold; someone who let outlaws lead her into the darkness, and who wondered how long the reverberations from his kisses would last.

The house, or what was left of it, had once belonged to the Russell family, members of the original Kentucky-born founders. Like many of the other abandoned first homes in the area, this one was on its way to becoming just a memory. The sod walls had lost their form, and the sod roof had tumbled into the interior. There was a fire pit only a few feet away from where she stood. The few lit embers cast just enough of a glow for her to see the bedroll and a few cooking utensils placed nearby. While he tied up the horse to an old wooden hitching post, then stooped to build up the fire, she watched him going about the task. He was precise and efficient, letting her know he did this often. She wondered how many times he'd made fires on the open plains and how many of them were so he could enjoy the company of a woman. She told herself it didn't matter; he had a past that had nothing to do with her or this time spent together, but parts of herself reasoned that his past did matter; Neil July knew much more about men and women than she, and out here alone with him she was vulnerable in all the ways a woman could be. Yet she didn't feel threatened. On every occasion he'd been a gentleman, and she sensed he would continue to be so.

Neil looked over at her framed by the now rising light of the fire. *What a beauty she is.* He'd spent most of his outlaw life amongst saloon girls, cathouse queens and nymphs du pave; women who knew their way around a man, and whose kisses and company came with a posted price, but tall, regal Olivia lived in a different world, and his greatest fear was that he'd scare her off or offend her in some way.

Walking over to his horse, he removed first the saddle, then the blanket beneath. He spread the blanket on the cleared ground next to the fire pit. "Have a seat if you'd like. Don't want you to get dirt on your dress."

Olivia was pleased by his chivalry and accepted the offer. When she saw him take a seat on the other side of the fire, she was disappointed but at the same time thankful for the chance to regain her composure.

Neil watched her for a few silent moments and noted how her look fled each time their eyes met. He wondered if she was having second thoughts about coming here with him. On the off chance that she was, he sought to reassure her. "I'll take you back whenever you want, Olivia."

Olivia watched the flames playing across his dark features. "I know."

He then rose to his feet, walked around the fire, and took a seat next to her, explaining, "I don't like sitting with my back to the night. Makes me jumpy."

Olivia had heard that men who lived by the gun always sat facing forward, and she supposed it made sense to want to see danger coming rather than have the danger creep up behind you.

He added, "It also gives me an excuse to come sit next to you."

"You don't need an excuse," she said, realizing she'd spoken the words aloud when she'd only meant to think them.

"Glad to hear that." The dark hid Neil's pleased grin. "You should probably talk about something, though—otherwise I'm just going to kiss you again."

That admission made her trembly inside. Her lips were still swollen and tender from their last bout. "What would you like for me to talk about?"

"I don't know—tell me about this fiancé you ran off from."

She reached down and absentmindedly toyed with one of the wooden buttons on her skirt. "His name is Horatio Butler, and he's my papa's business partner."

"What kind of business?"

"Timber. Papa and his men cut down the trees on our land and sell them to lumberyards."

"How long had you known him?"

"About a year. Never liked him, though. He and Armstead Malloy could have been hatched from the same egg. When he informed me that once we married he planned to sell my shop, I knew I couldn't marry him."

"Most women wouldn't have put up a fuss."

"I'm not most women."

"No, you aren't."

The timbre of his voice rippled over and through her, making her wonder if she'd ever be able to handle his presence in a nonchalant way. "Tell me something about you."

"I like to cook."

That got her attention.

He chuckled. "You seem surprised."

"I am. That was the last thing I expected you to say."

"Why?"

"A train robber who cooks?"

"Why not? Outlaws have to eat. I'm the best train-robbing cook you'd ever want to meet."

Olivia found both him and the statement amazing. "Outlaws aren't supposed to be domesticated."

"Says who?"

"The papers back east."

"Don't believe everything you read in the papers."

"I'm realizing that."

"Horatio ever kiss you?"

It was such an abrupt change in topics, she went still for a moment. "No."

"Why not?"

"I wouldn't agree to it."

He raised an eyebrow.

Olivia looked off into the dark. "My only explanation is that—he didn't move me." She turned back to Neil and tried to explain. "I know that society says women aren't supposed to be *moved*—we're supposed to just obey, but I couldn't obey a man who planned to stake his claim on my bank accounts, and I certainly couldn't kiss him."

"So you ran?"

"Yes."

Neil wondered what old Horatio had done upon learning his intended had flown the coop. Had he pined for her? From the short description she'd given, Neil tended to doubt it. "And here you are."

"Here I am, sitting in the dark with a very gentlemanly outlaw."

He chuckled, "Only because it's you. Any other woman would have her hands full."

She tossed back, "I find that hard to believe."

In response he pulled her onto his lap. "Do you?"

She was so startled and so affected by his bold move that she forgot for a moment what she was about. All she could do was look up into his dazzling eyes, brought to life by the glow of the dancing flames.

Setting aside his gentlemanly persona, Neil whispered against her ear, "Were you any other woman . . . I'd kiss you this way . . ."

He brushed his mustached lips across her jaw, then over the edges of her mouth. He sampled her lips with a series of short, lazy pressures, and Olivia began to drown. The tip of his tongue singed her earlobe. Her breath increased in her throat, and when his lips settled fervently on hers, she responded with a telling sigh of pleasure. She'd never sat on a man's lap ever in life, much less been kissed senseless, and that's how she felt—senseless.

The kiss deepened, and they fit themselves closer. Their tongues mated and played. His palm made slow circles over her back, and her body began to awaken to his call. Her nipples were tightening within her corset, and a warm yearning radiated between her thighs. He was now offering kisses to the small stripe of exposed skin beneath her jaw. Her head fell back limply, and she thrilled to the feel of his tribute.

"Dios, you're sweet. . . ."

The kisses were hot and arousing. He moved from her jaw to her lips to her ear and she descended further and further into the sensual maelstrom. Her eyes were closed. Her heightened senses responded to every caress. Now she knew why this sort of behavior was taboo. It was too good, too moving. Being in the circle of a man's arms while he plied you with eager, lingering kisses could make a woman forget all she'd ever learned about decorum and propriety; only sensation mattered.

And the sensations were wonderful. When he undid the upper buttons of her jacket, she forgot to protest. Her virgin's body wanted more, and he gave her more. She had on a collarless blouse beneath her jacket that seemed perfectly designed for him to press his lips against the blooming flesh at the base of her throat. His lips fit the space so perfectly, she moaned with delight. Women from good families were not supposed to let outlaws undo the buttons of their blouse, but Olivia did and was rewarded by the kisses he placed against the tops of her breasts pushing up over her tightly cinched corset and veiled by the soft lace of her camisole.

Neil wanted to ease aside the camisole, reach into her corset, and lift the twin beauties to his eyes and lips, but he held himself in check. Even though he was as hard as granite and the tastes of her soft skin made him harder still, she was a virgin, and her virginity was meant for whomever she married, not a train-robbing Texas Seminole. He kissed his way back up to her mouth and tried to content himself with whatever she was willing to give.

But he wasn't content. He ran a bold hand over her well-covered curves while he sampled the sweet expanse of her bare throat. He hated corsets, always had. A woman encased in whalebone was next to impossible to caress.

Olivia was having more and more difficulty controlling her breathing. The thrill of his hand moving over her bosom would have sent her into shock under normal circumstances, but this was not a normal occurrence. Her breasts were pleading in ways she'd never felt them plead before. There was a dampness between her thighs that had a call of its own, and she had no idea what the pleas and calls were about. All she knew was that she didn't want him to stop.

Neil didn't want to stop either—he hadn't gotten nearly enough of the beautiful, full-bodied woman in his arms—but he knew he should before things went too far. "We should stop . . . ," he whispered against her ear even as his hand continued to map her firmly encased curves.

She mewled a protest.

"If I don't, your corset is coming off and all hell is going to break loose."

Olivia was floating in such a haze of desire that his words seemed to come from far away, and she brazenly heard herself say, "I don't care."

He chuckled, "You will in the morning, Madam Mayor." He gave her another long, passionate kiss, then picked her up and set her beside him.

Their heightened breathing filled the silence of the night. Olivia felt boneless. Her whole body was throbbing and echoing in reaction to the passion he'd filled her with, and heaven help her, she wanted more. She turned her head his way and found him watching her. She wondered if he felt the same.

Neil said, "I could kiss you until the snow flies, Olivia Sterling."

"And I'd let you."

He leaned over and kissed her again. "Button your clothes . . . before you wind up without them."

Olivia dissolved.

"You've had enough for one night."

She kissed him back with a passion she hoped would haunt his days. "Says whom?"

He drew away and eyed her with amusement. "Sassy woman. You're going to be on your way to Texas if you aren't careful."

She bantered back, "That might not be too bad."

Neil was pleased by her playful side and added that aspect of her personality to the list of things he liked about the new mayor of Henry Adams.

Olivia reluctantly closed her clothing. He'd been right to end the tryst. However, her body continued to echo and pulse. *What would have happened had he taken her corset?* During her tenure at Oberlin, one of Olivia's fast classmates had possessed a series of small plates depicting men and women in the most suggestive and shocking positions ever seen by any of the other girls, including Olivia. At the time the plates had seemed revolting and vile, but now? . . . Unnerved by the direction of her thoughts, Olivia finished her buttons, then took a few deep breaths in hopes of achieving some measure of calm.

Neil sat beside her trying to create his own brand of calm. His manhood was not accustomed to being denied. Usually the women were willing and experienced and so was he. Tonight, however, a different set of circumstances were in play, but no matter how hard he tried to focus his mind elsewhere, he kept imagining her nude body arching and rising beneath his lips and his hands—the sounds of her, the tastes of her. It had been a long time since he'd wanted a woman this badly, but she was a woman he couldn't have. "How about some lemonade?"

"I'd like that." Olivia needed something for her parched throat and wondered if the beverage would also cool the heat in her blood. The memory of his lips on the tops of her breasts was going to keep her awake for weeks.

He retrieved the canteen from the saddle, and they took turns drinking. After handing it back to him, Olivia used her fingers to delicately wipe away the drops clinging to the corner of her lips.

Neil found the unconscious gesture to be so very sensual that he had to take another draw from the canteen. It came to him then that he should probably take her home. Granted, some men used a virgin's heady reaction to carnal play as a lead-in to seduction; a woman befuddled by desire might agree to whatever the man might choose to suggest, but Neil had more honor than that. "It's time I took you home."

Olivia didn't want to leave but knew it was for the best. Her reactions to his kisses proved just how wanton she could be, and after all she'd experienced tonight, she wasn't sure that newly awakened part of herself would return to the depths without protest.

Going home would keep her from crossing into far more dangerous territory.

He kicked dust onto the blaze until it died back to embers, then walked her and the horse back to the front of the house. He left the saddle hidden inside of the soddy and helped her mount to the horse's bare back. She sat sideways, and he mounted behind her. Without a word, Olivia leaned against his strong chest and hooked her arms around his waist. Cuddled against him, she closed her eyes and let him take her home.

When they reached her house, the night was just as silent as it had been earlier. The moon had risen, bathing the plains in a bright, soft light. She reached up and touched his face, letting her senses and touch memorize the strong planes of his face and the shape of his masterful lips. "I can't see you again, Neil." *If only he weren't who he was.*

"I know, darlin'. I know." And he did. He was an outlaw. She was a respectable woman who deserved a respectable man.

She leaned up and kissed him with all the regret and passion she could muster. "Good-bye, Neil."

He stroked her cheek. "Bye, Olivia."

He dismounted and helped her down. Without a further word, and without looking back, Olivia went into the house and closed the door.

Chapter 7

Olivia spent the days leading up to the Wednesday swearing-in ceremony sewing the finishing touches on a new ensemble she'd designed for the occasion and trying to forget the passionate Mr. Neil July. The first task was easy; the second seemingly impossible. No matter where her mind settled, he appeared, making her remember his smile, his kisses. By her estimate, she pushed away her yearning for him at least fifty times a day.

On Wednesday evening, dressed in her new blue walking suit and matching hat, Olivia left the house and headed to Sophie's, where the ceremony would be held, followed by a reception. On the walks, heading in the same direction, were men in their best suits and women in their Sunday hats. It warmed Olivia's heart to see so many people showing their support.

The atmosphere inside of Sophie's newly painted dining room was subdued, as befit the occasion, but everyone met her entrance with smiles. She smiled in return and accepted more rounds of congratulations before walking over to greet the Two Spinsters, who stood near Cara Jefferson and Sophie Reynolds. Hugs were shared, and as they waited for the ceremony to begin, Olivia did her best to control the butterflies flapping crazily in her stomach.

Asa stepped forward. "Miss Olivia, would you come up, please."

Applause filled the room. Feeling shy, nervous, and a bit embarrassed, Olivia walked to the front of the room where Asa stood. Once all the clapping died down, he held out a Bible and she placed her hand upon it. Then, repeating his words, she recited her oath: "I, Olivia Sterling, do solemnly swear to serve the citizens of Henry Adams to the best of my ability—to uphold the law and conduct myself in an honorable manner."

When that was done, applause rang out, and Olivia looked through the tears in her eyes at the faces of her jubilant neighbors. She was truly glad she'd chosen to start her new life here, and she planned to do them proud.

Neil was finally ready. Four days had passed since his last visit with Olivia, and he'd spent those four days debating with himself; should he leave, should he stay. Common sense said saddle up and ride out—be content with Olivia's memory and move on with his life. However, it was turning out to be a bit more difficult than that. In reality he knew so little about her that he didn't even know if she had a middle name, yet he was so infatuated with her that he couldn't sleep. Dreams of her haunted him each time he closed his eyes, and when he opened them in the morning, she was still there. He felt bewitched. The lure of her was stronger than a fully loaded gold train, and forcing himself to sit here and not ride over to her house for another taste of her sweet kisses had to be one of the damndest experiences of his life. He kept telling himself there'd be other women, but he didn't want another. He wanted Olivia Sterling.

With that in mind, and the fact that in the end she'd never be his, he was saddling up. In a few days, he planned to be at the border of Indian Territory. Maybe being with Shafts and their sister, Teresa, would help him forget. Neil was certain it would take time, but he planned to start today.

Seated in the saddle now, he took one last look around the camp to make sure he had everything. Only after he was sure did he turn his horse and ride south.

That evening, Olivia sat on her porch looking out over the plains and wondering about Neil. Had he finally ridden away? She assumed he had. Their bittersweet parting had struck her as final. She'd probably never see him again. The surety of that saddened her, but she knew it to be for the best. She couldn't hitch her star to an outlaw, a man who robbed trains for a living. It didn't matter why he'd taken up the occupation; he was wanted, and because of that, life with him had no future.

In Henry Adams there was no official mayor's residence. The mayor ruled from an old desk stuck in the corner of the sheriff's office. It had always been that way. Although Armstead Malloy had included the building of an independent space in his campaign promises, Olivia couldn't see spending the town's limited funds on something so cosmetic. So she was at the desk now, going through the items left behind by the late Mayor Stuckey.

Seated at his desk on the other side of the room, Chase said with a laugh, "If you find any gold in there it's mine. Martin owed me five dollars from a poker game."

Olivia smiled, then went back to her rummaging. She didn't find gold. She did find pens, a few old newspapers, a map of Topeka, and a program from last year's regional mayor convention. There were also personal items like a pair of socks and one cuff link. In the bottom drawer was a large ring of keys. "What are these?"

"Keys to all the businesses on Main Street. I have a set, too."

Olivia studied them. "Why does the mayor have a set?"

"Well, in case I can't find mine, and so Martin could go over and snitch cigars from Armstead Malloy's stock every now and then."

Olivia's eyes widened. "You aren't serious?"

He held up his hand. "I took an oath to tell the truth."

She laughed. "Well, as long as I'm in office, Malloy's cigars are safe."

She placed all of Mayor Stuckey's personal items in a crate. By rights they should go to his widow, but the young woman had left town the day after the funeral, taking with her every penny Stuckey had had in the bank. Olivia was just about to ask Chase where she could store the crate when Armstead Malloy strolled in wearing a brown-and-black checked suit. He gave both Olivia and the sheriff a patronizing smile, then said, "Good. I have you both here. I'm about to embark upon a new business venture."

Chase asked, "Which is?"

"Rebuilding the Liberian Lady."

"No," Chase said plainly.

"Why not?"

"Town doesn't need a saloon."

Malloy laughed. "Of course it does." He then turned his attention to Olivia. "I suppose you haven't changed your stance?"

"No."

"Well, since there's nothing in the charter that forbids it, I'm going to introduce my plan at tomorrow's Elders meeting."

Olivia's voice was cool. "That is within your rights."

"As is rebuilding that saloon. According to what some of the old-timers tell me, the Lady was originally owned by the son of the richest person in town. Man named Miles Sutton. Are they correct, Sheriff?"

"They are. And did they also tell you that it burned down one night because Sutton was a snake?"

Malloy tossed back, "Is that a threat, Sheriff?"

"No, Malloy, just some history. If I threaten you, you'll know it."

Malloy turned and looked up at the board on the wall that featured the faces and names of men wanted by the law. He seemed particularly interested in one featuring the Terrible Twins. "Anybody catch July and his Injun brother yet? Says here they're worth a thousand dollars apiece."

Olivia's lips tightened.

Chase replied, "Not that I know of."

Malloy asked Olivia, "You wouldn't know anything about July's whereabouts, would you, Miss Olivia?"

She didn't respond.

"Are you done here, Malloy?" Chase growled. "If so, there's the door."

"Just curious, that's all, Sheriff. We wouldn't want our mayor implicated in a scandal that may make her resign."

Olivia slowly folded her arms. The only scandal she was worried about was the one that would result from her feeding Malloy headfirst into the nearest horse trough.

Malloy gave them that patronizing smile again, touched his brown bowler, and exited.

For a moment, there was silence in the sheriff's office, then Chase and Olivia said in unison, "Nasty little man." They shared a look and laughed.

While Chase went home for lunch, Olivia sat at her desk and thought about Malloy. He was determined to make her job difficult. She was certain that his plans for the Lady would be the first in a series of proposals designed to vex her, but she was determined to stand her ground. The women in Olivia's family had always been active in their communities. Her paternal grandmother, Hattie, had been one of the founders of the nation's first female anti-slavery society formed in Salem, Massachusetts, in 1832. Olivia's mother, Eunice, had been a member of Philadelphia's famous Mother Bethel AME Church and had participated in the Free Produce campaign, the abolitionist marches and conventions. Olivia's activist parents began taking Olivia to rallies before she could walk. The parlor of their home was always filled with men and women discussing politics and the state of the Union. When she became old enough it was only natural for her to follow in the footsteps of her family, and she too did her part by volunteering to lift the race. She was certain those experiences would serve her well in her capacity as mayor if she could survive Armstead Malloy.

Friday night's meeting of the Elders turned out to be more fractious than she'd imagined. Everyone had an opinion on the resurrection of the Liberian Lady, and the meeting was descending into chaos. In an attempt to restore order, Olivia banged her gavel for what seemed like an eternity. This was the first community discussion on the subject, and she couldn't imagine what the subsequent ones would be like. "Order!" she yelled, but no one seemed to be listening. "Order!!"

Folks were arguing, yelling, and confronting those who disagreed with them. As a result, no one could hear anything. Olivia looked over at the sheriff and called out over the din, "Sheriff Jefferson, I want you to remove anyone not in their seat!"

He stood and yelled, "All right, who wants to be the first to go?"

One of the men shot back, "Take the mayor, she's the one who can't keep order."

To her dismay, a chorus of male voices said, "Amen!"

Olivia had had enough. "Sheriff. Remove that man."

Suddenly you could hear a pin drop on cotton. Olivia had come to the meeting determined to treat the representatives on each side of the issue with respect, but apparently there were those in the crowd who weren't operating under the same rules. She was aware that some of the men resented her victory, but she refused to turn tail and run because of it. Her papa had always said, Show a jackal your teeth and it'll back down. Well, they were about to see her teeth. The man she'd singled out, a prominent farmer, was staring at her as if she'd grown another head. "You can't have me ejected."

"Since I was duly elected, I can have you thrown in jail if I choose, Mr. Pierce."

He appeared stunned.

Olivia asked in a firm voice, "Are you leaving or staying, Mr. Pierce?"

He sat down angrily, and the silence in the hall grew.

Olivia looked over at Sophie, and the wink Sophie threw her way buoyed Olivia. Feeling more in control, Olivia told the large crowd, "Now, this is a very important issue, so let's discuss it as if it is. Mr. Malloy, state your position."

He stood and said grandly, "My position is: I have the money. There is nothing in the town laws that prohibits a saloon, so I see no need to discuss the matter further. I came to the board as a courtesy. That's all."

Olivia sighed with impatience. "Are you saying that you don't need the board's approval?"

"Yes, Miss Olivia. I'm saying I don't need your approval."

She turned to the Elders seated at their table in hopes they would verbally support her but received only shrugs instead. She plowed on alone, "We don't need a saloon here, Mr. Malloy." Much applause followed that statement. "Saloons breed disaster for the wives and children of those who imbibe too much."

"You don't understand," he replied slowly, as if talking to a child. "I am rebuilding the saloon. Unless you have the legal means to stop this enterprise, I'll see you at the ribbon cutting."

And he left.

Some of his supporters laughed at the dumbstruck

look on the faces of those who opposed the saloon, then they followed him out.

Olivia wanted to punch something.

Olivia and Chase spent Saturday morning poring over the town's charter, looking for a way to stop Malloy, but they found none. And because the Liberian Lady had existed in the past, the town really hadn't a leg to stand on in terms of precedent.

Olivia cracked, "I've been mayor less than three days and Malloy has already given me my first defeat. Who knows what other plans he has up his badly dressed sleeves."

Chase nodded his agreement.

Olivia gathered up the charter papers. "I'm going to take all this home. There has to be a way around Malloy, and I'm going to find it."

"Good luck. Lots of folks are pulling for you."

"And an equal number are not."

"True, but you didn't think being mayor was going to be easy, did you?"

"In a way, yes. The elders do most of the work— all Mayor Stuckey ever did was ride in the parades."

He smiled at her. "True, but things will work out. You'll see."

Not certain she shared the sheriff's optimism, Olivia went home.

But in going over the charter again and again, she had no better luck finding a way out of the dilemma than she had earlier. About an hour later, Cara entered the shop, and Olivia was glad for the distraction.

Cara took a seat on one of the chairs. "How are you doing?"

"Terrible. Malloy is going to win this round, unfortunately."

Cara's face mirrored her sympathy. "Well, with any luck somebody will burn it down like they did last time."

"You were living here then? What happened?"

Cara shrugged. "No one knows."

"Your husband said no one liked Miles Sutton."

"Miles Sutton was a snake. By the time the place burned down, not even his mother wanted anything to do with him."

Olivia wondered what kind of relationship Malloy had with his mother. "What happened to him? Did he pull up stakes and settle elsewhere?"

For a moment Cara didn't reply.

Olivia asked, "Cara?"

Cara finally met her eyes. "You may as well know. It's not as if it's a secret. Miles was trying to kill Chase, so to keep that from happening I shot Miles and killed him."

Olivia stared.

"It was an awful experience."

Olivia wanted to ask more, but she could see the pain in Cara's eyes, so she didn't press for more details.

Cara said, "I'll share the whole story with you someday, but right now, I have a question for you."

"Shoot."

"What is this I'm hearing about you night riding with Neil July?"

Olivia dropped her shears. "What?"

Cara smiled. "By your face I'm assuming it's true."

Olivia was speechless.

"The spinsters saw you."

Olivia's knees went weak.

"They won't tell anyone, but you should be more careful. Rachel and Daisy may not have been the only ones."

Olivia took in a deep breath.

Cara said, "I knew something was going on with you two the morning he came to see you after your heatstroke faint. I could feel the sizzle in the room."

Olivia was too embarrassed to meet Cara's eyes.

"No sense in being ashamed. Take it from a woman who knows—these things happen. Chase wasn't exactly suitable when he and I first met. Falling in love with him almost got me run out of town. I was dismissed from my teaching position. Biddies hissed at me in church."

Olivia looked up. "I'm not in love with him."

Cara held Olivia's eyes.

Olivia repeated, "I'm not. It's just—he's so different from the men I'm accustomed to meeting."

"And?"

"And I know better than to fall in love with an outlaw. I'm not that addled, but—"

Cara waited for her to finish.

Olivia had no idea how to explain to her friend the myriad emotions that connected Olivia to Neil July. "I can't explain."

"It's okay. I do understand. Chase hit me the same way."

"It's all so strange, Cara. Here I am, a fine, up-standing, well-raised woman, sneaking around with a wanted man. I keep telling myself that every woman has at least one man in her past who was un-suitable and that Neil is mine, but . . ." Once again she couldn't explain. "I suppose I'm having a hard time explaining it because I'm still trying to explain it to myself."

"Sometimes Cupid's arrow does the darndest things."

Olivia waved it all away. "It doesn't matter. I doubt I'll ever see him again, and if I do, he'll be out of my system."

"Okay," Cara voiced skeptically, "but if you need someone to talk to, I'm here."

Olivia nodded. "I know."

The two friends shared a silent look, then Cara got up. "Well, let me go and find Chase and Branch. We're having lemonade at Sophie's. I'll stop by on my way home."

"Thanks. You all have a good time."

After Cara's departure, Olivia sank into a chair and put her head in her hands. *She'd been seen.* Scandal wouldn't begin to describe the firestorm that would engulf her should the story ever get out. She prayed the spinsters had been the only wit-nesses, but Henry Adams was a small town. Al-though she knew the spinsters would guard her secret, somebody else might not be so discreet.

Lord. If Malloy ever found out, all perdition would break loose. She wanted to kick herself for letting lust overrule logic, but the die had been cast. There was nothing she could do but wait and see.

The Reverend Whitfield's sermon on Sunday was a fire and brimstone denunciation of demon rum and all its ancillary evils—gambling, loose women, and destitute families. Olivia was glad to have his support, but she noticed that Malloy and his followers weren't in church: The reverend was, as the saying goes, preaching to the choir.

The five mounted riders spread along the train tracks heard the rumbling train seconds before they saw it. As it came barreling around the bend, they could feel the earth shaking; could see the smoke belching and billowing from the stacks; could smell the brimstone in the air: but mostly they imagined what they were going to do once they divvied up all the gold the train was carrying.

Watching the beast approach, a familiar excitement filled Neil. The itch to start the chase was as strong in him as it had been a decade ago, when he took up train robbing; the only feeling better was the one found between a woman's thighs.

Neil waited for the train to charge closer. Train robbing was an art. The gang had an inner sense that let them know when the time was right. When the engine came close enough for him to see the engineer lean out, Neil yelled, "Let's get it!"

He whipped his reins across his mount's back and leaned into the saddle. His horse was fast—the fastest around—and he had no trouble moving to the lead. Not far behind him, a grinning Two Shafts leaned into his own horse. Beside him rode the wildly exuberant Teresa, whose high-pitched version of the Seminole war cry sounded as loud as the train. It had been years since they'd ridden together, and they were enjoying it immensely.

Neil urged more speed, and his horse obliged. By now they were even with the engine. Rocks shot off the wheels like fourth of July rockets, hitting Neil and his horse, but they rode on. The train sounded its whistle, filling the air like the roar of an angry beast, while the sparks from the stack fell like rain. The train was only carrying two cars—easy pickings in the old days. But today's trains were fast. Some were able to achieve speeds approaching fifty miles per hour, and Neil had the sinking feeling that this one might be one of those. He'd never seen one quite like it before. The design looked sleeker, the engine more powerful. The faster they rode, the faster the train seemed to be moving. In fact, Neil realized with wide eyes, it was pulling away from them. He cursed and dug his heels into his mount's sides, praying for more speed, but it wasn't to be. Blue uniformed soldiers stepped onto the porch of the last car, pointing and laughing at Neil's futile pursuit; some even waved. The distance between the train and the gang widened so much that the now angry and frustrated riders drew their horses to a halt and watched the train barrel down the track, taking the gold with it. Neil wanted to shoot something—the train, mainly. He hated progress.

Her long black hair and beautiful dark features hidden beneath her beat-up hat, Teresa threw the hat to the ground. "Dammit!"

Shafts looked disappointed, as did the rest of the gang. "Can't rob what you can't catch, little sister."

Teresa replied, "This is the second one this week."

Neil didn't want to be reminded of the failures. It was if the world had become unglued. He felt like an old man living in a new and changing world that was leaving him behind in much the same way the train had. "I say we get a bottle of tequila."

Teresa quipped, "Providing we can catch that."

Shafts said, "Don't worry, Neil. We'll get the next one."

Neil wasn't as optimistic, but he turned his horse and headed everyone back the way they'd come.

That night, after too much tequila, Neil lay outside on the ground behind Teresa's house, looking up at the stars. Thinking made his already pounding head worsen, but he couldn't turn off the memories of today's humiliation. How in the world was he going to make a living if he couldn't catch the damn trains? Neil's mother was a firm believer in signs, and by her way of thinking, not being able to catch two trains in one week qualified as something to be concerned about. He was now living in a world where trains could thumb their noses at outlaws and wave as the engine sped by. *Dios.*

He ran his hands wearily over his unshaven face. He was in the thirty-eighth year of his life—far past the age to be considering taking up a new occupation, even if he wished to. Yet that appeared to be what he was facing. When he resigned his commission with the Negro Seminole scouts nearly a decade ago, robbing trains had been a way to feed his family and pay back the army and the United States government for their broken promises to the Seminole Nation. The combined treachery of those two entities had filled him with enough anger and hate to fuel hell, but then, once his family's future was secured, robbing trains became fun. The underlying reasons still beat strong within him, but he loved the exhilaration and the excitement of the chase. Now he was lying here mystified by what the future might hold. The last thing he wanted was to turn into a model citizen and put his guns in a trunk for his descendants to marvel over. He had a lot of good years left in him, but he balked at spending them clerking or farming. So what were his choices? None that he could think of.

He struggled to his feet. It was time for more tequila. Then he was going to see Olivia.

Chapter 8

❦

Before Emancipation, free Black abolitionists and their White counterparts refused to celebrate July 4. They saw little reason to exalt the Declaration of Independence when over 3 million people of African descent were held in slavery. Instead they celebrated August First, the date Great Britain emancipated its slaves in the West Indies in 1837. Thousands of people in the United States and Canada participated in parades, lectures, and picnics in support of freedom and to honor the British edict. Some churches held night-watch services, while others offered speeches by prominent folks of the time. Once emancipation became law in the United States, many towns continued to celebrate August First, and Henry Adams was one.

The parade that officially opened the festivities

was set to begin at noon. As mayor, Olivia was required to be a participant, but she was dressed and ready by nine that morning because she had a ten o'clock appointment with Armstead Malloy.

True to his word, he'd rebuilt the Liberian Lady. Working the carpenters and their crews in twenty-four-hour shifts, the place had gone up in record time. The grand opening was slated for today, but the Board of Elders meeting last night had given her all the authority and ammunition she needed to put Malloy in his place. She couldn't wait to tell him the news.

She stopped by the sheriff's office first. Chase had been at the meeting last night and had promised to go with her to see Malloy. With him beside her for support, Olivia walked to the outskirts of town to confront her nemesis.

When they approached the new saloon, Olivia shook her head at its sheer size. Next to the Malloy Mercantile, the new Liberian Lady was the largest building in town. It had an imported Mexican bar, behind which hung a large, gilt-edged mirror reportedly from Italy. It also sported a linoleum floor and, at last count, six underdressed and overrouged girls working the place. Olivia couldn't pretend she approved of the enterprise, but Malloy had certainly put up an edifice that would lure folks from miles around just to see the place.

Women rarely entered saloons, so when Olivia swept in, the fancy-dressed piano player froze in the middle of his tune. Everyone in the place looked up—from the gaudily dressed girls to the bartender.

A few seconds later, Malloy came strolling down the staircase that led up to the private rooms leased by the girls. The dimly lit place housed at least ten tables, and there was enough liquor in the cabinets behind the bar to give Reverend Whitfield apoplexy.

"Well," Malloy said, showing his patented grin. "What brings you two here? Can I buy you a drink, Sheriff?"

"No thanks, Malloy. Miss Olivia and I are here on business."

Malloy looked between the two of them. "This isn't another attempt to shut me down, is it? I thought we agreed I was right and you all were wrong."

Olivia held onto her temper and said coolly, "The Board of Elders and I have designated this part of town a vice district, and as such it is subject to a series of town taxes."

He laughed. "You're pulling my leg." He turned to Chase. "She's fooling, right?"

"I am not laughing, Mr. Malloy. Many towns in the west have such laws on their books, and now Henry Adams has some of its own."

"Oh, come on now. Is this the best you can do? Taxes?"

Olivia didn't waver. "The Elders have established a five-hundred-dollar-a-year licensing fee for businesses in this district."

Malloy's eyes popped. "What?!"

"Added to that is an annual fifty-dollar federal excise tax, a monthly local business tax of fifty dollars, and a monthly ten-dollar liquor tax."

Malloy was now speechless.

Olivia then added, "We are also taxing your lady employees. In addition to assessing them ten dollars per month for their licenses, and an equal amount for their rooms, they are also required to pay Doc Johnson five dollars monthly for their physical examinations."

The women at the table protested loudly, but Olivia paid them no mind. Making the women visit Doc Johnson once a month would help them manage the virulent diseases associated with their trade.

Malloy's face turned mean. "I'm not paying it."

"Then the sheriff has the authority to close you down."

Chase's smile didn't reach his eyes. "And I would enjoy it. This place has a lot of bad memories for me and my wife, so please give me a reason to watch it burn again."

Malloy was so angry that his fists were balled up like an angry child's. "You can't do this!"

Olivia countered, "Ah, but we can. The charter which you were so dismissive of gives the Elders the right to enact any laws they see fit to promote the town's well-being. Regulating a vice palace falls under that category."

Olivia knew she had him over a barrel, and by the blaze in Malloy's eyes, he knew it, too.

"So when do I have to pay all these fines?"

"By the time the parade begins, or you do no business here."

His eyes widened once more. "I can't muster that much money on such short notice."

"Then I suppose you'll have to cancel your grand opening. Good day, Mr. Malloy."

Without further word, Olivia sailed out. A grinning Chase was right behind her.

Back at the sheriff's office, Olivia took off her gloves and set her handbag on her desk. "Was I firm enough?"

Chase nodded. "More than enough."

"He's such a little ferret."

"And you put the ferret in his cage. The town was right to elect you mayor. Once this gets around, your ladies will be wanting to run you for governor."

Olivia doubted that, but felt good knowing she'd found a way to bring Malloy down a few pegs. She'd gotten the idea from an article she'd read in a Fort Smith newspaper Cara Lee received by subscription. The article outlined the myriad fines and fees imposed by Fort Smith's town council to keep its red-light district under control. The next step for Olivia had been to share the information with the Elders and to come up with a similar fee structure for Henry Adams. The Elders, unhappy with Malloy's public denunciation of the town charter, had voted unanimously for Olivia's proposal. Even those members who had supported Malloy in the past had deserted him on this issue. She chuckled inwardly at the memory of Malloy's angry face and decided she liked being mayor.

The parade started promptly at noon. From the buildings on Main Street flew the standards of the United States, Liberia, and Haiti. Other buildings were decorated with the Kansas state flag and the banners of Henry Adams, Nicodemus, and the other Black townships in Barton and Rice Counties. The streets were packed, the smells of roasting hogs and beef were in the air, and everyone waited eagerly for the festivities to begin.

As always, the Civil War veterans were the first in line and received rousing cheers. The men were in uniforms, carrying the banners of their regiments. In years past, the procession had been led by Mr. Deerfield, the oldest vet in the valley, but he'd passed away last winter. His fourteen-year-old grandson, Mitchell, was wearing Mr. Deerfield's uniform and marching proudly in his stead.

Behind Mitchell were the men of the First Kansas Colored, and the crowds lining the street broke into earth-shattering cheers. The First Kansas Colored had fought for the Union even before President Lincoln had given approval for Black troops to enter the fight, and they'd distinguished themselves at the Battle of Honey Springs, one of the most important Civil War battles fought in Indian Territory.

Marching behind the Kansas regiment were uniformed men representing other Black units, including two members of the Fifth Massachusetts Cavalry, whose men had been among the first Union troops to enter Richmond after its fall to Union forces.

Once the soldiers marched by, the crowd turned its attention to the political societies. The Republicans drew the most cheers, even though the national party was no longer a staunch supporter of the race. The Democrats drew the most jeers for the continuing disenfranchisement of the freedmen. National leaders of the race were still calling for Black voters to change their allegiance so that the Republicans wouldn't take them for granted, but few heeded the call. Many of the valley's citizens had been forced from the south because of the terror and lynchings promoted by Redemptionist Democrats, and they weren't about to embrace them under any circumstances.

Cara and her students were next in the parade line. On their heels were the many church choirs that had come to town for the annual August First choir competition. Their melodic voices filled the air.

When the buckboard holding the Henry Adams town officials reached the middle of Main Street, the raucous cheers warmed Olivia's heart. She saw that many women were wearing Olivia Roses on their collars and lapels, and she couldn't have asked for a more moving tribute.

After the parade ended, the crowds dispersed to take a gander at all the other activities—the fastest pet contest, won again by fifteen-year-old Frankie Cooper and his pet rooster; the baked goods; the various bands now setting up in the field behind Handy Reed's livery. Later, those who cared to could head over to the church to hear a speech by the distinguished J. C. Price, president of the all-Black Livingstone College in North Carolina. Mr. Price, an articulate and rising national leader, favored education and self-help as ways to uplift the race.

By late evening, the festivities were still going

strong, but Olivia was exhausted. On her way back to her office, she stopped at an ice cream stand and purchased a small bowl. She'd just taken her first bite when Cara Lee walked up.

"Thought you might like to know that in lieu of opening, Malloy is charging fifty cents a head for folks to tour the inside of the Lady."

Olivia waved her spoon dismissively. "I don't care. I'm too tired to wrestle with him right now. Maybe tomorrow."

"I'm not finished."

Olivia sighed wistfully at the ice cream she was probably not going to get to eat, and asked, "What else is he doing?"

"Charging men two dollars to go around back and take a gander at the girls standing in the upstairs windows. They aren't wearing very much."

Olivia sighed again. "Okay. Have you seen your husband lately?"

"He's at Handy's."

Olivia handed Cara the bowl of ice cream. "You finish it. Life would be so much easier if Malloy would go out onto the plains and let himself be eaten by a bear."

"Amen."

"Thanks for letting me know."

"Thanks for the ice cream."

Olivia smiled, then headed toward Handy's to find Chase so she could sic him on Armstead Malloy.

Later, Olivia, Cara, the Two Spinsters, Sophie, and Sybil Whitfield gathered in Olivia's shop to go over the schedule for tomorrow's activities. All of the women were involved in making sure the celebration ran smoothly, and they were in the middle of discussing the choir competition at the church when Olivia heard a loud noise come from the back of the shop. It sounded like furniture being knocked over. Puzzled, the women looked at each other, but before they could get up to investigate, Neil July stumbled into the room. There was pain in his face. He had one hand on his side, and the other searched blindly for something to support his weight. "Olivia, help . . . me. . . ."

Startled, they all froze.

He stared into Olivia's eyes, letting her see the lucidity there, then he crumpled to the floor.

"Neil!" she screamed and ran to his side. Only then did she see the mass of blood staining the back of his brown leather vest. "Oh, Lord. He's been shot." And by the look of it, very seriously.

Cara was already out the door. "I'll get Chase!"

Sophie yelled, "Get Delbert too!"

The spinsters drew closer and knelt beside the barely breathing July. Rachel placed her hand on his forehead. "Get some cotton, Olivia, he's bleeding bad."

Olivia couldn't think. All she could see was the torn and bleeding flesh.

Daisy yelled, "Olivia! Move, girl! We have to staunch this blood!"

Olivia moved.

By the time Delbert and Chase arrived, the fabric the women had placed over the wound was saturated and useless. Delbert knelt quickly, saying, "You ladies move back, I need to get this vest off."

The sharp blade of Chase's knife made short work of Neil's leather vest. Delbert looked grim. "He's been back shot. I need to lay him somewhere so I can see if the bullets are lodged in the wound."

"Use my bedroom."

"Thanks. If we try and take him all the way to my place, I'm scared he'll bleed to death on the way."

There was so much blood that Olivia felt like swooning. Her heart in her throat, she watched Delbert, Chase, and the just-arrived Asa gingerly carry Neil into the back and place him on her bed. Once he was situated, the men closed the door, and Olivia began to pray.

It didn't take long for the news to spread, and soon most of the seven hundred people in town for the festivities were standing in front of Olivia's shop hoping to get a look at anybody connected to the whirlwind surrounding the infamous and popular Neil July.

Inside, Olivia was pacing and saying to the women, "I know he's wanted by the law, but who would shoot him in the *back!*"

That was the question of the hour. The code in the west was that only a coward shot a man in the back. A few moments later, Olivia's question was answered as Armstead Malloy burst into the shop. "Where's Jefferson?"

The women observed him with malevolent looks. Olivia replied, "The sheriff is occupied at the moment."

He grinned proudly. "I know. I came to stake my claim on the July reward money."

Olivia's eyes widened. "You did this?!"

He puffed out his chest like a bantam rooster. "If you're meaning did I shoot July, I sure did. Saw him ride by. Lucky I had my Winchester with me."

Sophie asked pointedly, "Was your aim that bad, or did you intend to shoot him in the *back?*"

Malloy flinched like he'd been slapped, then, recovering his swagger, he said, "Warrant said dead or alive. It doesn't say how to bring him in—just bring him in."

Sophie said, "So you bushwhacked him."

When Malloy didn't reply, Daisy said in disapproving tones, "Mr. Malloy, you have a lot to learn about living out here. Only a *coward* shoots a man in the back."

He appeared uncomfortable for a moment, then looked away.

Sybil Whitfield added, "I hope the money you collect will compensate for the damage this will do to your reputation."

Malloy sniffed. "He's an outlaw, ladies. You're acting as if July is someone of value."

Olivia had had enough. "Get out of my shop."

"I need to see the sheriff."

"Some other time, and don't worry, I'll let him know you were responsible. By this time tomorrow, everyone in the three-state area will probably know. I hope you enjoy the notoriety it brings." The fire in her eyes must have made an impression, because he turned on his heel and exited.

She snapped, "Nasty little man!"

Rachel said sagely, "Nasty little *bushwhacker*."

Olivia agreed on the truer description.

As one hour turned into two and the men still hadn't come out of the bedroom, Olivia was actively fighting her fear that Neil might die. *Where had he come from?* She thought he'd left the area weeks ago. She could still hear his plea for help, and the memory of his bloody, bullet-torn back would stay with her for a long time. Armstead Malloy needed a whip taken to him for such a cowardly act. No one deserved to be back shot—no one—yet Delbert Johnson was in there fighting to save Neil's life. She was sure he would do all he could, but would it be enough?

Three hours after Doc Johnson's arrival, he came out of the bedroom followed by Chase and Asa. All had blood on their shirts, and Olivia held her breath as she waited for Delbert's prognosis.

"If he survives the night, it'll be a miracle. I got the bullets, but he's lost a serious amount of blood. If anyone has a way of contacting his kin, it should be done."

Olivia bit her lip to keep the emotions from showing on her face.

Cara said to her husband, "Chase, Malloy shot him."

Chase turned sharply. "Malloy?"

She nodded. "He came by earlier to stake his claim on the reward money. Those are his words."

"You bushwhack a man, then you come in bragging about it? He's one of a kind."

Delbert shook his head in sorrow and amazement. "I'm going to spend the night here just in case I'm needed. Miss Olivia, you're welcome to stay at my place."

"No, I've another bedroom, and I'd prefer to stay. You may need someone to cook, wash linen—"

He eyed her. "I appreciate the offer, but you're an unmarried woman. It won't do to have the gossips trashing your reputation."

"Doctor, Neil July came *here* after being shot—my reputation is already being run through the mill. I'll stay unless the sheriff thinks it might be dangerous."

Chase shook his head. "July couldn't hurt a fly in the shape he's in, but it'll look better if I stayed around, too." He then turned to his wife. "You and Branch will be all right?"

She nodded.

Olivia silently blessed them both.

A short while later, Olivia's women friends decided to leave but vowed to stop by in the morning. There was still an August First celebration to oversee—Neil July or no Neil July, and they vowed to make certain the programs went smoothly. Olivia gave them all a strong hug, then saw them to the door.

Outside, the street was still filled with people. Many were holding lit torches so they could see in the thick Kansas darkness.

One of the farmers yelled out, "How's July doing, Miss Olivia?"

She knew the truth was best. "Not good. He was back shot."

A buzz of disbelief went through the crowd.

She added, "Armstead Malloy is claiming to be the bushwhacker."

More disbelief and a distinct grumble of disapproval could be heard.

"I'm asking that you all leave so Mr. July can have some peace. We'll know more in the morning."

To her surprise, the people dispersed without protest, and a grateful Olivia went back inside.

Chase met her at the door. "I'm going to talk to Malloy. I'll be back soon as I can."

She nodded, then went to join Doc Johnson's death watch.

Neil was floating through a lush green land he thought might be Florida. Although he'd never been there, his ancestral spirit assured him that this was indeed the homeland of the Seminole Nation. He saw orange trees and houses on stilts. There were children laughing and playing amidst the tropical forest, and women weaving vessels from the tall, fragrant grasses that grew in abundance. He saw men wearing the traditional colorful feathered turbans and ear ornaments working together to clear a portion of the forest so it could be turned into a productive field. One of the men was his grandfather, the old chief July. When he saw Neil approaching, he said, "Neil, my son."

"Greetings, abuelo."

Neil's grandfather looked healthy and strong. The other men stopped working and were viewing Neil with interest. Some of their faces were familiar: John Horse, the revered leader of the Black Seminoles, and Wild Cat, son of Seminole Chief Phillip.

In 1849, Chiefs Wild Cat and John Horse led the
Seminoles on the Great Trek, a nine-month walk
from Indian Territory to Mexico. Standing beside
John Horse was Adam Paine, a Seminole scout
who'd had the Medal of Honor bestowed upon him
for bravery, only to be murdered by a Texas sheriff
who shot Paine at such close range that Paine's
clothing caught fire. So, am I dead, too?

Before Neil could figure that out, or try and put
names to the other faces, his grandfather asked,
"Why are you here, Neil?"

"I'm not sure, abuelo."

His grandfather stated gravely, "It is not time for
you to join us."

Neil didn't understand.

"Go back, Neil."

The men turned away and resumed their work,
then Neil felt himself fading back into darkness.

Olivia awakened in her spare room, and it took
her a moment to remember where she was. Neil's
plight came back in a rush, so she got up and hur-
riedly grabbed a blouse and skirt. She prayed he'd
survived the night.

Delbert was in the kitchen pouring alcohol on
some of Olivia's stoutest thread when she entered.
"How is he?"

"He's alive, but for how long only the good Lord
knows. I need to repair some of the stitches."

"But you didn't expect him to live through the
night."

"No, I didn't."

"Then that's a good sign."

"Under normal circumstances, yes, but he has a long way to go. I wouldn't get my hopes up too high were I you."

Olivia nodded her understanding. "Where's the sheriff?"

"I sent him home about an hour after I sent you to bed."

The doc had shooed her off around 3 A.M. It was now six, which meant she'd gotten a whole three hours of sleep. She now understood why she felt so poorly and out of sorts. "When are you going to get some sleep?"

He shrugged. "I may leave for a few hours when Chase returns."

"I'll make us some fresh coffee, then. Are you hungry?"

"No, not really."

Olivia didn't press him. He had weariness stamped all over his face, and he didn't need her nagging him to eat.

While making the coffee she asked, "Has he regained consciousness?"

"Not really. He's been doing lots of mumbling—talking in his dreams, I'm assuming. Most of it is in Spanish."

Olivia was surprised by that revelation. She'd had no idea Neil knew Spanish, but when she remembered him talking about living in Mexico, it all made sense.

By the time the spinsters arrived at seven-thirty, Olivia was more awake, washed and dressed for the day.

Daisy asked, "How's he faring?"

"He's still here."

Rachel nodded. "The Seminole Nation fought the government almost two decades before their removal west. He comes from strong stock. Just keep praying."

As Olivia moved through the day, Neil was constantly on her mind. Asa and Sophie sat with him most of the morning, while Delbert went home to get a few hours' sleep. Olivia wanted to stop by and check on Neil, but the mayor was needed to open the choir competition. In the end she was glad to witness the event because of the inner strength she received from the holy music.

Everywhere she went for the rest of the afternoon, people stopped her to ask about Neil. She related all that she knew and was surprised by how many people claimed to be praying for his recovery.

Before heading home, Olivia walked over to the sheriff's office. Chase looked as weary as she felt. "How's our patient?" he asked.

"I haven't had a chance to check on him, but I'm assuming he is still with us."

"Someone would have let us know if he wasn't. So you survived August First."

Olivia sighed. The festivities were finally over for another year. "I'll let you know tomorrow."

"You did well, considering the circumstances."

"I know. A lot of people are praying for him. One would think folks wouldn't care one way or the other about an outlaw."

"True, but Neil isn't a run-of-the-mill outlaw. He and Shafts are larger than life out here. Folks admire them for their cleverness, their pranks, and their generosity."

He must have seen the confusion on her face, because he explained, "Neil and Shafts have been known to drop off their loot at orphanages, schools, veterans' homes. They've never killed anyone as far as I know, and folks respect that."

Olivia did too. "Did you talk to Malloy?"

"Yep. He's chomping at the bit for the reward money, but I told him he gets nothing until after the trial."

"Trial?"

He nodded. "Once the marshal in Topeka gets wind of Neil being here, he's going to want me to hold him until the trial."

"How soon?"

"Depends on when the circuit judge can fit us in."

She didn't like the sound of that. "Will Malloy be brought up on charges of bushwhacking?"

"No, unfortunately. Neil's the only one at risk here. The railroad and the army are going to lobby the judge for a long imprisonment. Neil's been a thorn in their sides for years."

"But Malloy goes scot free."

"And is entitled to the reward."

Olivia shook her head. She understood the army and the railroad's position on Neil, but she didn't think Malloy should be rewarded for his treachery. "Do you see any way out of this for Neil?"

"No."

Olivia didn't either. "Did you contact his brother?"

"I sent a wire to Wewoka in Indian Territory, one to Brackettville, Texas, and one to Nacimiento in Mexico in case some of his family is still there."

"What do you think Two Shafts will do?"

"Ride here and try to break him out. It's what I'd do if it were my brother. The Twins have only been captured once. I'm sure Shafts wants that record to stand."

"Will there be trouble?"

"More than likely. Shafts probably won't come alone."

Olivia felt a shiver of fear cross her skin.

Chase added, "I'm not so much worried about Shafts as I am about the bounty hunters who are going to come sniffing around."

"Bounty hunters?"

"Yes, the lure of the money on Neil's head is going to pull in every piece of horse riding trash from here to Texas."

"But doesn't the reward money belong to Malloy?"

"Only if he's alive to collect it and only if Neil stays put. Which he probably won't. The bounty hunters know there isn't a jail that can hold either of the Twins for long, and when he escapes they aim to be right on his tail."

Olivia found this more and more distressing.

"I told Malloy he might want to stop all his bragging and leave town until after the trial. Men who hunt other men for a living won't think twice about plugging him to put him out of the picture."

"What did he say?"

"He doesn't believe I know what I'm talking about . . . so . . ." Chase shrugged, as if that were explanation enough.

"Do you really think we're going to be overrun by bounty hunters?"

"Yep. If Neil lives, they'll start riding in by week's end."

"What are you going to do?"

"Call on a deputy marshal friend I know down in Wewoka to come up and add his guns to mine. Name's Dixon Wildhorse."

"Will he come?"

"I'm hoping so. Waiting for him to wire me back."

"Where do I go to resign as mayor?"

Chase chuckled. "Too late. In for a penny, in for a pound."

"I know." She felt like her head was spinning. "Well, I'm heading home. Maybe this won't seem so overwhelming after I've had some dinner." She headed to the door.

"Olivia."

She turned back. "Yes?"

"As long as Neil is alive, he's under arrest. If you aid him in escaping in any way, you'll be facing a judge, too."

She studied him. "I understand."

"Just so you do."

She nodded and took her leave.

Chapter 9

❧∽◦◦∽❧

Delbert and the Two Spinsters were at Olivia's house when she arrived. The doctor looked a lot less weary after having finally gotten some rest, and the spinsters, bless their hearts, had prepared a supper of roast chicken, corn, and collards. For Olivia, the combined forces of no sleep, the festivities, and Neil's crisis had her so worn down that she wasn't sure she could stay awake long enough to eat the meal. "How is he?"

Delbert replied glumly, "Nothing's changed."

It wasn't good news, but in Olivia's mind, it wasn't bad news either. Neil was still breathing, and that in itself was a blessing. Although she dearly wanted to see him, she didn't know how the doctor would react to such an improper request, so she kept the wish to herself and sat down to eat.

Neil was floating again, but unlike the lush green forest he'd visited before, his surroundings were harsh, the earth parched and cracked, reminding him of the mountainous regions of Texas. Up ahead he saw a woman cooking beans over a fire. She was dressed in red. It was his mother. When she looked up and saw him, surprise livened her face. "Neily, is that you?"

"Yes, Mama."

"You are bleeding."

For the first time, Neil noticed the blood pooling at his feet. A look behind him showed the trail of bloody footprints leading to the spot where he stood. The sight disturbed him, but he wondered why he didn't feel any pain. "Where am I, Mama?"

"In my dreams, Neily."

He tried to make sense of that but couldn't.

His mother gave him a sad smile. "I will send your brother to fetch you home. Hang on to your soul."

Neil had no idea what she meant by that, but being the good son that he was, he said, "Yes, Mama."

And she was gone.

Neil stayed in dreamland for seven days. He hunted jaguar with the Great Chief Osceola, hiked the mountains of Texas with his father, and dined on peaches and rattlesnakes. Neil and his horse chased trains that always left them behind, and he saw Olivia's face shimmering in a clear pool of water at the base of a waterfall. Through it all he could hear the sounds of hushed voices nearby, and he wondered if they were the voices of the Seminole gods.

On the eighth day, he haltingly opened his eyes and saw Chase Jefferson asleep in a chair beside the bed. Neil wasn't totally lucid, but he had enough awareness to know he was in a strange bedroom. His attempts to sit up were slapped down by the excruciating pain that exploded in his back. Breathing harshly, he tried to will the hurt away, but the burning was so intense that he moaned.

Then Chase was standing over him, and Neil's eyes met his.

"Neil?"

But before Neil could reply, he slipped back into the arms of dreamland to seek shelter from the flames licking at his flesh.

Olivia stood in the doorway of the sheriff's office and watched the latest bounty hunter ride slowly down Main Street. His battered hat and dusty clothing sat on a frame that was average height but rail thin. His swagger and cocky grin exuded such menace that everyone on the walks stopped what they were doing to watch him pass by. Olivia frowned. He was the third one so far. The sheriff's estimate of their arrival had been off by only two days. It had taken eight days for the first one to ride in, and now, on the tenth day, she knew the elders needed a means to corral the strangers before all perdition broke loose.

She noted the man's many contrasts. Unlike his shabby clothes and hat, the black leather gun belt around his waist gleamed with care. The chamber and pearl handle of the gun glinted in the sun. She assumed he was heading to the Lady, where the others had taken rooms. For the life of her, she couldn't imagine what Malloy must be thinking, to house men who might be hunting him before it was all said and done, but Malloy seemed determined to go his own way, so everyone just watched and waited. Many of the citizens were looking to her for assurance that their quiet lives would return, and the burden of trying to make their wishes a reality was keeping her awake at night.

And always in the back of her mind was Neil.

"Miss Olivia?"

The voice interrupting her reverie belonged to Liza Pierce, daughter of the farmer Olivia had threatened with jail during the meeting concerning Malloy's decision to open the saloon. Standing with sixteen-year-old Liza were two of her young friends. "Girls. How are you all?"

They exchanged pleasantries for a few moments, then Liza handed Olivia a small embroidered pillow. "I made it for Mr. July."

Olivia was caught by surprise. "I see."

"Will you make sure he gets it, and tell him it's from me, Pearl, and Sylvia?"

Olivia eyed the silent but eager-appearing Pearl and Sylvia. "I most certainly will. I'm sure he'll be real appreciative."

"We think he's *so* handsome."

"And dangerous," Pearl added with a smile and a shivery move.

Sylvia added, "With him being in your house and all, I'm betting you get to see him all the time, don't you, Miss Olivia?"

Olivia wasn't sure whether to be appalled at the girls or to howl with laughter. "No, not really. He's still under Doc Johnson's care."

Liza said, "Will you please tell Mr. July that me, Pearl, and Sylvia send our regards."

"I will."

That seemed to make the day complete. "Thank you," they squealed and left giggling.

Olivia glanced at the pillow and wondered what on earth would happen next.

When Olivia got home that evening, Asa and Sophie were playing checkers at her kitchen table. Their Winchesters were leaning against the table within easy reach. Chase wanted everyone armed in the event the bounty hunters tried to take Neil by force.

"Evening," Olivia called, setting down the pillow and her handbag before untying the ribbons of her beige bonnet. "Who's winning?"

Without looking up from the red-and-black board, Asa and Sophie answered in unison, "I am."

Olivia chuckled. A quick look at the board showed they were even, at least so far. "How's the patient?"

Asa answered, "Sleeping, last time I looked in."

Olivia knew that last night, Neil had awakened long enough to speak to Chase for a few minutes. According to Delbert, the flesh around the gunshot wound was beginning to heal, but because Neil was under arrest and because it was improper for an unmarried woman to be at a man's bedside, she hadn't had any time alone with him. In reality she would have gladly traded her own need to see him for news that he was out of the woods and finally on the mend. She noticed that she hadn't seen Delbert, though. "Is the doc in with him?"

While studying her options on the checkerboard, Sophie replied, "No. He rode over to Nicodemus to deliver a baby. Their doc is back east burying his mother, and the midwife is gone to Topeka for the christening of her new grandson."

"Is he returning tonight?"

"No. Said if the birth was easy he'd be back tomorrow afternoon. Said July would be okay until he gets back."

Asa snarled playfully, "Come on, woman. Move. We don't have all night."

"Hold your peas, old man. I'm thinking."

Olivia poured herself a cup of coffee and smiled at them as she brought the hot brew to her lips. According to the gossip, Sophie and Asa had met in New Orleans, before the war. Sophie Reynolds was the elegant quadroon owner of a well-heeled sporting house, and Asa, an escaped slave. In spite of the differences in their stations, they'd fallen in love and had been together now almost thirty years.

Olivia had once asked Sophie why she and Asa had never married. Sophie replied that one, she was too old, and two, her love for Asa didn't need the blessings of a government that couldn't even uphold the Constitution.

Neil could hear the voices of two women and a man drifting in from somewhere beyond his room. He didn't recognize the man's, or one of the women's, but the other woman's voice was so painfully familiar his heart began to pound in his chest.

When Olivia heard Neil calling her name, she thought she imagined it at first, but when the call came again, she shot Sophie and Asa a confused look even as she hurried to her bedroom.

Inside, her steps slowed at the sight of him awake.

"Welcome back," she said softly. It was easy to see he was still in pain, but his lopsided smile lit up her heart.

"Glad to be back," he whispered thickly. "Where am I?"

"My bedroom."

He gave her a knowing look. "Not exactly the way I planned it, but I'll take it."

Olivia sensed Sophie and Asa behind her. She wished them gone so she could touch him to make sure he was indeed alive, but she set aside the selfish thoughts.

He croaked, "I could use some water if there's any around."

Olivia went to the pitcher on the nightstand and poured him a cup.

Sophie said, "Olivia. Asa and I think we hear prowlers outside. We'll be back in a quarter of an hour."

Olivia dropped her head to hide her smile. What friends she had. "Okay."

And they slipped out but left the door open.

Olivia took a seat on the edge of the bed and guided the cup to his lips. He drank a few sips, then dropped back against the pillows to catch his breath. She waited a few seconds and then asked, "How are you?"

"Hurting, but I'll make it."

Neil then reached up and slowly traced a bent knuckle down her cheek. He wondered if she had any idea how good it felt to be alive and to see her again. "I dreamed about you. I was at a waterfall and your face was reflected in a pool of the clearest water I've ever seen."

The whisper in his voice was as soft as his touch, and both left Olivia shimmering. She said to him, "That first night—we didn't think you were going to make it to morning." She would never forget how scared she'd been for him.

"I'm glad I did."

"So am I."

Neil felt as if he could watch her for every minute of every day for as long as he lived. "Tell your friends out there thanks for letting us have this time."

"I will, but I won't stay long. I don't want to tire you out."

"It'll be a good tiring out, so don't worry."

He took her hand and placed it atop his heart, then covered it with his own. He closed his eyes, seemingly content. After a few silent moments passed, he asked, "Do you always sleep on lace-edged sheets?"

Enjoying him holding her hand, she smiled. "Yes. Something wrong with them?"

"No. They're just real soft. Never been on sheets this soft, or pillow slips."

"Glad you're enjoying them."

Neil wondered how it might be to make love to her on these lamb-soft sheets, but he pushed his mind away from that. He couldn't even make it to the privy alone. "Chase says there's bounty hunters in town."

"Three so far."

"Waiting for me to make a run for it." For a moment, he quieted again, then said with a subdued laugh, "As long as that Bible-quoting Preacher doesn't show up, everything should be fine."

"The sheriff said the Preacher is the only bounty hunter to ever bring you and your brother in."

Neil's eyes were closed, but he smiled. "Sure is. Stayed mad at him for months afterward. Finally forgave him when Shafts and I went down to Texas to help Griff and Jessi Rose get rid of some varmints. Preacher was a big help."

He rolled his head in her direction so he could see her face, then, before he could say anything else, his eyes slowly drifted closed once more. "Looks like we won't get to use that whole quarter hour after all," he said with sleepy amusement.

"That's okay," Olivia assured him in a tender tone. "Rest. I'll see you soon."

He gave her hand a little squeeze. She leaned in and placed a feather-light kiss on his forehead.

He smiled and was asleep before she left the room.

A few evenings later, the Board of Elders met. Chase and Olivia proposed a new town ordinance that would require all strangers in town to surrender their weapons as a condition of being on town property. The weapons would be returned when they rode out. Anyone who refused to obey would be given the choice of not entering town or going to jail. The ordinance passed unanimously.

The next morning, a worried Olivia paced the sheriff's office. Chase, Handy, Asa, and three other newly deputized men were over at the Lady informing the bounty hunters of the new weapons ordinance. Her worry stemmed from whether the strangers would comply. Chase had been gone over an hour, and although she hadn't heard any gunfire, she kept steeling herself for the sounds.

In the end, Chase returned. His face was grim. "None of them wanted to surrender their guns, so they're leaving the Lady."

"Good."

"Not good. They're camped outside the town limits."

She stared. "What?"

"I escorted them off town property, and that's as far as they have to go. We can't regulate them on land that doesn't belong to the town."

Olivia sank into a chair. She had been so sure the men would leave when faced with the ordinance, it never occurred to her they'd know how to circumvent it.

Chase explained, "We're not the first town with ordinances these men have faced. They know how to skirt the law, but at least we got them out of town."

Olivia acknowledged the small victory, but the war remained. "Did you ever hear from Marshal Wildhorse?"

"Yes. He and a few men will be heading up as soon as the marshal finishes testifying in a case."

She sighed with relief.

"His guns will be a big help, but his presence will go a long way towards making sure my badge is respected."

Olivia didn't understand.

"A couple of those men out there are rebs, and they weren't real happy having to deal with me and my deputies."

She understood now. " 'We have no rights which a White man was bound to respect,' " she said, quoting the infamous line from the ruling against Dred Scott in 1857. Every man, woman, and child of the race was familiar with that ominous phrase because of its continued effect on their lives. In many areas of the country, peace officers who were men of color weren't allowed to enforce the law if the lawbreaker wasn't a member of the race. "Is Wildhorse a White man?"

"No. Black Seminole, but he was appointed by Hanging Judge Isaac Parker, and Parker has made it well known that the officers under his jurisdiction can arrest *anyone*, no matter the race."

Olivia was glad to hear that. She'd read about Judge Parker in the newspapers. He was a tough, no-nonsense jurist, and outlaws were terrified of him; he wasn't called *Hanging* Judge Parker for no reason. "I'll be glad when the marshal arrives."

"So will I. In about a week or so, Neil should be strong enough for me to move him here to the jail."

Chase must have seen the displeasure on her face, because he said, "It's for his protection, Olivia, and he is supposed to be under arrest, remember?"

"I do."

He studied her for a moment. "You have feelings for him, don't you?"

"I don't know. I haven't been with him long enough to find out, but something's there."

"My wife thinks so, too."

Olivia gave him a little smile. "Your wife talks too much."

He laughed aloud. "Been telling her that for years—but she won't believe me."

Olivia chuckled. "Well, whatever happens with Neil, my first priority is the safety of Henry Adams and its citizens."

He nodded, "And you're doing a bang-up job."

"Thanks. Have you seen today's *Nicodemus Cyclone*?"

When he shook his head no, she handed him the two-sheet daily.

Chase looked at the drawing of the smiling Malloy on the front page and shook his head, then read the banner headline: "Henry Adams Merchant Brings Down Neil July." "Soon as this gets around Malloy's going to be known from here to St. Louis. Hope he'll like being famous."

"I hope he gets eaten by a bear."

Chase chuckled and went off to do his rounds.

When Olivia reached her home that evening, the sight of three mounted men watching her house from about two hundred yards away gave her pause. She could only assume they were bounty hunters. She hurried inside to alert Asa, who was sitting with Neil. When she and the armed Asa stepped back outside, the men had vanished.

By the fifteenth of August, Neil was able to walk around, albeit slowly. His strength was returning with a steadiness that pleased Doc Johnson, who finally gave him permission to venture outside. Because Neil was under arrest, and with concerns for his safety mounting now that there were six bounty hunters holed up at the makeshift camp outside of town, he was confined to the back porch, but he didn't care. The elation of being alive far outweighed any restrictions.

And now he was seated in the old upholstered chair on Olivia's back porch, enjoying the rising wind. "Feels like a storm comin'."

Daisy, sitting on the edge of the porch with Rachel and Olivia, looked up from the doily she was crocheting to say, "Lord knows we need some."

Rachel took her pipe out of her mouth and shaded

her eyes as she peered toward the western sky. "Does look like something's on the way."

Olivia, shelling a bowl of peas, hoped it poured. It hadn't rained in weeks, and for the past few days, each succeeding one had been hotter and stickier than the one before. The citizenry, however, had a novel way of dealing with it. "Sophie told me this morning that she and Asa have been sleeping in the storm cellar to get away from the heat."

"So have we," Daisy proclaimed. "It's too hot to do anything but perspire."

Neil enjoyed Rachel and Daisy's company, but he only had eyes for Madam Mayor. The quick, shy glances she kept shooting him from beneath her long lashes had his heart beating like a Seminole drum. He wanted to be alone with her so that he could talk to her about the things gurgling inside. She had on a navy skirt that was bordered by a band of pleats and another one of her long-sleeved blouses with a frilly collar that highlighted the beautiful, angular lines of her face. He was sure she was roasting in all those clothes, but she looked real fine doing it.

The wind rose a few more notches and the grass began to whisper in response. The sky was slowly filling with fat gray clouds.

Daisy scanned the sky, but instead of remarking on the weather, she said instead, "So, Mr. July, what are your intentions towards our Olivia?"

Olivia howled, "Daisy?!"

Rachel said to her, "Hush, Olivia, and let the man answer."

Neil was so caught off guard that all he could do was laugh.

Daisy voiced firmly, "This is not a laughing matter, Mr. July. It's very easy to see you two are smitten, but nothing will come to fruition if you continue to *rob trains*."

Supposedly concentrating on her peas, Olivia took a quick look up at Neil to gauge his reaction and found him watching her with the most serious expression on his face she'd ever seen.

"I know," Neil responded quietly; he did because the issue was causing great debate within himself. "If I could court Olivia openly, it would mean more to me than all the gold I've ever possessed. . . ."

Olivia went weak. The latent power in his voice touched her like a hand.

The Two Spinsters were smiling. Then Rachel said, "The last time this town had such goings-on, the place was in an uproar for months."

Daisy nodded. "That Chase and Cara Lee kept us on the edge of our seats."

"Sure did," added Rachel.

"Now that was a grand passion."

Olivia, still reeling from Neil's passionate declaration, barely heard the bantering spinsters.

Rachel said, "Daisy, we need to get home. I don't like the looks of that sky."

The wind had picked up again, making the sleeves on Olivia's blouse ripple in response.

Suddenly a mounted Chase appeared. The wind was increasing in such fast increments it was now whipping the women's skirts. He yelled, "I'm telling everybody to head for the cellar. Got a wire that a cyclone just tore up some farms about fifty miles west of here. It should be right on top of us within the hour."

He then looked at Neil. "I can't spare anybody to babysit you or protect you, and I doubt you're strong enough to ride all the way out to my place where I can look after you, so you'll have to stay here. You got to give me your word that you won't run off while this storm is going on."

Neil looked his friend in the eye. "You have it."

"Good. Then take this just in case," Chase tossed Neil his gun belt.

Neil caught it deftly.

Olivia's voice was concerned. "If the situation is that dangerous, maybe I need to be at the mayor's desk in case—"

Chase tossed back, "In case what? In case the cyclone flies you to Topeka? No," he countered firmly. "Stay here."

She started to protest.

Chase cut her off and turned to Neil. "She is not to leave the house. If you have to sit on her, do it. Olivia, you are so much like my wife sometimes, it scares me. Let's go, Spinsters. I'm escorting you home."

Rachel and Daisy gave Olivia hugs good-bye. They were about to head to their buggy when Rachel stopped and said to Neil, "We are all expecting you to conduct yourself like a gentleman with our mayor, Mr. July."

"I will, ma'am."

Daisy said, "And if anyone asks, we were here with you, Olivia. You know how folks like to talk, but your cellar isn't large enough for four, and ours isn't either."

Olivia nodded.

Chase said, "Come on, ladies. We'll get our lies in a row after the storm."

With a wave, the Two Spinsters drove off across the grass. Chase stayed behind for a few seconds and held Neil's eyes for a long, speaking moment. Seemingly satisfied, he turned his mount and galloped to catch up with the buggy.

Olivia had seen the exchange and asked curiously, "What was that all about?"

"He was telling me the same thing the Spinsters did. Only a bit firmer."

"I see." Knowing she might be alone with him for hours made Olivia as aware of him as she was of the thunder that could be heard grumbling off in the distance.

Neil's awareness of her was just as acute; he wanted to kiss her like a man home from war, but they had preparations to take care of first. Chase would hang him personally if the Madam Mayor wound up in Topeka.

Olivia said, "Let's get you in the cellar, then I'll fetch candles and things."

"I can help." The male in him refused to be treated like an invalid even if he was still almost one.

The grasses were bowing and scraping, and lightning flashed across the eerie, green-black sky. The wind was loud enough to be heard, and Olivia knew she didn't have time for male ego. She handed him the lantern she kept on the porch and said over the wind, "Hold that, I'll be right back."

Neil looked down at the small light. He turned to tell her that he could certainly carry more than that, but she'd already disappeared into the house.

Inside, Olivia ignored the wind-whipped curtains standing out like flags and hastily grabbed up some candles and matches. In the bedroom, she threw open her cedar chest and snatched out a blanket. She also grabbed a pillow from the bed and hurried outside to the sound of booming thunder.

Olivia handed Neil the bundle of goods. She knelt and lifted the heavy door that led to the underground cellar. "You go first," she said. "There are five steps to the bottom."

Neil was glad for the information because it was as dark as Hades inside and he couldn't see a thing. It took Olivia three tries to light the lantern in the wind, but once it caught, she handed it to him. "Take this."

Neil smiled. "Remind me to keep you around."

She chuckled, "Will you go on."

He started down the steps, and she ran back to the house.

For a moment, he stood there astonished that she was not going to follow him down, but, shaking his head, he began his descent.

Once on solid ground again, Neil waved the lantern around to see what he could see. He saw jars of put-up fruit and vegetables resting on shelves carved into the earth. There was a bag labeled Potatoes leaning against the wall, and in the corner a small cot rested on a short-legged wooden frame. On the floor beside the cot stood a large lantern. The space was a twin of most root cellars he'd seen, but he'd never used one to ride out a storm.

Walking haltingly, he went over to the cot and sat down. He was not as strong as he wanted to be yet, so he needed to catch his breath. The sound of something hitting the ground startled him. A sheet wrapped around he knew not what lay at the bottom of the earthen steps. He assumed Olivia had tossed it down ahead of her descent, so he waited for her to appear and reveal the contents.

She showed herself only a few moments later. "I hope I thought of everything. We may be down here just a short while, or it may be until morning."

He nodded, loving the sight of her.

Outside, the wind was howling like a banshee. Olivia grabbed onto the rope suspended from the heavy open door, then, using all of her strength, she pulled the rope until the door slammed shut. It was so quiet that, had it not been for the light of the lanterns, the space could have passed for a tomb. She knelt to unwrap the two sheets and pulled out the items she'd brought along.

Neil watched, then laughed. "You brought a ham?"

"It was in the icebox and we may get hungry."

Neil was hungry all right, but not for food.

Olivia could see the glitter in his eyes, and she hastily went back to unpacking. When she was done, she lit a few of the candles to help the lanterns beat back the gloom.

Neil asked, "Won't the candles burn up all the air?"

She shook her head. "There are pipes in the ceiling that lead to the ground above us. The 'dusters got the ideas from the stovepipes they used in their dugouts."

When the founders had settled Henry Adams, they hadn't had time to build homes before winter arrived that first year, so most had lived underground in dwellings called dugouts. Rachel once told Olivia that the settlers preferred living underground in Kansas to living above ground in the Redemptionist South.

Neil took the lantern by the cot and peered up into the shadowy ceiling, but it was too dark to see the pipes.

Olivia said reassuringly, "Don't worry. They're there."

Neil took her word for it.

Where once there was silence, they could now hear rain pelting the door like rocks.

"Hail," Olivia said.

Neil nodded. "Good size too, from the sounds of it."

For the last few days they'd both been pining to spend some time together, and now that it was here they were both a bit awkward—especially Olivia. Her reputation would be in shreds should it ever become known that she'd ridden out the storm with him. Alone. But since she had no control over that now, she decided to enjoy his company. "Where were you on your way to when Malloy shot you?"

"Is that who shot me?"

"Yes. You didn't know?"

"No. I guess I was so busy recovering, and you all were so busy taking care of me, that no one mentioned it. Wait until I get my hands on that little bug."

"Shooting you in the back didn't make him many friends."

"Well, he's going to wish he had a few when I'm done with him." He went silent for a moment, then said, "Malloy, huh?"

Outside, they could hear the muffled screams of the ferocious winds. The rain and hail hadn't let up either. The flames of the candles danced crazily in response to the gushes of air pushed down the pipes by the storm, but they didn't go out.

Neil eyed her standing in the center of the dirt floor. "You're going to get awful tired standing up like that. Come sit, I won't bite unless you ask me to. . . ."

Chapter 10

The tone of his voice set Olivia reeling. Her nipples tightened shamelessly, and the pulse between her thighs came to life. Her wish to be with him had finally come true, and she was so overcome that she couldn't move.

"I promise not to compromise you in any way, Olivia, but I want to kiss you so bad, it hurts."

The lure in him drew her across the floor to the cot. There, in the candlelit darkness, trying to keep her breathing even, she stopped before him and beheld the man who filled her with emotions she didn't quite understand. Seemingly of its own accord, her hand rose to cup his bearded cheek, and his skin trembled. That surprised her—that he could be so stirred by her inexperienced touch. Emboldened, she leaned down and pressed her lips to his, one more bold move in the many she'd made since meeting him.

Neil eased an arm around her waist and guided her down onto his lap, all without breaking the seal of their lips. When she settled down, the bullet wound in his back kicked up a bit, but he ignored it and pulled her closer so he could kiss her like he'd dreamed of doing—sweet, lingering, mouth-parting kisses that left them both limp, breathless, and hungry for more.

He worked his hand into her hair, and her fingers moved over the back of his neck. He nibbled her lip and Olivia slid her tongue into his mouth, savoring the groan he made. Their tongues danced, parted, and danced again. Still drawing on her lips, he ran a slow hand down the front of her blouse, and it was her turn to moan.

Neil kissed the bare skin beneath her chin that was visible above her lacy collar and moved his hands over her corset-encased breasts. The image of holding her in his hands, taking her into his mouth, and feeling the nipples harden under his tongue flared his desire. "I want to touch you, Olivia. . . ."

The heat of his hands penetrated Olivia's clothes; her breasts were hard, pleading to know more, so when he began undoing the buttons of her blouse, she didn't protest—nor did she when he gently spread the fabric aside and brushed his lips over the bare, trembling hollow of her brown throat. The scented nook was treated to a series of short, smoldering licks that sent ripples clear to her toes. This was lust, plain and simple. The other emotions they felt for each other weren't as developed or as strong as this hot, carnal wanting, and Olivia didn't need to know why; she didn't care. His skillful hands, magnificent kisses, and heated whispers made her feel like a woman, and she was of a mind that every woman should experience lust at least once in her life.

"*Dios,* you're lovely. . . ." Neil confessed thickly. His lips traveled over her jaw, her ear, and sucked gently on the lobe, while his hands roamed her body like a man blind.

Olivia lost track of time; she had no idea if it was still raining, dawn, or two days past. She did know that his hands and kisses were magical and she didn't want him to stop.

Neil's only plans were to pleasure her until she screamed his name. He would never forget this interlude, and he wanted her to remember, too.

He freed more of the small black buttons, and his eyes and lips feasted on the soft brown tops of her breasts temptingly displayed above the strapless, low-cut French corset. His hands moved to the hook-and-eye fastenings, and he slowly began to work them free.

Olivia was so entranced that every one of her senses seemed heightened. His hot tongue on the skin between her breasts made her groan low in her throat. His lips greeted each newly bared expanse of skin with sensual salute until she was bare and held in his big, warm hands. When he brushed his lips over the pleading nipples, she melted, and her head fell back. He pleasured her slowly, surely, taking the buds into his mouth and teasing them with the tip of his tongue. She was dissolving, keening. He ran his large palm over the now damp tip, then raised up to recapture her mouth.

Neil wanted to ease her back onto the cot and ready her like a man readies a virgin bride, but she was not his bride. This sweet-breasted lady mayor was destined for a man much finer than himself, and he forced himself to honor that. "We need to slow down a minute, darlin'."

Olivia was in such a hazy world, it took a moment for her to hear him. "Why?"

He ran a finger over her berry hard nipple, erotically framed by the half-opened corset. "Because this is about to get out of hand, and I promised Chase, the spinsters, and you that I'd be good." Unable to stop himself, however, he kissed her again, and then again before finally, reluctantly breaking the seal of their lips.

Still caught in the haze of desire, Olivia said, "But you're being *very* good. . . ."

He ran his eyes over her passion-filled features and chuckled, "Brazen woman, you know what I'm talking about."

She met his eyes and said seriously, "But I don't. Not really. That's why I don't want you to stop. . . ."

He studied her—the tender swelling of her lips, the glitter of desire in her eyes—and hated the idea that someday another man would hold her as he was doing now. "Your full knowing will come with the man you marry, Olivia. Not with me."

She touched his cheek. "And what if I want it to be with you."

Neil ducked away and stared over her head into the shadows. "You don't know what you're saying."

"I'm not fishing for a husband," she said earnestly.

"If we don't slow down, you're going to need one."

"Why do men insist on telling me I don't know my own mind."

"Virgins *don't* know their own minds."

She tossed back sarcastically, "Thank you very much, Neil July."

It was easy to see she was becoming more and more frosty, but he was getting a kick out of watching her huffing and puffing. "Olivia, darlin', you are something."

She met his eyes and said quietly, "I told you when we met, I doubted I'd marry—"

"But you never know, sweetheart, and I don't want you to be shamed by a night in a cellar with an outlaw."

She understood his chivalrous intentions; the respect he had for her was unequaled in her life, but she didn't want to fight with him and ruin the rest of the time they had together because she was suddenly greedy for pleasure. Maybe he was right and she didn't know her mind, maybe it was because his kisses made her out of her mind.

Neil held the silent Olivia against his chest. Content, he kissed the top of her hair and willed his manhood to be silent, too.

The wind continued to howl and the rain pounded

against the door like it wanted in. Olivia had no way of knowing if her house was still standing, or if everything had been sucked up and blown away. She dearly hoped no one had been injured or was in need of assistance.

Neil asked quietly, "Penny for your thoughts."

"Wondering how much damage the town is taking on."

He chuckled.

"What's funny?"

"At a time like this, a man hopes the lady on his lap is thinking about him."

She dropped her head sheepishly. "Sorry. I'm new at this sitting on a man's lap business."

He squeezed her gently. "No need to apologize. Just shows how special you are, Olivia Sterling." Then he asked, "Do you have a middle name?"

"Jean. What's yours?"

He shook his head. "I don't have one." Then, as if trying the sounds of the name on his lips, he echoed, "Olivia Jean. I like that."

She settled back into the cocoon of his arms. "Is your wound bothering you?"

He shrugged. "A little."

She straightened, concerned. "I should look at it." She made a move to leave his lap, but he kept her where she was.

"We'll look later. Right now, I want to know everything about Olivia Jean."

She cocked her head at him and her eyes sparkled. "Such as?"

"I don't know, start at the beginning."

"Okay." And she began by telling him when and where she was born. "Which makes me an ancient thirty-two years of age."

"Six years younger than me, though, so you're not that ancient. What was it like at Oberlin?"

She thought back for a few moments. "Very interesting. The trustees let women of color attend, but there were very few places in the city we could board, and even fewer places to find employment. Some of the other students treated us atrociously, but I was given a good, solid education."

She looked up at him and added, "In fact, one of my teachers told us that the war would be the defining moment in our lives, so he made us do interviews with people we met and then chronicle their experiences. It's an exercise that stuck with me, because the experiences were so fascinating and varied. Now, whenever I meet someone, I always ask. So, now I'm asking you. Where were you and what did you do during the war?"

"Well, let's see. I was in Indian Territory when it began but wound up in Kansas."

He went on to explain that because Chiefs Billy Bowlegs and John Chupco had refused to sign with the Confederacy as some of the other Seminole town chiefs had, the Reb cavalry had come to round up everyone who'd refused to take them into custody. "But when they got to the towns we were gone. Almost two thousand men, women, and children—mostly Seminoles and Creek—left to follow the old Creek chief Opotheyohola up through Cherokee country and into Kansas."

"Did you make it?"

"Barely. It was winter and most of us were walking. The first two times the Rebs rode down on us, we battled our way clear, but the third time they captured over a hundred and fifty of the women and children."

Olivia's heart stopped.

"The rest of us had already lost everything we owned during the other battles along the way, so by the time we did reach Kansas we were destitute and hungry. But once we were settled, every man strong enough to pick up a rifle signed up with the First Kansas Colored and went to war to fight the Rebs. I had to wait until '64 when I was fourteen, but I went gladly."

"What happened to the captives?"

"Many of them were sold. Slave catchers had been nipping at the Black Seminoles like a pack of hounds since before the removal, making false claims of ownership to any court that would listen, kidnapping when they could. They hated the idea that they couldn't round us all up and send us back to wherever they thought we belonged."

"So, do you consider yourself a Black man or an Indian?"

"I am Seminole. I will always be Seminole no matter what the government or those within the Seminole Nation now denying our claims to our land and our heritage say."

"Your people are having problems?"

He nodded. "Since the war, many of the full-bloods have conveniently forgotten the sacrifices my people made to the Nation. Contributions of men like John Horse and Gopher John are being conveniently forgotten, as are all the African-descended Seminoles who negotiated on behalf of the full-bloods with the Spanish and Americans because we spoke all three languages. They definitely don't want to discuss all the battles we fought together so that everyone could be free. The full-bloods have bought into the Redemptionist idea that we of African Seminole descent have no rights."

"That's terrible."

"Yes, it is. I think they're hoping the wind will magically blow us away and take our claims with it so we can stop being a thorn in their side, but we aren't going anywhere. We'll make them recognize us if it takes us three hundred years."

Olivia had had no idea such racial discord was rife among the tribes. Slavery had poisoned the waters of the country so pervasively that it seemed no group was immune. She wondered how much longer the issue of race would scar the lives and the land of a nation supposedly founded upon freedom. "What about the Blacks in the other tribes?"

"All the other so-called Black Indians have found themselves on the outs with the full-bloods, too—be they Creek, Cherokee, or Choctaw." Neil could feel the old anger rising and sought to dampen it by changing the subject. "What was the most memorable event in your life besides the war?"

Olivia took the abrupt change in topic as a signal

that he didn't want to talk about that part of his life anymore, and she respected that. "Coming to Kansas."

"No, before that."

Olivia pondered her past for a silent few moments. "Probably my graduation from Oberlin. I'd never been so proud in my life. My parents were proud, too. My papa strutted around with a big grin on his face for weeks." Thinking about her father made her wonder how he was faring. In spite of their differences over the arranged marriage, she loved her father very much. Her disappearance probably had him worried to death. She decided the time had come for her to let him know where she was, and that she was safe. Burying her daughterly guilt for now, she tightened her hold on Neil's waist and asked, "What was your most memorable event?"

"Besides meeting you, and being shot because of it?"

She smiled in response to the humor in his eyes. "Yes, besides that."

"Probably eating peaches and rattlesnakes."

"Is that some kind of Seminole delicacy?"

"No, we were on a campaign in the Texas desert, and that's all we had to eat. The peaches were in our packs. The snakes we caught."

"Was this during the war?"

"No, during my time as a Seminole Negro scout."

Olivia was quite surprised. "You were a scout? For how long?" The Seminole Negro scouts were very famous.

"Until the army broke its promises, took our

homes, and left my people to fend for themselves. I resigned and started robbing trains."

Olivia searched his eyes. What a life he'd led—and how much sorrow to make a man with such a storied ancestry descend into crime. She still didn't think that his choice to be a train robber was justified, but she hadn't spent her life being hunted and hungry, so she really had no right to be judgmental. Nevertheless, she said, "Robbing trains is wrong, Neil."

"So is bringing two hundred women and children from Mexico to Texas, promising them they would be cared for and fed if their men fought Comanches and Apaches, and then turning your back on them. I wasn't going to let my family starve."

She nodded sadly.

"How about we talk about something else," he offered in a soft, yet hardened, voice.

She agreed.

He raised her chin so he could memorize the lines of her face and the lush bow of her lips. "Let's not fight over something that has no bearing right now."

"But it does."

His lips tightened. "You're tenacious, if nothing else."

She offered a small smile. His choice of occupation impacted any future they might want to have. "Kiss me then—"

"And you know how to end an argument, too." He traced her lips. "Don't you?"

She gave him a little wink, and he laughed and brought his lips down to hers. All other matters were set aside. Neither wanted to fight or argue when passion could be shared instead.

Neil undid the remaining hooks on her corset so he could bare her fully to his hungry eyes and hands, then dallied and feasted until her hips took on a sensual rhythm. He dragged his lips up her nakedness until he found her mouth. While he plundered her lips and sucked the tip of her tongue, his hand kept her breasts wanting, then slipped down to possessively map her hips and the front of her skirt-covered thighs.

The heat between Olivia's thighs had never known life until Neil. The warm, strong hand moving purposefully over her made her want to part her legs so she could feel more. He obliged her by exploring their trembling inner lines with a slow urgency that sent the fabric sliding sensually up and down the sensitized skin. Her passion was building, her nipples hard, her mouth parted under his deepening kiss. She was damp, yearning, and her virgin's body instinctively knew what would come next, so when his hand moved between her legs and cupped that spiraling space, the sensations were too much and she exploded with a loud, strangled cry. Clinging to his hand, her body convulsed with a pleasure she thought might blow her apart. His fingers continued a slow tease, and she cried out again; trembling, dying. Then he was kissing her and her legs were open as wide as the Kansas plains so he could do to her what he may.

And what Neil *mayed* was to touch her fully. To facilitate that he slid his hand beneath the skirts and snow white slips, caressing and squeezing the whole way until he found her drawers. He could feel how wet the vee of the undergarment was, and he smiled like a lover at the sight of her rising to the play of his hand. He acknowledged how hard his manhood had become in appreciative anticipation, but he concentrated on pleasuring her. He circled the bud put there by nature for her pleasure and for his, and her thighs widened even more.

Olivia was in a world where nothing existed but sensation; the sensations of her drawers being tugged down her legs; the sensations of being naked beneath her skirts; the sensation of his bare hand gliding like silk over her bare thighs. It was heady, wanton, and so very divine she didn't want to leave his lap ever.

Neil could feel a spreading spot of dampness on his back that had to be blood, but he put off investigating it for now. Instead, he swung their bodies around and gently laid her down on her back on the cot. Seated above, he looked down into her eyes and slid his hand back beneath her skirt. His gaze held her captive as he played and coaxed and teased. When her lids fluttered shut in response to the simmering contact, he pushed her skirt up her legs so he could see her in the candlelight. Her hair was dark, soft, wet. When he brushed the tip of his finger over the swollen, trembling temple at the apex of her thighs, she sucked in a breath and her hips rose invitingly. Soon they were rising shamelessly; openly. Unable to resist the sweet offering, Neil lowered himself to his knees and kissed her there.

Olivia shot up off the cot, her eyes wide. "What are you doing?" She backed up until the dirt wall prevented her from going any further.

He grinned. "If you come here, I'll show you. . . ."

Her eyes did not diminish in size.

"Thought you wanted to know . . . all . . ."

"I do, but—"

He whispered, "Then come here, woman." He reached for her and felt the pain in his back flare and the stitches burn like tiny pokers. By sheer force of will he gently took hold of her waist and pulled her closer. Neil and his pain were running a race to see who would win. The pain had a good head start— Neil could feel the throb at the center of the wound deepening to red like coals in the bottom of a fire pit, but the need to show Olivia just how magnificent desire could be made him endure. Running his hand down her luscious breasts, he whispered in the half dark, "You want the man you marry to love you this way, Olivia . . . you want him to touch you, stroke you. . . ." He leaned over and nipped each bud with lover-soft teeth. "Bite you . . ."

She groaned and twisted.

Neil worked his hand between her thighs. She was running with desire, and because he had prepared her so very, very well, he knew she was ready. With his hands he teased her until her thighs parted, and then he leaned in and kissed her sweetly. "You want a man who can do this. . . ."

Neil sucked the citadel into his mouth, slid a finger into the warm recesses of paradise. As the orgasm grabbed her and flung her to Topeka, Olivia screamed loud and long. But he didn't stop. While she convulsed and arched and felt herself going mad, he dallied, licked, touched, and played until he'd had enough. For now.

Sitting on the floor, as hard as he'd ever been in his life, Neil turned and rested his back and head on the edge of the cot. He wanted her so badly, but he let the pain he'd suppressed until now rise to the surface so it would kill his need to sink between her legs and love her until the earth was no more. *Dios!* He let the memories of loving her sing in his mind for a moment or two longer, then felt the agony. And once he did, every breath he took sent knives through his back, so he took in short, shallow breaths instead.

Olivia, still reeling from his exquisite loving, was floating in a pulsating reverie when the sound of his breathing rose on the silence. She sat up and moved to him. "Are you okay?"

"Nope. I'm bleeding, I think. Could use a few slugs of willow tea, too, if there's any around."

Worried by his revelation, Olivia scrambled off the cot and picked up the lantern. With a gentle hand she made him turn his back to her so she could see. Sure enough, the entire base of the shirt tucked into his denims was dark with blood. "Move up onto the cot so I can get a better look."

Neil did so and decided lying down was wonderful. When he could, he undid his belt buckle so that she could tug his shirt free.

Olivia eyed the wound. "You've torn some of the

stitches. I'll go see if the storm is over. You may need the doc."

Before she could run away, he grabbed her hand. "Whoa, Madam Mayor. Hold on a minute. I just need you to put something on it to stop the bleeding, and the tea."

Willow bark tea was a standard remedy for Doc Johnson's patients. It was an Indian remedy he'd learned from Chase Jefferson. It worked so well on dulling pain that he prescribed it for everything from toothaches to gout. There'd been a steady pot of it brewing for Neil since his injury, and Olivia had brought a jar of it into the cellar with the other supplies.

She took him the now tepid jar of tea, and he drank a long swallow. The bitterness of the brew showed on his face when he handed it back. She sealed the lid, then set it on the floor near her feet. "Now let's look at your back again."

He raised up so she could turn up the tail of his shirt, then she brought the lantern closer. She gently removed the bandages. Had she been a woman with a weak constitution, the sight of the fluids and blood oozing from the stitching would have sent her into a faint, but since she was not light-headed (unless the temperatures climbed into the nineties), she dabbed at the oozing with the clean cloths from the aid kit. "It was probably bleeding more profusely earlier, but it seems to be slowing."

"Probably all that kissing and hugging."

She chuckled softly. "Probably." She put a clean

bandage over the wound. Now that the potential crisis appeared under control, she let herself remember all that he'd done to her and all that she'd felt. It was mind boggling. "Well, there'll be no more kissing and hugging for you for a while, Mr. Seminole. You need to rest."

"You're such a cruel mayor, Olivia Jean."

He eased over so he could see her face. He reached out and teased the nipple bared by her still open corset. "So did you learn enough tonight?"

The heat of embarrassment flooding her face matched the heat of arousal that flooded her thighs. She tossed back softly and sassily, "For now."

He tried not to laugh because it hurt to do so.

Olivia leaned down and kissed him. "I'm going to see if the storm's over. It sounds pretty quiet out there now."

"Better do up your clothes first," he pointed out.

She peered down at herself. She'd totally forgotten her disheveled state. A bit embarrassed, she fastened her corset and the buttons on her blouse. "I can see now that being around you is going to turn me into a pagan."

"But a beautiful one."

She didn't bother with her drawers. She admittedly liked the wanton feel of being naked beneath her skirts. Shocked by her outrageous thoughts, she climbed the stairs. The overhead door was heavy even for a woman of Olivia's size, and it took her a moment to get it up. She raised it a bit higher so she could see out. Rain. Gray. The cool air felt good. She raised the door a bit higher to see if her house was there. It was, and so was the working end of a rifle less than six inches from her face.

"If you move you'll have a closed casket at your funeral."

Olivia didn't dare breathe. Suddenly the door was whisked out of her hand, and there stood Two Shafts wearing a beat-up rain slicker. He looked grim but wasn't armed.

The voice behind the gun said, "Where's my brother!"

The person came into view, and Olivia looked up into the dark, angry eyes of a hat-wearing, outlaw-smelling, black-leather-wearing woman who could only be Teresa July. Olivia hid her smile and gestured, "Down here."

Neil heard Teresa threatening Olivia, and he struggled to his feet with the intentions of calming her down before she recklessly shot the mayor. However, sitting up made the pain in his back burn like wildfire, and he was still sitting on the edge of the cot when they reached the floor of the cellar.

Teresa ran to him and looked down into his pain-filled face. "Neily, you okay?"

"I've been better, but it's good to see you." He acknowledged his brother with a smile. "'Bout time you showed up."

"Didn't get the wire from Tamar until a few days ago."

Tamar was Neil's mother. Neil suddenly remembered the dream. Tamar had always been a magical, mysterious woman. That he had somehow wandered into her dreams was not so far-fetched to those who knew and loved her.

Teresa asked, "We came to take you home. Are you ready? Where's your horse?"

Olivia watched and waited. She assumed he would be going, and there was nothing she could do to prevent the leaving. Even though he'd given Chase his word, there was a judge coming who might remand him to the territorial prison. Given the choice, Olivia didn't think he'd keep his word. He was an outlaw, after all.

Teresa asked again, "Neil?"

Neil was studying Olivia standing over there so silently. If he left, he'd be breaking his word not only to Chase but to her as well. He still didn't know a whole lot about her, but what he did know, he liked. He liked her smile, her wit, her sense of purpose. When he first met her, he'd told himself she was a woman who could make a man lay down his guns, and dammit if he hadn't been right. His eyes met Olivia's and held. "I'm staying here."

Relief closed Olivia's eyes.

"What do you mean, you're staying here?" Teresa sounded stunned.

"Just what I said. I gave Olivia my word."

Eyes filled with disbelief, Teresa looked from Olivia to Neil. "The judge is going to put you in prison, Neil."

"Maybe. Maybe not."

"Probably. Yes," she contradicted firmly. She then looked over at Olivia. "Has he been drinking?"

"Just bark tea."

Teresa said, "Get your gear. Where's your horse?"

He laid back down on the cot. "Tee, I'm not leaving. There's some bounty hunters in town hoping to tag me and bring me in. Be real appreciative if you could add your gun to the sheriff's until the judge arrives."

"Neil, this is loco."

"Maybe."

Teresa threw up her hands and said to Shafts, "You talk to him."

"Not me."

"Shafts!"

He shook his head.

Neil said, "Tee, I need to sleep. Can you yell at us from outside?"

Exasperated, she turned on her heel, climbed her leather-clad body up the steps, and disappeared.

Olivia watched her leave and was concerned.

Shafts assured her, "She'll be back after she cools off. I'm going to find Jefferson."

Olivia asked, "Isn't there a warrant out for you, too?"

"Yep, but I think I can convince Chase he'd rather have me shooting with him than at him."

"Can you assist your brother back up to the house before you go? His needlework needs repairing."

But when Olivia glanced Neil's way, she decided moving him would have to wait. He was asleep.

Chapter 11

◦━━◦◦━━◦

While Neil slept, Olivia went to check on her house. Back in Chicago, cyclones were relatively rare, but out here on the plains they were a deadly menace from spring through fall. The previous year, a twister had torn through the town of Prescott, leaving sixteen dead and two hundred and fifty people injured.

Olivia saw Teresa July sitting on the edge of the porch, but Teresa had such a disagreeable look on her dark face, Olivia passed her by without a word and went inside.

During the onset of the storm Olivia had been so focused upon getting Neil into the cellar and gathering supplies, she hadn't time to close the window shutters. As a result, she found damp floors, walls, and furniture. Panicked at the thought that she

229

hadn't closed the shutters in the shop either, she quickly went to see. They were closed. Her precious fabrics and dress forms wearing their half-finished ensembles were all dry. She sent praises to heaven and returned to her living quarters.

The house smelled clean and fresh after the rinse-out by the wind and rain. She looked into her bedroom, where Neil had been recuperating, to see if it needed any tidying before his return. Casting her eyes to the bed, she thought about him and all that had happened since they'd sought shelter from the storm. The memories came flooding back, reminding her of his dazzling lovemaking and her shameless enjoyment; of how he'd touched her, and how and where he'd placed his kisses. It had been an erotic, eye-opening encounter that still had her tingling and craving more. Chastising herself for being greedy and scandalous, she left the room to join the Julys in the cellar.

On her way, she scanned her roof and saw that some shingles had been ripped away by the high winds. She made a mental note to talk to Handy Reed about handling the repairs. Teresa was nowhere in sight, and Olivia wondered where she'd vanished to. She looked across the field to see if there was any movement around Rachel and Daisy's place and was pleased to see their buggy heading her way. She stopped and waited.

When they reached the house and put on the brake, she went around to help them down. Daisy said, "Are you all right, dear?"

"Yes, ma'am."

"And our outlaw?"

"Sleeping."

Rachel nodded. "Any damage in town?"

"I won't know until I go and see. Neil's brother and sister are here."

Both women stopped. "Did they come to break him out?"

"Yes."

Rachel went back for her rifle, which was lying on the backseat.

Olivia chuckled at the determined set of Rachel's face. "You can leave it there, Miss Rachel. He told them he was staying."

Daisy raised an eyebrow. "Really?" She said then, "I knew he was the one."

Olivia looked confused. "The one for what?"

Rachel gave her an exasperated tongue a click. "The one for you. We had this same problem of not understanding when Chase was courting Cara Lee. She said the same thing."

Olivia wasn't certain she understood any of what they were fussing about, but it didn't matter. Chase rode up.

"Everyone here okay?" he asked.

The women nodded and Olivia asked, "How's my town?"

"No real damage. Shingles blown down here and there. Some of the livestock ran off, but nothing monumental. Main Street's a mess, though."

It was to be expected. A hard rain always turned the unpaved street into a sea of mud that took days, sometimes months, to dry up, but she was glad to hear there was no real structural damage. "Two Shafts is in the cellar and their sister is here too, somewhere."

His face turned grim and he dismounted. Pulling his rifle free from the saddle, he announced, "You all get in the house."

Olivia quickly reassured him, "It isn't what you think. They came to help him escape, but he told them he's staying. Said he'd given us his word."

Chase looked surprised.

"I was impressed, too."

"How'd they take it?"

"Shafts accepted it. His sister was so upset she stomped off."

"I'm not surprised. Everything I've ever heard about her says she's a real hothead."

"Neil told them about the bounty hunters. Asked them if they'd add their guns to yours. Shafts wanted to talk to you about it."

Chase quieted for a moment, as if mulling over the idea. Before he could put his thoughts into words, Shafts and his sister climbed out of the cellar. Chase cocked the rifle and pointed it their way. "Hands up."

Both looked surprised to see the sheriff.

Teresa snapped, "I told you we couldn't trust her. First thing she did was run to the law."

Shafts ignored his sister and nodded a greeting Chase's way. "Sheriff Jefferson."

"Two Shafts. Miss July."

She didn't respond.

Chase asked, "What brings you to Henry Adams?"

Shafts answered truthfully, "Came to get Neil, but he doesn't want to go."

"Kind of a problem."

Shafts nodded. "Yep."

"The mayor here says you had a proposition for me. You can drop your hands. Neil told you about the bounty hunters?"

"He did."

"I'm hoping the storm ran most of them off, but I doubt it. The lure of that money would make most of them wade through hell. Sorry, ladies."

Shafts asked, "Think they're waiting for him to escape?"

Chase nodded.

The two men spent a few moments discussing the number of bounty hunters, then Chase told Shafts about the men seen watching Olivia's house.

"Sounds like they're getting impatient. They may try to snatch him and take him somewhere else to claim the reward there."

"My thinking too."

"Do you want my gun?"

"The marshal in Topeka is an old Reb. He'll want the Elders to take my star if I deputize you."

"Maybe not," Shafts said easily. "Neil and I were made deputy marshals in Texas a few months back."

Olivia and Chase stared at him as if he'd turned into a two-headed calf.

Chase stuttered, "What? By whom?"

"Hanging Judge Parker."

Chase's eyes widened. "Parker made you a deputy marshal?"

"Yep. Griffin Blake needed our help—"

Chase interrupted again, "Griffin Blake, the train robber? I thought he was in the territorial prison."

"He was, but Marshal Wildhorse got him freed in April so he could help Judge Parker with a problem down in Texas. Let me show you something." Shafts took a moment to walk over to his mount, which was tied up to the porch. He searched the contents of his war bag. He came back with a marshal star and handed it to Chase.

Chase studied it closely before raising his eyes back up to Shafts. "This is real."

"Sure is. Parker gave us a pardon for our sins, too."

Chase handed the star back wordlessly.

Olivia wasn't sure she understood all the twists and turns in Shafts's story, but apparently Neil and Two Shafts were not only outlaws but, courtesy of Hanging Judge Parker, U.S. deputy marshals as well.

"So how long was your appointment?" Chase asked in a voice still filled with amazement.

Shafts shrugged. "'Til he takes it back, I'm guessing."

Olivia could see that Chase was terribly confused. She was too.

Rachel asked, "Do the railroads and all those folks offering money for your head know about this?"

Shafts shrugged again. "No way of knowing."

Olivia thought this quite the conundrum. How would this surprising revelation affect Neil when he went to trial? Would there be a trial? He was still wanted, but Judge Parker's influence was long. If he could make two well-known outlaws like the Terrible Twins officers of his court and send them to Texas on his behalf, could he have the warrants for their arrest voided as well? The railroads were powerful and influential too. What would they do when they found out that their most wanted man may or may not be under Judge Parker's protection? Surely Parker wouldn't condone their train robbing. She realized she was getting dizzy trying to sort it all out, so she stopped.

Chase said, "Well, no sense in lying. I really could use your guns."

"All yours."

Chase looked to the beautiful Teresa. "And you."

"To keep my brother alive. I'll throw in, too."

"We'll let Judge Parker sort out your warrants, because right now the safety of this town is my only concern."

Now that the details had been settled, Olivia asked Two Shafts, "Is Neil still asleep?"

Shafts nodded.

She thought about the wound on his back. "He needs to be in a bed. Can you help him?"

He nodded. Chase and Teresa went to help. The spinsters followed Olivia into the house.

Rachel said, "I never met a lady outlaw before."

"I haven't either."

Daisy said, "Do you think she's really an outlaw or just a girl playing at being one?"

Olivia had no way of knowing. She did know that Teresa didn't like her—not that it mattered, but Olivia was a bit perturbed that Teresa believed Olivia would betray Neil.

Neil entered the bedroom under his own power. He was slow, but he managed. His eyes found Olivia's and held them, making her remember all that had passed between them. As if reading her mind, he threw her a quick wink, then eased himself to a seat on the edge of the bed. Now gingerly lying down, he warned his sister in a tired voice, "No yelling, Tee."

Teresa smiled—the first one Olivia had seen.

"I'm not escaping," he added tiredly. "Promised Olivia."

Olivia could see many eyes turned her way. She tried to ignore them, but she couldn't ignore the increased beating of her heart.

Lying on the bed on his stomach, he closed his eyes. A few moments later he said, "Chase, they came to take me home, but I told them no. Kept my word."

Chase said, "I knew you would."

Neil had a tired smile on his face. "Good. Going to sleep now."

And he did.

They'd just closed the door on the sleeping Neil when a loud knocking on the back door filled the house. A concerned Olivia hurried to answer it.

It was Armstead Malloy. "Where's the sheriff?"

He looked very distressed. Olivia let him enter. "He's here."

She ushered Malloy into the shop, where the rest of her visitors were gathered.

Upon spotting Chase, Malloy gushed, "Oh, thank God! Sheriff, you gotta come."

"Where?" Chase asked skeptically.

"The Lady! They've taken over."

"Who?"

"The bounty hunters."

Chase looked as confused as Olivia felt. "What do you mean, taken over?"

"They're drinking all my whiskey, eating all of my food. They won't pay and they won't leave. They're threatening to kill me if I don't renounce my claim to the July reward."

Shafts pivoted swiftly. "You're the one who shot my brother in the *back*?"

Malloy's eyes widened in fear, then he calmed himself and said haughtily, "Isn't there a reward out on you, too?"

The taunt had no sooner left his mouth than Teresa's gun magically appeared between his eyes. "There's a reward out on me, too. Want to try and collect it in hell?"

Malloy gave an involuntary squeal of fright.

Teresa gave him a cold smile, then drew the gun back. "I thought not." She put the Colt back into her belt and returned to Shafts's side. The contempt on her beautiful, dark face was easy to see.

Olivia guessed the question had been answered: Teresa was indeed an outlaw and not just a woman playing at being one.

Chase asked Malloy, "So what do you want me to do?"

"Make them leave. You're the law around here."

Chase studied him for a moment before saying, "I'll be there directly."

"Not directly," Malloy demanded. "Now! Or do I have to wire the marshal in Topeka?"

Chase shrugged. "Wire anybody you like, Malloy. You had no business letting them bunk at your place in the first place, and I told you it wasn't a good idea to keep bragging about that reward money."

Malloy hazarded a look in Shafts's direction, but the Comanche's deadly glare made him turn back to the sheriff. "They were paying customers then."

"And now they're not."

Malloy's face showed his frustration. "They're threatening to kill me!"

"You said that," Chase reminded him casually. "Is there anything else?"

An angry Malloy turned to Olivia. "You're the mayor. Make him act."

"He said he'd investigate, and he will."

"I am a tax-paying citizen, and I demand satisfaction."

Olivia said, "And you'll receive it. Were I you, I'd sleep elsewhere tonight."

"I can't! Haven't you been listening? If I'm not back in twenty minutes, they're going to torch the place. They said they're holding me hostage in exchange for July."

Rachel asked, "Then what are you doing here? Just don't return."

"I am not letting those ruffians burn me out. Do you know how much money I've invested in that place!"

Olivia knew Malloy was stubborn, but this was over the top. "You're going back?"

"Of course. Since the sheriff won't do the job he was elected to do, I'll have to handle the matter alone." Flashing with fury, he stormed out.

Everyone in the shop shook their heads at his single-minded stupidity.

Chase said finally, "Guess I should get over there before the doc has to treat Malloy for busted suspenders."

"Good luck," Olivia said genuinely.

Chase, Neil, and Teresa departed. Olivia and the spinsters sat down to wait.

About twenty minutes later, they returned.

Chase said, "Well, Malloy really is a hostage now. They won't let him leave, and they want to exchange him for Neil."

"Are they aware that they're going to be stuck with Armstead?"

Shafts chuckled and Chase grinned. "Tried to tell them that, but they want to talk to you."

"Why me?"

"Malloy has them convinced that he's such a big-wig around here, the town will do anything for him, even give up July, so they want to talk to the mayor and negotiate the matter."

"When do they want me to come?"

"Soon as you're ready."

Teresa was staring at Olivia as if she'd never seen her before. Olivia asked, "Something wrong?"

"You're the mayor?"

"I am."

Teresa's face was still confused.

Olivia put on her beige everyday bonnet and took up her handbag, wondering what was going on in Teresa July's head.

Teresa stayed behind to watch over Neil while Olivia rode behind Chase on his horse. Arriving at the Lady, she could see that Malloy's palace had already sustained considerable damage. Some of the fancy windows were shattered, one of the elegant swinging doors hung by a pin, but its twin was missing. There was broken glass from windows and drinking glasses littering the ground. She said to Chase, "I don't suppose this is storm damage?"

"Nope."

They dismounted, and Olivia adjusted her skirt and bonnet. The swish of her skirt made her remember that she was still without her drawers. She forced that startling realization out of her mind and turned her attention to the man now stepping out of the door of the Liberian Lady.

He was a Black man, bearded, medium brown skin, medium height. Olivia noted that his clothes were as dirty and tattered as the ones worn by the other bounty hunters she'd seen ride into town before the ordinance had been put into effect, and she wondered what had made him turn into a man hunter. He took one look at Olivia and asked Chase, "Who's this?"

"Mayor Sterling."

"What?! She's a woman. What kind of town is this?"

Olivia answered, "We are an historic town, Mr.—"

"Name's Charles."

Olivia nodded. "Well, Mr. Charles, this town was founded in 1879, and the people who founded it did so to escape the Redemptionists."

He looked at her oddly, but she continued, "In order to reach Kansas, many of them sold everything they owned to come to a place they'd never seen. Whole church congregations traveled here, and when they arrived, they had to live underground the first winter."

"Why are you telling me all this?"

"So that you will know the strength and resolve of the people who live here. If the people here were brave enough to face down the Redemptionists and live underground, do you really believe we will succumb to men like you and your friends?"

He looked so surprised that Olivia heard Chase cough to hide his laugh.

Olivia pressed on. "The answer is no." She continued, "For the record, Mr. Malloy is a thorn in the side of everyone in town. I know that isn't very Christian of me, but it is the truth. If I weren't the mayor, I'd tell you you could keep him until Christmas, but since he is a citizen, his release is my responsibility."

"We want July."

"You can't have July. Are you familiar with United States Deputy Marshal Wildhorse?"

"Yeah," Charles answered. "He's the big Seminole marshal in Indian Territory. Why?"

"Is he someone you want to cross swords with?"

He didn't answer.

"I'll take that to mean you don't. He's on his way to Henry Adams to add his guns to this fight."

The man's eyes widened just long enough for Olivia to see it. "I would advise you and your friends to let Mr. Malloy go or face the marshal."

The man said angrily, "We want July."

Olivia turned to Chase and Two Shafts and said, "Gentlemen, I'm ready to return to my shop."

While the man named Charles stared on in what looked like shock, Olivia was helped to the back of the horse. Chase mounted, then Olivia and her guns rode back the way they'd come.

Back at her shop, Chase escorted her inside. He laughed. "Did you see the look on his face when you gave him the history of the town?"

Olivia removed her gloves and bonnet.

Teresa came out of the kitchen. Chase and Two Shafts told her the story of Olivia's encounter, and when the telling was over, Teresa stared Olivia's way. "You don't look that brave."

"I'm not, really, but I was angry at having the people around here endangered all because of that nasty little Malloy."

Two Shafts nodded. "He'd better hope the bounty hunters keep him."

Chase said warningly, "You're an officer of the law now, Shafts. Remember that."

"I haven't forgotten, but I won't always be."

Teresa tossed back, "And I haven't sworn to uphold anything but the July name."

Olivia could see that she and Chase were sitting on a potential powder keg. Olivia hoped there might be some news soon on the marshal's arrival and the arrival of the judge. "Where are Rachel and Daisy?"

"They went home," Teresa said.

Olivia wished the bounty hunters would do the same.

The next day, news did arrive, but it wasn't the news she'd been expecting. It came in the form of a letter from her mother.

Dear Olivia,

Disaster has struck. Your father discovered your letters hidden in my bureau and all perdition has broken loose. We will be leaving for Kansas today on the nine o'clock train. Accompanying us will be Horatio Butler. Your father and Mr. Butler are determined to see you married. Mr. Butler has obtained a writ of some sort that he boasts will force you to honor his suit. We are scheduled to arrive . . .

Olivia looked at the date and felt sick to her stomach. They'd be in Henry Adams tomorrow! "Oh, no!"

Chase was seated at his desk. "What's wrong?"

"My parents are coming!"

The confusion on Chase's face made her tell him the story.

When she was done, he stared, amused. "You ran away from home?"

She nodded and read the letter again, hoping the wording would change. It didn't. "My lord. What am I going to do? With all my other worries, now this?"

Marrying Horatio Butler was the last thing she wished to do. What she knew of him she couldn't abide, and she was very concerned about this writ he'd supposedly armed himself with. Could it really compel her to marry him, and under what penalty should she refuse?

Footsteps entering the office made them both look up. A big, dark-skinned man wearing a Stetson and sporting a topaz stud in his ear stood on the threshold.

Chase grinned and jumped up. "You made it!" He shook the man's hand. "Thanks for coming, Dix. Olivia. Marshal Dixon Wildhorse."

"Welcome, Marshal. I'm Mayor Olivia Sterling."

He touched his hat. "Nice to meet you, ma'am. You're the mayor?"

"Yes, I am."

He smiled. "Not many lady mayors outside Indian Territory."

Whatever he was about to say next was interrupted by the entrance of three more men. Dix said to Chase, "These three were visiting and decided to come along."

The sight of one of the men seemed to catch Chase by surprise. "Jack? Jack Blake!"

"Been a long time." The two men embraced like

old friends while Olivia looked on with a smile. Jackson Blake was as handsome and dark as Neil.

Jackson said, "Don't know if you know my little brother. Griffin Blake, meet Chase Jefferson."

"Only by his Wanted posters."

The redheaded Griffin Blake laughed and shook Chase's extended hand.

The last man walked over to Olivia and said, "These heathens have no manners. The lady is always supposed to be introduced first. I'm Vance Bigelow, ma'am. Folks call me the Preacher." He was dressed all in black. He had brown skin and luminous green eyes.

Olivia couldn't hide her surprise. "I'm Mayor Olivia Sterling. Pleased to meet you."

"Likewise," he returned politely, then he said, "you seemed surprised when I gave you my name. Has Neil been telling lies again?"

Olivia couldn't tell whether he was kidding with her or not. "I've never known Neil to be a liar."

Griffin Blake burst into laughter. Olivia turned to him in confusion.

The Preacher explained. "Don't pay him any mind. He's known Neil a long time, and the Neil he used to know is probably not the one you know."

Griff took offense, "What do you mean, used to know? When they left Texas, they took a carpetbag of my gold."

Dix scolded, "I'm sure the lady doesn't care about that."

Griff saw the stunned look on Olivia's face and said, "You're right. Sorry, ma'am."

Had Neil taken Blake's gold? Olivia reminded herself that Neil was an outlaw, but surely he didn't rob his friends, too?

Dixon switched the conversation. "So tell me about these bounty hunters."

Chase and Olivia took turns telling parts of the story. When they were done, Griffin Blake asked, "And this Malloy is the man who shot Neil in the back?"

"Correct," Olivia said.

"Let the bounty hunters have him, I say."

"I agree," Olivia replied, "but Chase and I have a duty to protect the citizens, and he is one of them."

Dixon Wildhorse thought for a moment, then said, "How about I go down and give them a talking to?"

"Fine, but answer me a question first. Are the Twins really marshals?"

Dix nodded. "They were."

"Well, Shafts is here, along with Teresa July."

Dix raised an eyebrow. "They come to break Neil out?"

"Yep, but he turned down the offer."

Griffin said, "What?! You sure we're talking about Neil July?"

Chase nodded. "He gave me and Miss Olivia his word, and he kept it."

"Well, I'll be," Dix responded.

The men all studied Olivia. She held their gazes for as long as she could, but the speculation in their eyes made her change the subject. "Marshal Wildhorse, do you think the bounty hunters will leave?"

"If they have any sense, they will," Jackson Blake cracked.

Griffin said, "After we talk to the bounty hunters, I want to see this new and improved Neil July. The Neil I know would never turn down an opportunity to escape the law, and you say Teresa's here, too?"

Olivia nodded.

Dix said, "Been after her for months now. Don't suppose I should arrest her if she's on our side."

Preacher turned to the marshal and quoted quietly, " 'Touch not my anointed, and do my prophets no harm.' Psalm one hundred and five."

Olivia had no idea how to take a Bible-quoting bounty hunter.

Griffin said, "That's why we keep him around. Shall we go?"

Neil was on Olivia's back porch talking with Teresa and Shafts. Teresa was still upset about his refusal to hightail it out of town, and he was attempting to make her understand. "I'm thirty-eight years old, Tee. I'm tired of running." Neil glanced over at Shafts, who met his gaze emotionlessly. "Tired of sleeping on the ground, tired of always having to look over my shoulder. Times are changing."

"I understand that, but what will you do if they send you to prison?"

"Probably have you break me out," he said with a small smile. "Spend the rest of my days in Mexico."

"Then why not leave now?"

Olivia's face floated across his mind's eye. "I can't. I need to work out something here first."

"Is it the woman?"

Neil didn't hesitate in his answer. "It's the woman."

Teresa shook her head. "Don't tell me you're in love."

He shrugged. "Don't know." And he didn't. What he did know was that leaving Henry Adams without a clear understanding of how Olivia might fit into his future would haunt him for the rest of his life if it wasn't resolved. Frankly, he was more surprised than anyone else by his decision to turn down the escape. Only time would tell if the choice had been sound, but there was a peace within him that made him feel it was. He met his brother's eyes. "Do you think I'm loco?"

Shafts replied solemnly, "No. We're both feeling our age. Every morning I wake up with the call of my land in New Mexico in my bones, and every morning it's getting harder and harder to resist. Think I may want to answer it now. We had a good run, you and I."

Neil's face echoed his brother's words. "That we did."

"Time we start acting like old men." Shafts added wryly, "We need sons, though."

Neil chuckled. Olivia's face shimmered by once more. He wondered if the call of Shafts's land was as strong and as sweet as the call of the Madam Mayor.

Teresa looked at both of them with a mixture of pity and disgust. "I need a drink." She stepped from the porch and walked to her mount. As she rode away, the laughter of her brothers followed in her wake.

Chapter 12

Olivia accompanied the long-striding peace officers down the walk to the Liberian Lady. They were an impressive sight with their heights, good looks, and stars pinned to their shirtfronts. The Preacher, striding beside them clad in his flowing black duster, added to the effect. The townspeople shopping and conducting business on Main Street stared. An eerie silence descended, and the only sound Olivia could hear was the death knell-like cadence of the lawmen's boots on the wood. Even folks standing in the middle of the street trying to coax their wagons and buggies out of the mud stopped what they were doing and followed the procession with their eyes. Soon people began to follow the men with the stars. Others ran for cover, while others ran to alert their neighbors of the confrontation to come.

The lawmen stopped across the street from the Lady's front entrance. Marshal Wildhorse said to Olivia, "Ma'am, I'm going to ask you to get behind that buckboard over there."

The buckboard was one of many vehicles parked near the walk. Olivia picked up her skirts and hastened to safety.

Chase turned to the small crowd that had gathered. "Go home before you get hurt."

No one moved.

He repeated himself, louder this time, but nobody paid him much mind.

Olivia saw Doc Johnson, bag in hand, running toward them. He took up a position behind the buckboard with Olivia. He was out of breath. Olivia was glad he'd arrived.

Since no one would take Chase's advice, he gave up. He turned back to the Lady and called out, "Send out Malloy! Then come out with your hands high!"

The answer was gunfire, and the lawmen scrambled even as they opened up with their own weapons. The few panes remaining in the Lady's upstairs window were broken out by the men inside so they could add their lead to the fray. Bullets were flying and pinging everywhere. The male citizenry hidden behind the vehicles drew their Colts and Winchesters, adding them to the fight on the side of the lawmen.

Olivia tried to see the action but was forced to keep ducking down to avoid the bullets peppering the buckboard. A quick look up showed a man firing from a window on the second floor. She saw him take a slug in the chest, then slowly pitch forward out of the window and spiral to the ground below. The gut-wrenching sight made her hold her heart and pray this would end soon.

The two sides exchanged bullets for what seemed like an eternity. Olivia hugged the wood of the board and tried to keep out of the way. Amidst all the noise, she heard Griffin Blake let out a loud curse followed by, "I've been shot!" On the heels of that he declared angrily, "All right. I'm tired of this. Cover me!"

To her dismay and surprise, she saw him zigzag his way through the mud and a hail of bullets toward the Lady. Guns blazing, he barreled through the single hanging door and disappeared inside.

The citizens and the lawmen continued their fierce firing, providing Jackson Blake the cover he needed to follow his brother. Chase followed him. Then, to Olivia's complete astonishment, Teresa July ran toward the door, firing from Colts in both hands! Teresa took a second to blast a man on the roof. The hot lead spun him around and made him cry out in pain. Teresa was already inside by the time he landed on the ground. It was a jaw-dropping show of marksmanship. Olivia shared a stunned look with Doc Johnson, then trained her attention back on the fight.

Gunfire continued to erupt from the saloon's interior. Added to it came the sounds of crashing wood and glass, leading Olivia to believe they were fighting with their fists now. The sounds of mayhem continued for another few minutes, then it stopped. Silence echoed from the scene. Those outside drew down their guns, and they, along with the townspeople, waited and watched tensely.

Moments later a grim-faced Chase came out, followed by a line of angry bounty hunters, whose wrists were bound together with rope. Bringing up the rear were the Griffin brothers, Teresa July, and a very dirty Armstead Malloy. Beside him were the crying but happy saloon girls.

The crowd's cheers were as loud as thunder, and the grinning Olivia was sure the celebration could be heard in Topeka. She was so glad this was all over. *So glad.*

When she walked out to congratulate the victors, her smile met Chase's. "Excellent job, Sheriff Jefferson. Excellent job."

"Thanks."

Griffin Blake had blood staining the sleeve of his blue shirt from the bullet he'd taken in the arm. "Not bad for a day's work, wouldn't you say, Dix?"

Dixon nodded, then addressed the lady in black leathers hanging back a bit. "Thanks, Teresa."

"Anytime," she said. "Now, figure out a way to get my brother off his hook and I won't tell Mrs. Wildhorse that this town is run by a lady mayor."

Dix stared.

Jackson laughed.

Olivia didn't understand.

Dix explained. "Miss Olivia, my wife, Katherine, is so filled up with marching for women's rights I've spent most of my marriage either putting her in jail or bailing her out of jail."

Olivia began to laugh.

Dix continued, "If she ever finds out nontribal women can be mayors, she is going to start her own campaign to change the laws at home, and neither I nor the men in Wewoka will get any peace."

He then turned to Blake and said, "I don't know why you're laughing. Your banker wife, Grace, is no wallflower either. What do you think she'll do if she finds out there are places she can run for mayor?"

Jackson hung his head, apparently conceding the point.

Dix then eyed the smiling Teresa. "I'll see what I can do."

Teresa gave Olivia a satisfied wink, then disappeared into the still excited crowd.

It took most of the afternoon for the lawmen to mop up. The eight uninjured ruffians had their guns confiscated by Marshal Wildhorse, then they were given the choice of either going to jail for firing on a deputy marshal or leaving the county. The bounty hunters grumbled, but all chose the latter. The three injured men, including the two who'd tumbled to the ground, were treated by Delbert and put up at his small hospital. When they healed, they too would get to pick which option they preferred.

To honor the lawmen, Sophie Reynolds offered them free lodging for the remainder of their stay in Henry Adams, and she passed the word that she would be throwing a party for them at her hotel that evening. The whole town was invited.

As for Armstead Malloy, he charged into the sheriff's office late that afternoon and declared angrily, "I demand the Elders pay for the damages to my establishment."

Olivia sighed. One would think that after such an ordeal, Malloy's personality would have tempered. Apparently not. "Which establishment are we speaking of, Mr. Malloy?"

"The Lady, of course."

Olivia shared looks with the lawmen standing around the room before asking Malloy, "Why should the Elders pay?"

"Because the sheriff didn't do his job."

Dixon asked, "Did the sheriff tell you not to return to the saloon after the bounty hunters moved back in?"

"Yes, but—"

"You have no case. And if you take it to court, I will come and testify on the town' s behalf. Good day, Mr. Malloy."

Malloy balled up his fist again, steamed for a silent few moments, then stomped out.

Everyone was glad to see him go.

An hour later, Olivia finally headed home with the lawmen and the Preacher in tow. They all wanted to see Neil.

Neil, Shafts, and Teresa were on the back porch drinking lemonade. When Neil saw Olivia come into view with a smile of greeting, he thought his heart would beat out of his chest. When he saw the men she had with her, his heart began to pound for other reasons, and he grinned. "Well, if it isn't the four laziest sheriffs and marshals this side of the divide."

He eased himself up out of the chair and greeted each of his old friends, even Preacher, with a warm embrace.

A pleased Olivia went into the house and left the men to visit.

She was pouring herself a cup of coffee when Teresa entered. Olivia held up the pot. "Do you want some?"

Teresa shook her head negatively. "No. Hate the stuff."

Olivia took a seat at the table and gestured for Teresa to join her.

"I'll stand."

Olivia didn't press, but she sensed the young woman had searched her out for a reason. Olivia took a sip of the hot brew and set the cup down on the tabletop. "That was some fine shooting you did out there today. On behalf of the town, thanks."

Teresa nodded. "You're welcome."

Silence.

Then Teresa said, "May I ask you something?"

"Sure."

"How do you feel about my brother?"

Olivia hadn't expect that, so she answered cautiously, "I enjoy his company."

"Is that all?"

Olivia scanned the young woman's face. "Why the questions?"

"Because he's very taken with you."

Olivia smiled inwardly. "To be honest, I'm taken with him also."

"You don't mind that he robs trains?"

"Yes, I do."

Teresa studied the serious set of Olivia's features. "It's not fair of you to ask him to risk jail for you."

"I've never asked your brother to do that for me."

"Then why is he talking about not being an outlaw anymore."

"Maybe because he is old enough to make his own decisions in life."

Teresa July's jaw tightened, and she looked off Olivia's steady gaze.

Olivia asked kindly, "How old are you, Teresa?"

"I'll be nineteen next month."

"One day, when you get much older, life will call upon you to make decisions others might not understand, but you will follow your own conscience. Just as your brother seems to be doing."

This was the first Olivia had heard about Neil's planning to change his direction in life. It pleased her and gave her hope that maybe they could explore a future. At the moment, her own future was clouded by her parents' arrival tomorrow with Horatio Butler. She still had no idea what to do. Had she married one of the farmers who'd come courting when she'd first arrived in Henry Adams, Butler and his writ would be thwarted. An idea popped into her head, but it was so outrageous that she forced it away.

When she looked up, Teresa was gone. Olivia went back to her coffee.

By the time the cup was empty, Olivia had made a decision. Setting the cup in the sink, she went outside to talk to Neil.

She was surprised to find him alone. "Where'd everybody go?"

"Sophie's to get cleaned up and ready for the party. Hope they all remember they're married men now—well, everybody but Shafts and the Preacher. Teresa went with them."

He looked up at her and said, "Come sit awhile. Let me hold you."

She crossed to him without hesitation and took a seat on his lap, raising her lips for his kiss. He obliged her, then held her against his heart.

He said, "Shafts and I are mad we missed all the shooting."

She chuckled, "I bet you are, but there were enough bullets flying as it was."

"Chase told me how good Teresa was."

"She upheld the family name well."

"Are you tired?"

"Exhausted."

"Then just sit and relax."

"Wish I could, but I've a problem." She straightened so she could see his face. "I need you to marry me."

He blinked. "Whoa, we didn't go that far, did we?"

She dropped her head to hide her embarrassed smile. "I'm not carrying, Neil, but my parents are arriving tomorrow. Along with Horatio Butler. Mother's letter says he has a writ that'll force me to be his wife."

"That's mighty manly of him." Neil was sure he wasn't going to like this Butler.

"I know this is sudden and probably loco, but I don't see any other way around it. If I'm married he'll have to look elsewhere for a wife."

"True."

She searched his eyes. "I'm not seeking to stay married to do this ''til death do us part.' I know you aren't wanting to put down roots here. Once they go back to Chicago, we can call it off."

Neil studied her and wondered what she would say if he announced that he *wanted* to marry her until death do us part. "You really want to stain yourself this way?"

"I'm not staining myself, I'm saving myself." She searched his face. "What do you say?"

Regardless of the circumstances, Neil didn't want to see her with another man, and the idea that she would be his, even if for only a short while, pleased him. "If it'll keep you out of the clutches of Horatio Butler, yes."

She threw her arms around his neck and jumped up and down with joy.

He put his hand on her waist. "Whoa, no jumping. I'm still an injured man."

Olivia was kissing him all over his face, whispering, "Thank you, thank you, thank you."

He grinned. "So when will the I-dos take place?"

"It'll have to be tonight."

"So soon?"

"They're arriving tomorrow."

Neil supposed that made sense. "What do I need to do in the meantime?"

"Nothing. Leave everything to me."

She kissed him again, infusing the deepening kiss with her gratitude. He kissed her back, sparking a fire that still smoldered from the time together in the cellar, and she had to pull away or drown.

Her voice softened by the rekindling of her desire, she said, "I hope you're well rested, because it will be our wedding night, and I plan to learn all. . . ."

Neil stared.

She grinned, gave him a provocative wink, then left his lap to go back into town to arrange the wedding details.

Neil waited until he was sure she was out of earshot before yelling at the top of his lungs, "Hallelujah!"

Olivia found Cara Lee in Sophie's big kitchen helping the staff and an army of local women prepare for the evening's festivities. Everybody greeted Olivia with smiles and calls of greeting. She acknowledged them all, then said, "Need to borrow Cara Lee for a moment."

Cara, shucking ears of corn, dried her hands on her apron and followed Olivia outside, saying, "I'm mad I missed all the excitement. Heard Teresa July shot nine men off the roof."

Olivia began to laugh. "She shot one man on the roof."

Cara asked, "You sure?"

"I was there, Cara."

"Okay, okay. That's what I get for living in a small town. Rumors."

Their steps carried them out to the open plains behind the hotel and Cara asked, "What can I do for you?"

"Will you stand up for me tonight at my wedding?"

Cara looked at her strangely. "What wedding?"

Olivia explained the events leading up to her decision to marry and who she had chosen to be her husband.

Cara's eyes widened. "Neil July?! Have you been out in the sun again?"

"No."

"Olivia . . . ." Cara couldn't seem to find the words she needed.

"I know, but this is my only option."

"But he may be in prison soon."

"I am aware of that."

Cara looked at Olivia as if she'd never seen her before. "Couldn't you have found someone else? What about Delbert?"

"With Delbert comes Delbert's mama."

Cara said, "True, and she's already made it plain that she's the only woman in his life. Are you sure you can't talk to your parents and this Butler? Seems to me if you just explain your position—"

"A man armed with a writ isn't coming for a discussion."

Cara quieted for a moment. "Hadn't thought about it that way." She searched Olivia's eyes. "I will always be your friend, so if you want me to stand up with you, I'd be proud to, but are you sure this is what you want to do?"

"No, but I can't see any other way out."

Cara asked, "Who's going to say the words?"

"I planned to ask Reverend Whitfield, but I thought he might balk."

"And give a sermon on women who marry outlaws for convenience."

Olivia chuckled.

"Sheriffs and marshals can perform weddings, and we have a silo full of them in town right now, so take your pick."

"I prefer your husband."

"Then I'll find him and tell him he has one more official duty to perform tonight before he can put away his star. Who else are you inviting?"

"The spinsters. Neil's family. His lawmen friends. Sophie and Asa, if they can get away."

"No Armstead Malloy?"

Olivia cut her friend an amused look that made them both laugh.

Cara, still laughing, asked, "What time and where?"

"My back porch." Olivia glanced at her watch. It was now almost 7 P.M. "Around ten?"

"That's fine." Cara then added in a more serious tone, "The Elders may make you resign because of this. They can be pretty provincial when it comes to town officials marrying wanted men."

"I know."

"The next few weeks may be tough."

"I'm prepared." She wasn't really, but she planned to be so by the time she had to face the populace.

Cara gave her tall friend a strong hug. "I'm with you no matter what."

Olivia hugged her back. "You're the best. Would you ask Chase to let the other marshals know that they're invited as well, and Sophie and Asa too, when you see them?"

"Sure will."

"You don't think we can keep this a secret, do you?"

"We can try, but it isn't going to matter. Remember the nine men on the roof? Before it's over the gossips are going to have you married to Neil *and* his brother Two Shafts."

They both smiled.

Olivia said, "Then I will see you at the house. Thank you, Cara."

"You're very welcome."

Olivia waved good-bye, then went to seek out Shafts and Teresa.

She wanted to talk to Shafts before she spoke to the volatile Teresa. After questioning a few people on the walk as to his whereabouts, she found him coming out of one of the local bath houses. His long hair was wet and gleaming, and he looked cleaner than she ever remembered seeing him. The sculpted features of the big Comanche were as handsome as his brother's. "May I speak with you for a moment, please?"

"Sure. I'm heading back to the hotel. We can talk on the way."

"I'll get right to the point. I asked your brother to marry me."

Shafts stopped and stared. "When?"

"Just a little while ago."

She explained her dilemma to him and waited for his reaction.

"So, you plan to stay married to him for how long?" The disapproval on his face was plain.

Olivia was disappointed by his unfavorable reaction. "Not very long. Just until my parents leave."

"And he agreed to this?"

"Yes."

Shafts looked out over the landscape for a long moment. He then turned back to her. "Do you care for my brother?"

"I do."

He studied her face as if seeking the truth. "Teresa and I will be there in time to get him ready." He walked away.

Olivia wasn't certain what had just transpired, but at this juncture she had so many other worries that she had no room for another.

She swung by the Two Spinsters' house and explained to them the pickle she was in and what she'd decided to do about it.

Rachel asked, "What kind of man uses the courts to force a woman to be his wife?"

Daisy replied, "Sounds like a bounder to me. Marrying Neil might be a good idea in the long run,

Olivia. You may need him to protect you from this Mr. Butler."

Olivia chuckled, "I don't believe it will come to that."

"It doesn't matter what you believe, dear. Just be careful."

Walking home, Olivia felt buoyed by the support of her elderly friends, but their concerns added to her worry list.

But when she entered her house through the back door and saw Neil seated at the kitchen table eating dinner, all of her worries melted away like snow in April.

Neil thought she looked pretty chipper for a woman intent upon sullying her reputation by marrying him, but her spirit was another one of the attributes he liked about her. "Why so happy?"

"Because when I'm with you there are no squabbles between neighbors to settle. No arguing by telegraph with snippy little clerks in Topeka over the correct amount of taxes the town owes the state. No bounty hunters terrorizing citizens. It's just us two, and the silence."

Olivia noted that coming home to him was different than coming home to a house with no one. It wasn't better, per se, just different.

"How're the wedding plans coming along?"

"Everything is in place. Chase is going to do the honors, and I've invited your brother and sister, Cara Jefferson, the spinsters, all your lawmen friends, and the Preacher, of course."

"Of course," he echoed quietly.

Olivia noted the desire flaring in his eyes. In response, her corset-encased nipples began their shameless blossoming. "Oh. I also asked Cara to let Sophie and Asa know. I'm not sure they—"

Her voice slid to a stop because he was beckoning her with a crooked finger. His gaze had already set her afire, and the intensity glowing in it now was akin to adding kindling. She went to him willingly, though—very willingly.

When she reached him, he used two fingers to trace her lips. The sensations filled her, and her lids fluttered closed. The fingers trailed down her chin and over the bones in her jaw before traveling lower to her throat. Moving with sensual intent, he teased the hollow, making her skin react, then drew a line down the valley between her breasts, and then lazily up again.

Olivia's lips were parted, her breathing changing. The fingers circled each nipple with such a light yet arousing pressure that the familiar quickening began pulsing in the secret places between her thighs. He leaned up and kissed her then, softly, gently, still toying with her breasts.

He slid his hand gently between her thighs and rubbed her skirt erotically, murmuring, "You should go get ready before I put you on the table and have you for dessert. We'll finish this later. . . ."

She thrilled to his hot voice and touches, but even more to the promise. "Do you promise?" She spread her legs a bit wider to accommodate his idle play.

He raised her skirt and sought the straining bud hidden within her drawers. "Promise what? . . ." he asked with a whisper, moving his hand through the back slit in her drawers and caressing the soft skin of her behind. "To put you on the table, or to finish this . . ." and he slid his finger across the temple of her desire, making her arch and raise herself to him for more.

And he gave her more; more dallying, more touching, until she was wet with desire. The pressure built and built, and then an orgasm broke over her. She hollered hoarsely. Watching her with eyes hardened by his own desire, he smiled.

In the silent aftermath, he whispered, "Man likes a woman who's easy to please. . . ."

They shared one last humid kiss, then Olivia floated off to prepare for the wedding.

In the spare room where she washed up, the still throbbing Olivia paid no attention to the voices in her head. They wanted to debate the issue of this marriage and question her sanity, but she refused. She was on the verge of marrying a man who made her body sing, and she planned to concern herself only with that.

She went to her wardrobe to seek something appropriate to wear and settled on a fine lawn blouse and her purple satin suit. For the first time in her life, Olivia didn't put on a corset. The reasons were selfish and scandalous: She wanted to feel Neil's touch and wanted him able to feel her in return. A corset prevented that. The other advantages, such as being able to breathe freely, made her understand why more and more women eschewed the confining garment. Olivia had always worn one because her mother had, and because society deemed them proper. As Olivia slipped on the purple satin jacket over the thin lawn blouse, she decided that a women who went without corsets, rode out storms while making love to outlaws in a cellar, and confronted bounty hunters while wearing no drawers beneath her skirts had left the realm of propriety long ago. Patting her saucy little hat, she approved her reflection in the mirror, then left the room.

"Are you loco?"

Neil fixed the suspender and surveyed his brother. "Maybe."

They were in Olivia's bedroom. Neil was dressed in a white shirt loaned to him by Chase. He would have preferred to be gussied up for the wedding, but an outlaw rarely traveled with a formal set of clothing, and Neil was no exception. "She's in a fix. I can help."

"That the only reason?"

"You know it isn't, so why even ask." Neil's feelings for Olivia were becoming more and more complicated, and more and more entrenched.

"Testy, are we?"

"Yep, because this isn't something we need to be arguing about."

"She's using you."

"And the point of that is?"

Neil faced his brother. "Do you see that beautiful woman out there. A woman like her wouldn't be with a man like me for all the gold on all the gold trains. She's smart, independent, she's the mayor, for

Pete's sake, but there's something going on between us. I don't have a name for it, and I don't think she has one either, but she picked me, Shafts. If this farce of a marriage only lasts two days, I'll take it."

"You're gonna get your heart broken."

Neil shrugged. "I'm a big boy, Shafts, but your prediction is noted."

Shafts quieted while Neil took a brush to his hair. "Anything else?"

Shafts shook his head, but then said, "She's a good woman. Hope it works out for the best."

Neil paused in midstroke. They'd never been able to stay upset with each other, even when they were boys growing up. "Thanks."

Shafts nodded and left the bedroom.

Chapter 13

~⟡~

Out on the back porch, Neil waited for Olivia to make her grand entrance. Torches had been lit, and the soft light bathed the darkness with a romantic glow. Waiting with him were Two Shafts, Marshal Wildhorse, the Sheriffs Blake, and the Preacher. No one had seen Teresa. Although Neil was concerned about her absence, he figured she'd show up once she got done pouting.

A rustle of sound caused the men to turn. Neil focused his attention on the door and noted that anticipation had dampened his palms. First to appear were the Two Spinsters, followed by Cara Jefferson and Sophie Reynolds. Sophie had tears in her eyes even though the event had just begun. After them came Chase, Asa—whom Olivia had asked to give her away—and finally, Olivia.

Neil thought she looked beautiful in her purple suit with the bustled skirt and the confection of a hat perched saucily upon her head. She was carrying a bunch of pink and white hollyhocks. He took a quick look at Two Shafts, and his brother flashed an approving grin. As she took up her position at his side, Neil fought down his nervous trembling. It wasn't every day an outlaw married a good woman. He waited for her to give her bouquet to Cara before reaching down and taking her hand in his. He gave her a little squeeze, and she gave him one in return.

The service took only a few minutes. When it was done, and Chase declared, "You may now kiss the bride," Neil kept it tasteful and short so as not to embarrass her in front of her friends.

The new Mr. and Mrs. Neil July faced their friends and were showered with congratulations and applause. After tastes of the cake supplied by the spinsters and some coffee, the visitors offered their good-byes. The Two Spinsters went home to their beds, and the others returned to Sophie's hotel for the rest of the party in the newlyweds' honor.

Soon, Neil and Olivia were alone. Their eyes met in the sputtering light of the torches. He held out his arms, and she went to him and let herself be enfolded. More than anything she wished this moment were real, and that they were actually committed to each other, but there was nothing that said she couldn't pretend.

Neil was pretending too; pretending that there were no barriers to them being together, no looming trial, no differences in their stations. In his mind, they had a lifetime—not days—to explore whatever it was they were feeling for each other. Holding her against his heart felt as natural to him as breathing.

He walked her into the house, and they doused candles and lamps as they went. The distant sounds of voices and music from the goings-on at Sophie's hotel floated through the velvet silence, but Neil and Olivia barely heard them, because there were about to be goings-on in the living quarters of Miss Olivia's Dressmaking Emporium that were of an entirely different nature.

In the bedroom, she stood before the mirror and removed her hat. Placing it on the wooden bureau below the mirror, she raised her eyes back to the glass and saw him reflected behind her. Even though he was on the other side of the room, she felt as if he were much closer; so close she could feel the warmth of his breath teasing against her neck and his trail-hardened thighs against her own. Anticipation thickened the air. Nothing needed to be said; they both knew.

Feeling bolder than ever in life, Olivia held his eyes and untied the strings of her cameo she'd worn in honor of her mother and set it on the bureau top. Next came the silky ascot around her neck and the large gold broach accenting it. His eyes in the mirror fairly glowed with desire, and it spurred her on. The rhinestone buttons snaking down the front of her cinch-waisted jacket were freed one by one. The Eve awakened inside of herself made Olivia disrobe slowly, purposefully. Off came the jacket, followed by her skirt. Her own eyes smoky, she watched him watch her remove the apronlike bustle with its stair-case of steplike pleats. As she undid the buttons of her blouse, the intensity of his interest and the arch-ing heat made her fingers tremble.

She turned her head so she could see him truly, and the moment was so vivid that it was as if time had slowed.

Then he came to her and fit himself close behind her. He placed soft, humid kisses up the plane of her throat. His hands came up to cup her breasts. Her eyes closed, and she arched against his strong chest. He played with her in and out of the camisole, mak-ing her nipples answer to his fevered call and her moans rise in the silence.

Neil's discovery that she wasn't wearing a corset sent him soaring; he was filling his hands with warm woman flesh, pressing his lips against the side of her perfumed neck, and that hardened him even more. "Open your eyes, Olivia. Watch your husband make love to you. . . ."

Reflected in the mirror, there she stood in her camisole, drawers, stockings, and shoes. He was be-hind her, his kisses on her neck, his hands sensually moving the camisole over and around her breasts. Fingers teased, circled, and rubbed. The nipples were berry hard, and the tableau was so very scan-dalous that she had to close her eyes or explode.

The rest of her clothes were taken next; slowly, lazily, his hands stroking and teasing as the gar-ments magically melted away.

Neil wanted to move over to the bed but found it impossible to stop touching and stroking her satiny skin. He figured he could stand with her just this way for the rest of his life. The citizens of Henry Adams were in danger of ever seeing their beautiful mayor again, because he was never going to let her go.

Olivia had expected to be modest and embarrassed in the marriage bed, but Neil had her so enthralled that being a shrinking violet was the furthest thing from her mind. He was teaching her the smoldering joy to be found in uninhibited loving, and she was a student willing to learn every lesson in the curriculum.

He led her to the bed, kissed her, then left her for a moment to turn down the lamps.

When he returned, she looked up at him from her seat in the middle of the bed and felt nothing but wonder. She rose on her knees, and her hand tenderly captured his bearded jaw. With her kiss, she drew him down to join her, and he didn't protest at all.

Olivia was lying on her back. For the first time in her life, she was naked to the sweep of a man's hand. Had she not been so overwhelmed by the caresses moving over her like a sculptor fashioning clay, she might have been able to put the experience into words, but she was floating in such a hazy world of desire, and the sensations were so blissful the words wouldn't come. She was hard in some places and damp in others. She opened her legs when his touch soundlessly invited her to, then arched while he brazenly lingered within the dewed folds of her passion-swollen core.

Neil knew that if he didn't have her soon he was going to hurt himself; she was hot, wet, and more lush than he'd ever imagined. He undid his belt buckle, then struggled out of his borrowed shirt. So as not to neglect the tight-breasted mayor reclining on the bed, he lowered his head and took a ripe nipple into his mouth. He toyed with it until she moaned softly. Satisfied, he straightened and rid himself of his trousers.

Olivia tried not to stare, but she couldn't help looking at him in all his dark Seminole glory. She grazed her eyes across his chiseled arms and shoulders and his trim waist. That brought her attention to the hard proof of his need, and she thought it better to concentrate on his mustached face instead.

He asked with quiet amusement, "Something wrong?"

Now she was embarrassed. "No."

Getting onto the bed, he felt the springs adjust to his weight, and he lay on his side and faced her. Leveraging himself on the elbow of one arm, he used the other hand to trace her bottom lip. "Some women find it kind of strange-looking at first . . ."

She glanced down and then up quickly. Suddenly she was not as uninhibited as before. In fact, for the first time tonight she felt like the virgin bride she knew herself to be, wondering if she really would enjoy the marriage bed.

"You'll be fine," he whispered, as if reading her mind and trailing a finger over her gorgeous breasts.

Olivia confessed, "I've never seen a nude man before—"

"I would hope not," he replied with a soft chuckle.

She thought back for a moment and corrected her

earlier statement. "Well, I have, I guess." She then told him about the erotic postcards she'd seen at Oberlin.

"Oh, really?" he said, sounding surprised. "And here the country's thinking you young ladies are there learning mathematics and how to speak French."

Olivia's eyes were closed because he was tracing imaginary circles and lines over her sensitized skin. She was realizing it was hard to keep her thinking clear when he was around.

He kissed her, deepening it until she melted into the feather bed beneath her back and he murmured, "You'll have to tell me about them one day soon . . ." Right now, Neil didn't need any added stimulus—he was just this side of exploding as it was—so, kissing his way down her full brown body, he prepared her for their ride to heaven. Touching his tongue to the circle of her navel, he asked, "Are you ready, Mrs. July? . . ."

In response to the fingers now moving over the damp, hot place between her thighs, she breathed, "Yes."

Neil loved watching her feed on his loving; loved the way she arched, loved the way her candy-hard nipples rose so invitingly. "Are you sure? . . ." He bit a nipple with love-gentled teeth.

"Yes . . ."

His voice was as hot as she, and twice as hushed as the room. "Let's make sure. . . ."

When he leaned down and placed a gentle lick against the place he'd been preparing so marvelously, she let out a strangled moan.

"What's the matter, *novia?*" Neil opened her gently, then feasted slowly; lingering, dallying. He reached up until his fingers captured both nipples. Giving them a tender squeeze, he circled his tongue around the lodestone that made her woman, and she twisted and opened her legs in wanton invitation. He gently sucked the temple into his mouth, slid two fingers into the palace walls, and the release shattered her.

Neil decided that making her come was even more exciting than train robbing. While she rode the last waves of her orgasm, he fit his manhood gently inside and pushed. Her eyes opened and held his. Forcing himself to go slowly, even as his organ screamed for the full taking, he teased himself in and out; coaxing her, enticing her. "It may hurt, *querida,* but only this first time." Her lids fluttered closed, and passion tightened her face.

Unable to hold back any longer, Neil pushed past the barrier and, using all the discipline he had, held still.

Olivia wasn't sure she cared for this part; he was big, he felt foreign, and the push that had taken him past her virginity hurt.

Neil wanted this night to be one of pleasure, not pain. In his mind, no woman should eschew lovemaking because their first time hadn't been good. Concentrating on her pleasure, he began with gentle strokes, moving his hands over the soft skin of her waist and the hardened nipples of her breasts. He kissed her lips, her jaw, his hand continuing its sensual mapping in hopes that her passion would be revived. A moment later, he felt her responding; felt the rhythm in her hips tentatively rising to meet his. He knew she would be all right, and because he did, he increased the pace.

Olivia decided she'd been wrong; she did like this. Her body seemed to have adjusted to his size, and his stroking had extinguished the hurt. Now, things were as they were before; her body was being rekindled by kisses and touches, and the feel of him inside her was glorious indeed—so glorious, in fact, the fullness signaling the path to orgasm was increasing steadily. Who knew this way could be so moving, so wondrous?

Neil had reached his limits. The rise and fall of her body, the sensations of her tight heat sheathing him made him want nothing but pleasure. He forgot about her virginity, forgot about the wound screaming in his back. He filled his hands with her hips and steadily increased the speed of his thrusts. They became faster, deeper, faster. He was soon stroking her like he'd never make love to her again, and when the thunderous orgasm broke, he threw his head back and yelled out his release, dark hips pumping.

Feeling his crisis in every part of her body, Olivia thought nothing could top the pleasure he'd already given her, but this heated coming together drove her into an orgasm that was by far the strongest. The brilliant power made her twist, cry out, and ride the hard root of passion with no thought to propriety or societal dictates. As he continued his rapid thrusts, she shattered again and somewhere, off in the distance, heard herself hoarsely screaming his name.

In the silence that followed, Mr. and Mrs. Neil July left the stars and slowly drifted back down to earth. They were both breathing harshly, the echoes of their completions pulsing still. He reached for her hand, she threaded her fingers through his, and they slept.

By the time Neil stumbled awake the next morning and made his way to the kitchen for a cup of the coffee whose aroma was filling the air, Olivia had bathed, dressed, and done her hair. She was a bit sore in all the tender places he'd made love to, but at the moment, seeing him come into the kitchen, she was the happiest outlaw wife in the nation.

"Mornin'," he croaked, pouring himself a cup of coffee. "You look real fetching, Mrs. July."

"Why thank you, Mr. July." She had been very particular in her choice of attire today because her parents were coming. She had on a dark blue jacket and a matching bustled skirt that sported a plethora of pleats on the hem. It was her wish to look businesslike and prosperous so that her parents would see that she was doing well. That he would remark on how she looked endeared him to her.

Neil studied her mayoral loveliness over his cup and drawled, "You wouldn't want to take all that off and come back to bed with me, would you?"

She chuckled, "I would love to, but—no. I can't run the town from bed."

"Sure you can."

"Your middle name should be Temptation."

He smiled over his cup. "Neil Temptation July. I like that."

Olivia found him to be as tempting as his offer. Spending a leisurely day with him so they could learn more about each other, play with each other, and make love was tantalizing. Last night's interlude came back in a heated rush, making her remember all they'd shared. Her nipples tightened as if saying Amen. However, she had town issues to handle, including the arrival of her parents, and she doubted they'd approve of finding her in bed with her skirts rucked up around her waist.

Neil said, "Well, since I can't convince you to stay here, go on and do your job. Do me a favor, though, and send Delbert around so he can look at this wound."

"Is it paining you?"

"No," he lied. "Just want him to take a look."

"You want me to take a look at it?"

He shook his head negatively. "You head out. I'm going back to bed. I was with a woman last night who did so much screaming and hollering I didn't get much sleep."

Smiling, she tossed back, "Well, you do that, because that screaming, hollering woman guarantees you won't get much sleep tonight, either."

He raised his cup. "I can't wait." Then his voice changed. "Come here a minute first, though."

She walked over, and he placed his cup on the sink. He took her in his arms and looked down into her eyes. "I didn't hurt you last night, did I?"

She shook her head. "No."

"Good." And then he kissed her so slowly and masterfully that she was soon breathless and weak. Reluctantly breaking the seal of their lips, he said, "Now you can go. . . ."

He turned her loose, and Olivia floated off to work.

Although Olivia felt as if the sun were shining inside her, the skies above were dreary and gray. There was a distinct coolness in the air, a harbinger of the autumn to come, and she was glad she had on her jacket.

Olivia took the long way so she could stop by Delbert's and give him Neil's message. She was met at the door by Delbert's mother, Sally. Sally Johnson had come from Wisconsin to live with her son eight months ago. She was a bitter old hag whose contrary attitude made her someone most folks in town avoided. Delbert didn't have that luxury, however. Like most sons, he loved his mother, but her presence was beginning to make him see red. Lately, he'd become particularly riled over her refusal to accept Muriel Harrington as the woman Delbert loved. Sally had declared loud and long that Muriel, a cook at Sophie's, wasn't socially fit to marry her doctor son.

Sally had that perpetual sour look on her face as she studied Olivia for a moment before announcing, "Doctor Johnson isn't in." And she closed the door.

Olivia stared at the closed door and bit back her

temper. With a shake of her head, she left the porch and headed to the sheriff's office.

Inside she found the place crowded with lawmen. They all applauded when she entered, and a very embarrassed Olivia curtsied and went to her desk.

Chase said, "We got the court date for Neil. The judge will be here the day after tomorrow."

Olivia stilled and felt a chill cross her soul. "Do you know who it will be?"

"Yes, Hanging Judge Parker."

Olivia's heart sank.

Chase looked glum too. "He wired to say he has a special interest in this case, so the other judges on the circuit are going to let him handle it."

"That's not particularly good news, is it?"

Griffin Blake answered, "No. He's going to be real irate that Neil and Shafts have gone back to their robbing ways, after making them deputies."

Clouds descended on Olivia's previously sunny day. "Is there going to be a jury?"

Chase shrugged. "Parker will call the tune when he arrives."

A deflated Olivia sighed. "Are you all going to stay around?"

Dixon Wildhorse nodded. "And we'll do what we can to try and get Neil a light sentence."

Olivia didn't want to think about Neil standing trial or the sentence he was likely to receive. The railroads and the army wanted his hide, and she didn't see the judge letting him off with just a slap on the wrist.

The Preacher's glowing eyes found hers, and he quoted, " 'Deliver my soul from the sword; my darling from the power of the dog.' " Psalm Twenty-two. Verse twenty."

Olivia responded with a quiet "Amen."

In the thick silence that followed, Chase said to her, "We're going to ride the perimeter to make sure our bounty hunter friends really did leave the area. We'll be back in a few hours."

Olivia nodded.

Jackson Blake spoke up. "My brother has something to say before we leave."

The stern look on Jack's face made Olivia wonder what this was about.

Griffin began by clearing his throat; he looked embarrassed and chagrined. "Well, last night, I had a little too much to drink at the celebration, and I stood up in the middle of the place and proposed a toast."

Olivia still didn't understand. "What kind of toast?"

"To you and Neil."

Olivia's eyes widened.

Marshal Wildhorse looked grim. "I know you wanted to keep this a secret, at least for a few days, but the cat's out of the bag."

Griffin seemed to be studying his boots. He looked up. "I'm real sorry, Miss Olivia. Were my Jessi Rose here, she'd probably take a black snake to me, and I'd deserve it."

Olivia sighed. He looked so contrite that she almost felt sorry for him—almost. "The news was bound to get out sooner than later—that's the joy of living in a small town. But thanks for telling me."

They exited. Alone, Olivia dropped her forehead to the desktop and tapped it lightly a few times, wondering if this day could possibly get any worse.

"Mayor Sterling?"

She looked up to see a short, skinny, brown-skinned man she didn't know. He was dressed in a green-and-black checkered suit that could have come straight from Armstead Malloy's wardrobe. "I'm Mayor Sterling. May I help you?"

He grinned and came in fully. "My name is Wilson Young. I'm a reporter for the *Nicodemus Cyclone*. I'd like to interview you about your marriage to Neil July."

Olivia lowered her head back to the desk and groaned.

It was now a bit past noon, and Olivia was on her way home for lunch. She needed to tell Neil about the imminent arrival of Hanging Judge Parker and that their marriage was going to be front-page news in tomorrow's edition of the *Cyclone*. The reporter had been as nosey as a gossip, but she'd known that if she hadn't been forthcoming with her answers, he would have printed whatever he'd wanted, and that it probably would have been more lurid than the admittedly lurid truth. She prayed for strength and went into her shop.

The sight of all the projects needing her attention only added to her mood. Two months ago, life had been calm and uneventful; she'd had her sewing and her committee work. Now, life was filled with so many dramatic twists and turns she may as well be an actress on the stage.

Neil looked up at her entrance and knew by the furrows in her brow that she was troubled by something. "Your parents here already?"

"No." She then related all that had happened in the four and a half hours they'd been apart.

"You've had some morning."

"I want you to shoot Griffin Blake the next time you see him."

He grinned, "Yes, ma'am."

"I'm serious."

"I know." He walked over and eased her back against his chest. Wrapping his arms around her waist, he placed a tender kiss on her temple. "You weren't too hard on him, were you?"

"No."

"Good, because he would walk through fire for me and I for him. And don't worry about Judge Parker either. What will happen, will happen, but I won't go to prison. Not willingly."

She turned to face him. "What will you do if you're sentenced?"

"Head for the Mexican border."

She studied his eyes.

"I spent most of my life under some entity's thumb—not adding the state of Kansas to the list."

"Neil—"

"Your parents will be gone by the time Parker gives his ruling, so what happens to me won't affect that."

But it would affect me, she wanted to say. She didn't, though, because this marriage was just pretend and they both knew it. "Well, I came home to eat. Did Delbert drop by?"

"Yeah. He checked the stitches and said he should be able to remove them in a couple more days."

"That's good news."

"I thought so, too."

He gave her a kiss on the neck and said, "Let's get you fed. You're going to need your strength tonight, Mrs. July."

His words made her sparkle inside. To reward him for taking her mind off her troubles, she gave him a long, sweet kiss.

He made her a ham sandwich. She added a cup of coffee, along with a small slice of leftover wedding cake, and declared it a meal.

Neil sensed that his plan to go to Mexico didn't sit well with her, but his mind was made up. He'd already done his time: on disease-filled reservations, in degrading government-run schools, and as a member of the Negro Seminole scouts. None of those experiences had been positives ones, and he knew a stay in prison, no matter the length, would not be either.

Olivia finished her food, then stood. She wasn't looking forward to returning to her office, but she had no choice. "Has your brother visited you this morning?"

Neil shook his head. "No. Not yet. I figure he'll show up soon enough."

Olivia decided he was probably right, but she wondered if Two Shafts would follow his brother to Mexico. "Well, I need to leave."

Neil nodded her way. "Everything will work out for the best, you'll see."

"I wish I had your optimism."

He walked over and gave her a kiss, then murmured, "If you need me, send someone."

"I will," she promised, then departed.

Old Man Gardner's coach usually arrived from the Ellis train station around three in the afternoon, and as the time neared, Olivia grew increasingly nervous. How angry would her father be? Would her marriage to Neil be enough to send Horatio Butler packing for good? Whose side would her mother take? So many questions and no answers. She was tempted to run home and get some of Neil's kisses to help raise her spirits, but she knew that for all of their magic and power, they couldn't delay the inevitable.

At ten minutes past three, Olivia heard the horn blast that signaled the coach's arrival. She put on her hat, drew on her gloves, and, after picking up her small fabric handbag, left the office.

The big brown coach was parked in front of Sophie's hotel. Olivia saw a few passengers disembark, then stop and peer around, as if attempting to evaluate the surroundings. Then her father stepped out. He was dressed in a dark blue suit, and his fat mustache made her smile. She watched him assist her mother, and Olivia's heart swelled seeing them again. When her mother looked up and met Olivia's eyes, she smiled, and Olivia hurried to greet her.

They embraced each other with a rocking motion. Olivia's eyes were wet with happy tears, and her mother's brimmed with the same.

Eunice gushed, "It is so wonderful to see you, child."

"It's wonderful to see you, too."

Then she looked at her father. His icy demeanor told all. "Hello, Papa."

He nodded, but before he could speak, Olivia's attention was grabbed by Horatio Butler alighting from the coach. He looked prosperous in his reverend black suit, his walking cane, and bowler hat. He peered around at the storefronts and the people strolling on the walks, and as his face took on a look of disdain, Olivia's temper began to simmer.

He seemed to finally notice Olivia standing there. The coolness in his gaze mirrored her father's, but Butler's eyes had a quiet fury in them as he beheld her.

"Olivia," he said, raising his chin. He was ten years younger than her father, and the gray in his hair was almost as prominent as his receding hairline.

The chin-raising motion was as much a part of him as his other personal habits. Olivia guessed he thought it made him taller, but it didn't matter; she still towered over him enough to look down onto the top of his head. "Mr. Butler."

Her mother, trying to keep the peace, said, "What a quaint town."

"We like it."

"Is there a boardinghouse where we might get a room and freshen up? Then I want to see your shop."

Butler once again looked up and down the street, then quipped sarcastically, "Talk about running away to the ends of the earth."

Olivia snarled inwardly, but outwardly her face was placid. "You might prefer the hotel here. Sophie Reynolds runs a fine establishment."

Her father scanned the ornate front on the Henry Adams Hotel and asked, "They don't rent to whores, do they? The newspapers say the hotels out here are full of them."

The unexpected question took Olivia by surprise. Because his remark was rooted in an ignorance of the town and of Sophie, she held onto her calm. "No, Papa. No whores."

Before she could usher them inside, up the walk came sixteen-year-old Liza Pierce and her friends, Pearl Dobson and Sylvia Simmons.

"Mayor Sterling," they called out.

Olivia didn't look to gauge her father's reaction to the title; if he had indeed read her letters to her mother, he knew she'd been elected and would no doubt voice his thoughts on the subject later. She didn't care about Mr. Butler's reaction. "Afternoon, girls."

"How's Mr. July?" Liza asked. Remembering her manners, Liza nodded a greeting to the man and woman standing beside the mayor.

"He's recuperating."

"Did you give him the pillow?"

"Sure did," Olivia lied—she had no idea where the thing was. She gave the girls a nod, then moved to escort her visitors inside when Pearl asked in an awed voice, "Did you and Mr. July really get married last night?"

Olivia froze.

Sylvia gushed, "I think that is so romantic, you marrying him."

Liza offered, "I do too, but my pa said he'd take a strap to me if I ever even thought about marrying an outlaw like Mr. July."

Olivia's father began to cough violently. Olivia heard a thump behind her. She turned. Her mother had fainted! Ignoring the fury blazing on Butler's face, Olivia knelt beside her mother and yelled out, "Sophie!"

Chapter 14

Smelling salts revived Eunice a few moments later. Still a bit disoriented, she looked around. When her eyes found Olivia, she said in a trembling voice, "Olivia Jean, how could you?"

Olivia swallowed her guilt. "Mother, let's get you inside."

By now, half the town was staring on curiously. Delbert, who'd come running after being informed of the problem, closed up his bag and asked, "Mrs. Sterling, can you walk on your own?"

"I believe so."

Sophie said, "Then let's get you up."

Eunice was soon on her feet, but Olivia noted how pale she appeared. James Sterling took her elbow and escorted her inside. Olivia thanked Delbert, looked at all the curious faces viewing her, and tried not to think about all the gossip this too was going to generate. Praying for strength, she hurried to join her parents and Horatio Butler.

Sophie's hotel was very grand. The frescoes on the walls and the beautiful chandeliers rivaled any establishment back east. Olivia could see her parents staring around like rubes at the fair.

Eunice said, "Never expected such a beautiful place way out here—"

"In the middle of nowhere," Butler cracked.

Olivia saw Sophie give him a studied glance before turning to Olivia's parents and saying, "Mr. and Mrs. Sterling, I'm putting you in the Presidential Suite."

Eunice looked surprised. "How much will that cost?"

"Not a cent. You're my guests."

James and Eunice appeared shocked.

Sophie glanced Butler's way. "Are you family as well, sir?"

"No," he said importantly. "I'm Horatio Butler, Olivia's fiancé."

Sophie scanned him from the top of his black bowler to the soles of his store-bought oxford shoes, and Olivia noted that Sophie Reynolds didn't appear impressed. "Fiancé, huh? I can't wait for Neil to meet you."

Butler puffed up his chest, but that didn't impress Sophie either. "Your room will be a dollar fifty a night."

He looked offended.

Sophie said coolly, "It's the special *fiancé* rate."

James interrupted, "May we go to our rooms, please. My wife would like to lie down."

Sophie nodded. "Certainly."

She rang the bell on the desk for the porter on duty. Young Frank Cooper Jr. appeared, dressed in his blue-and-black uniform. "Frankie, please show Mr. and Mrs. Sterling to the Presidential Suite. Mr. Butler there will be in Room five."

She then addressed the Sterlings. "Frank will bring up your trunks and bags."

James nodded. "Thank you." He then turned to Olivia and said tersely, "Once your mother is settled, I wish to speak with you."

Feeling all of ten, Olivia nodded. "Yes, Papa."

Frankie led them to the stairs, and an unhappy Olivia followed. Sophie offered Olivia a smile of encouragement, but Olivia found little to smile or be encouraged about.

As far as Olivia knew, the Presidential Suite had never housed anyone as august, but the spacious, well-appointed suite of rooms offered a sweeping view of the countryside. It was also the most expensive room to let in town.

After Frankie left them in the main sitting room, departing with the promise to return with their trunks, Mr. Sterling settled Eunice into the bedroom. He returned, quietly closing the door connecting the bedroom to the main sitting room.

James then turned his thunderous visage on Olivia. "Now, miss. I demand that you explain yourself. Do you know I thought you dead?!"

She lowered her eyes. "I'm sorry for the distress I caused, Papa, truly, I am, but I had to leave."

"Why?"

"I didn't want to marry."

"Apparently you overcame that aversion," he returned sarcastically. "Is this man truly an outlaw?"

An angry Olivia turned her eyes to the window and then back. "My aversion was to Mr. Butler, not the institution, and yes, Neil robs trains."

Her father's eyes widened. "Then it's true?"

Since she had already confirmed that, she simply nodded.

"How could you disgrace us that way? You run away like a spoiled child and then you marry someone like that! Is he wanted?"

"Yes."

Butler snapped, "We had an agreement."

Olivia turned on him slowly. "You had an agreement with my father—never with me."

Butler's eyes narrowed. "How dare you use that tone with me."

Olivia didn't respond.

"Apologize, Olivia," her father demanded.

"I will not, Papa."

James stormed over and latched onto her arm.

"Take your hand off my wife!"

The soft, deadly voice grabbed the attention of everyone in the room, and they swung their eyes to the doorway. There stood Neil July, his steel-blue Colt drawn. Dressed in black leather, he looked ominous indeed.

"I'm her father," James snapped.

"I'm her husband, and unless you want to be buried in that suit, you'll do as I ask."

"I will not be threatened by the likes of you."

Neil pulled the hammer back on the Colt, and in the tense silence of the suite, the brittle click was as loud as a tree falling in the forest. "You might want to rethink that."

James slowly relinquished his hold.

Olivia had forgotten about this side of her outlaw lover, but this demonstration served as a grim reminder. "I'm all right, Neil. Don't shoot him."

"You sure?"

A small smile peeked through. "Positive."

Neil swung his arm and trained the Colt on the terrified-looking Butler. "Who're you?"

Butler cleared his throat a few times as if trying to make his voice work. "Horatio Butler."

Neil looked the short and slightly trembling man up and down before saying, "Ahh, the writ-bearing, *former* fiancé. Can I shoot this one?"

Olivia surveyed the man who'd come to Kansas to allegedly force a marriage upon her. "Maybe later."

"Good enough for me."

He lowered the Colt and said to James, "Name's Neil July. Want to invite you and your wife to have dinner with me and Olivia after you get rested up. We can talk after."

Olivia saw her father take a quick look at the now docile Colt, then back up at Neil.

"Where and what time?" James asked. There was

less force in his voice, but it was obvious that he remained angry.

Olivia answered, "At my shop. Around seven? Sophie can tell you how to get there."

Her father nodded tightly. "Is Mr. Butler invited?"

Olivia didn't hesitate. "No."

Her father's lips thinned. "Very well. Seven."

Neil asked, "Are you ready to go home, *querida?*"

"Yes." She turned to her father. "I will see you at seven, Papa."

When he pointedly looked away, a saddened Olivia let Neil escort her from the room.

Outside on the walk, Olivia could see people stopping and staring. She supposed it was to be expected; it wasn't every day that the town's mayor married a wanted man. "Thank you, Neil."

"Anytime. I'd come to meet them hoping we'd start out on the right foot. Guess not, huh?" He looked down at her.

"Guess not. Too bad, really. Because I believe they'd like you given the opportunity to know you."

"Well, I'm not sure that will ever happen now, but I'm glad I got there when I did."

"Me, too."

"I expected your fiancé to be taller."

"He wishes he were."

Neil chuckled, and they walked the rest of the way smiling.

Two Shafts and Teresa were sitting on the back porch when Neil and Olivia returned to the shop.

Shafts asked, "Where've you been? Doc know you up and around?"

Neil quipped, "Yes, Mother. Doc gave me permission today."

Olivia said, surprised, "You didn't tell me that earlier."

"Wanted to surprise you."

"Well, you certainly surprised Papa," Olivia noted.

Teresa asked, "Your father's in town?"

"Yep. My mother, too."

Neil added, "And a little bug claiming to be her fiancé."

Shafts said, "Sounds interesting."

Neil replied, "Very. Stay for dinner and see how much."

Teresa nodded. "Count me in."

At ten minutes to seven that evening, James Sterling drove up to the shop in a rented buggy. Seated beside him was his wife, and seated beside her was Horatio Butler.

Two Shafts, standing on the steps with Olivia, asked, "That the bug sitting next to your mother?"

A tight-lipped Olivia replied, "Yes. His name's Horatio Butler and I specifically told him he wasn't invited."

"Well, if he acts up, he can always be the after-dinner entertainment."

Olivia grinned and looked up into his twinkling dark eyes. She studied him for a moment, then confessed, "I don't know who is more outrageous, you or your brother."

"Definitely Neil," he told her with a straight face. "I've always been the quiet one."

The amused Olivia shook her head and waited for her parents to come up the walk.

When they got halfway to the porch, their steps slowed. Olivia could see them staring at Two Shafts.

Shafts said to them, "Welcome. Name's Two Shafts. I'm Neil's brother."

Her father's lips thinned, but he nodded a curt greeting.

Her mother looked a bit afraid but responded with a polite "Good evening."

Then Olivia turned her eyes on Butler. She wanted to yell at him for being so rude as to invite himself when he'd been told to stay away, but she decided to take the high road. As Shafts noted, Butler could always be the after-dinner entertainment. She looked away from him and said, "Come on in, everyone. Dinner's just about ready."

Since cooking was Neil's forte, he'd prepared the meal. There were two fat roast chickens, green beans flavored with ham and onions, and ears of sweet corn. Teresa, who apparently shared her brother's acumen in the kitchen, had just put a large pan of biscuits into the oven when Olivia escorted her parents and the bug into the kitchen.

Neil, wearing one of Olivia's aprons over the shirt and denims he'd worn to the wedding, had just set the steaming, golden-brown birds on a platter. "Evening," he said.

Eunice had the oddest look on her face. It was as

if she were having difficulty reconciling this apron-wearing version of Neil with the terrifying version her husband had described back at the hotel. "Good evening, Mr. July," she said haltingly. "I'm Olivia's mother."

"Evenin', Olivia's mother," he responded with that dazzling smile of his. "Welcome to Kansas."

"Thank you. Smells mighty good in here."

"Thank you, ma'am." Neil thought the tall Eunice as beautiful as her daughter, and he now knew where Olivia had gotten her good looks. "Soon as Teresa's biscuits are ready, we can eat."

He then nodded at Olivia's father. "Mr. Sterling."

James nodded back.

Olivia could see her mother eyeing Teresa standing with her arms crossed by the back door. Eunice was trying not to stare at the beautiful woman in the black leathers wearing a gun belt, but she was doing a poor job of it. "Mother and Papa, this is Teresa. Neil and Shafts's sister."

Teresa inclined her head. "Evenin', folks."

Olivia's mother turned a very confused face to her husband. He responded with a solemn shake of his head.

Neil asked, "How was the train ride out, Mrs. Sterling?"

"Long," she sighed.

Butler said, "And we weren't robbed." It was an undisguised slap.

Teresa drawled, "Olivia, how about I just shoot him now and save us all the trouble."

Eunice clutched her husband's arm in fright.

Olivia turned blazing eyes on Butler. "Either be respectful or leave."

He inclined his head regally. "My apologies. It was a joke."

Nobody believed him for a moment.

Neil studied Butler silently. It occurred to him that the bug was going to get stepped on before this was resolved; the man was too arrogant and disrespectful for a tenderfoot who'd just gotten off the train from Chicago. Neil just hoped not to have to arm-wrestle Tee and Shafts for the honor when the time came.

Olivia gestured toward the table. "Please. Sit."

Because Butler's presence hadn't been planned on, the table was short one chair and one table setting. "Mr. Butler, I'll have to get you a stool and a service. Excuse me, everyone."

Shafts went with her to carry the stool.

Neil, attempting to make nice, said, "Mr. Sterling, Olivia tells me you're in the timber business."

"I am."

"A man could get rich shipping timber here. Not many trees on the plains."

James said, "I noticed the lack on the ride here," but said no more.

So much for small talk, Neil thought to himself.

Olivia and Shafts returned. She placed the plate and tableware on the counter near the sink, and Shaft set the high-legged stool beside it. Butler would have to eat apart, mostly because he deserved to and because the table was so crowded now that there wasn't room for him.

Still keeping a wary eye on Teresa over by the door, Eunice said to Olivia, "You've set a lovely table."

"Thank you." Olivia had used her best tablecloth and her company china and tableware. The center-piece, a tall lead glass vase, held the pink and white hollyhocks she'd carried as her wedding bouquet last evening. *Had that really been only last night?* Olivia felt like days had passed since then.

The small hourglass biscuit timer finally emptied itself, and Teresa took the biscuits out of the oven. They were fat and beautifully browned, and the aroma added to the kitchen's fragrant air.

When Teresa took her seat, James Sterling said, "Shall we say grace?" He looked across the table at Olivia and asked pointedly, "You do still say grace, don't you?"

Olivia didn't flinch. "Yes, Papa. And I attend church every Sunday."

James turned his eyes to Neil. "Mr. July, would you do the honors."

Silence.

Olivia simmered. Everyone in the room knew that her father assumed Neil knew nothing about such things and was attempting to embarrass her husband. She was not happy about it. She made a move to say something but was touched on the arm by Shafts sitting beside her. He gave her a tiny shake of his head and directed her attention back to the encounter.

Neil held James Sterling's mocking eyes and knew that the other man was certain he had Neil over a barrel. Apparently, Butler thought so too, if the snicker he'd just let out was any indication.

Neil ignored Butler, but Teresa placed her hand atop Olivia's and pleaded, "Please let me shoot him. Please."

Olivia wanted him shot now, too, but she told her sister-in-law, "Later."

Neil and James were still staring each other down like opposing gunslingers. Neil said finally, "Let's bow our heads."

Olivia could see the sarcastic little smile on her father's face.

Neil began. " 'And Solomon made affinity with Pharaoh king of Egypt, and took Pharaoh's daughter and brought her into the city of David.' "

He raised his eyes to James, and in the shocked silence that followed, added, " 'Blessed be the Lord my strength which teacheth my hands to war, and my fingers to fight.' Amen."

Eunice couldn't have looked more stunned had she encountered a talking rabbit. James's chin was thrust out angrily; it was obvious he'd not expected to be so eloquently shown up and put in his place. Olivia was certainly floored. She knew the Preacher often quoted the Bible, *but Neil?* Shafts had a look of quiet amusement on his handsome Comanche face. Teresa threw a mocking glance at Horatio Butler.

Olivia met her husband's sparkling eyes. "Thank you, Neil."

"Anytime."

As everyone began filling their plates, Eunice continued to stare openmouthed at the Bible-quoting badman married to her daughter.

James Sterling had little to say during the meal,

but Eunice attempted to keep the gathering on an even keel by making small talk about the goings-on back in Chicago and the disposition of some of Olivia's friends. "You remember Doris Carson, don't you, dear?"

Olivia did. They'd sung together in the church choir. "How is she?"

"She had twin boys in April."

"Oh, my. I must send her a belated christening gift."

"That would be wonderful."

Neil realized that in the scheme of things, the rough-and-tumble Julys had no business breaking bread with the elegant Sterlings, but the scheme had been set on its ear when Olivia had proposed they marry. Neil watched and listened as she talked with her mother. Olivia was the rarest, most brilliant light in his life, and he planned to enjoy that radiance for as long as Olivia kept him around, whether her parents approved of him or not.

When the meal was finished, James Sterling said, "Olivia, I would like to speak with you, if I might. Privately, if you don't mind, Mr. July."

Neil glanced over at Olivia. She gave him a short nod of approval, so Neil said, "Be my guest."

Olivia stood. "Let's step outside, Papa."

Father and daughter headed out the door, and the remaining people in the room eyed their departure silently.

Outside, on the porch, Olivia noted that the gray skies were gone. Now that the day was ending, the sun had finally broken through and was sinking into the horizon like a brilliant red-and-orange jewel. She glanced over at her father's wintry face. "Come, walk with me."

He stepped off the porch and they walked out into the prairie. For a time there was silence, then Olivia asked, "Do you remember the day I received my certificate from Oberlin?"

"Of course."

She thought back. "It was a beautiful blue-sky day, and you seemed so proud."

"I was very proud."

"You encouraged me in everything I'd ever attempted to do. You insisted I read the weekly papers, that I familiarize myself with Shakespeare and the writings of Fred Douglass. You even made me stand up for myself when the boys in the school named me The Giraffe."

She saw the small smile that momentarily crossed his lips, then she added sincerely, "All that I am is because of you. Mama taught me the womanly things like committee work, how to dress, and how to set a table. But you, Papa, you gave me all the things I am inside."

She held his eyes. "Yet in light of all of that, you arrange a marriage for me with someone like Horatio Butler? How could you?"

He looked away.

"Butler doesn't care that I can balance a ledger, or read, or even *think*, for that matter."

"I'm your father. I'm supposed to provide for you."

"I am aware of that," she conceded earnestly, "but you raised me to provide for myself, Papa.

When Mrs. Barth died and left me the building and business, you loaned me the funds I needed to make repairs. Why would you then turn around and give my hand to a man determined to sell that business as soon as the ink dried on the marriage certificate?"

"Girls your age are supposed to be married."

"Many successful women go to their graves without the benefit of a husband."

"I didn't want that for you. It's so hard being a woman on her own."

Olivia saw the truth in his eyes. "And I appreciate that as well."

"But you married an *outlaw*, Olivia. A wanted man."

"To keep from marrying Mr. Butler, I would have married the town drunk had there been one around."

"Olivia!" he gasped, scandalized.

"I'm sorry, Papa, there's no sense in me lying. I fled to *Kansas*, for heaven's sake. That should be an indication of how upset I was."

He looked up at the sky for a few silent moments, then back down into her face. "I thought I was doing what was best for you."

"I understand that. I just wish you had broached the subject with me beforehand."

He thinned his lips. "In hindsight, I wish I had too. Maybe then you wouldn't be in such a scandalous marriage."

"Neil's a good man, Papa."

"He drew his gun on me!"

"He thought you were trying to harm me. I did, too."

"I was very angry."

"Yes, you were."

James sighed his frustration. "You're not going to admit you were at fault in any of this, are you?"

"My only fault was in sneaking out in the middle of the night. I apologize for worrying you."

"And for marrying a man no one back home is going to accept? What about that?"

"I don't care about the folks back home. Henry Adams is my home now."

He studied her as if seeing her for the first time. "What happened to my modest, always-obedient daughter?"

"She's grown up. Just like you raised her to do."

"I'll *never* accept him in our lives."

Olivia was disappointed by that statement, although it was expected. Neil was an outlaw, after all. "Then let's go back inside," she said quietly, "because never is a very long time."

As they reentered the kitchen, Olivia saw the questions in her mother's eyes and in Neil's. Olivia shrugged. Her mother looked disappointed by the response. Neil's face was emotionless.

Later, as Olivia and Neil lay together in the bed in the dark, she said, "I did my best with Papa, but he's determined to believe this is all my fault."

"He's your father. If I had a daughter and she married a man like me, I'd be concerned, too."

"Would you?"

"Yep. I'd be concerned about all the screaming and hollering she might be doing."

Olivia grinned. "I was trying to be serious."

"I am being serious."

They listened to the silence for a moment, and then she said, "Your Bible quoting surprised me. My parents too, by the way my mother's jaw dropped."

"Thank the government Indian schools. When they weren't calling us savages, they were making us pray. For hours on end."

"Doesn't sound like you enjoyed school."

"Nope. I'd run away, they'd hunt me down. I'd run again, they'd drag me back. After awhile they threw up their hands and I went home for good."

"Where was the school?"

"Army fort about sixty miles away from the Texas border. Soldiers rode into the village one day and rounded up the children like cattle. Our parents had no idea where they were taking us. The soldiers told them nothing more than the children had to go to school."

He went silent for a moment, then said softly, "I'd never been away from my parents, not even for a night. None of us had."

"Must have been frightening."

"It was, some cried the entire way." He turned so he could see her face. "I was one of them."

"How old were you?"

"Almost ten."

He went on to tell Olivia about his first days there. "There were many children from many tribes, and before we were allowed to enter the buildings, those with long hair had it cut and their braids were tossed in a pile on the grounds behind the school. I remember children on their knees begging to keep their hair."

Olivia listened in silence.

"Then the little medicine bags our mothers had placed around our necks for protection were taken, along with our clothing, ear ornaments. Everything tied to our lives as members of our tribes was placed in that pile and burned."

Olivia turned to him in shock. "My Lord," she whispered.

"We weren't allowed to speak the language of our parents—only English. You were punished if you did. I saw a teacher throw a young Apache across a room and into a wall for speaking Indian to his friend. Broke his collarbone."

She shook her head in sadness and disbelief. "No wonder you ran away."

"Again and again, and again."

Neil pulled her to him and kissed her on the neck. He was finding that holding her eased the pain of the past. It was his hope that if he held onto her long enough, he might one day heal. "Enough about that." He slid his hand over a nightgown-covered breast and whispered in her ear, "How about some screaming and hollering?"

She grinned, and then purred, as the warmth of his hand slid her gown up over her hips. "Thought you'd never ask . . . ."

Chapter 15

Olivia was in her office the next morning studying the town's ledgers. She and the snippy male clerks in Topeka were still going back and forth over the town's tax bill. The numbers were in dispute because the clerks refused to consider the possibility that their calculations might be wrong. Tossing the ledger aside, she thought about her parents. Her hopes that she could somehow breach the chasm that divided them had not borne fruit. Last night her father had left her house as stone-faced as he'd been upon arriving. Apparently her attempts to explain herself had not swayed him, and she was sorry for that, because she did love her father.

Tomorrow's visit by Judge Parker also weighed heavily on her mind. How severe a sentence would he hand down? Would the decision prompt Neil to flee? In spite of all the Wanted posters and myths surrounding her husband, with Olivia the infamous Neil July had been nothing but kind and gentle. He'd shown concern for both her welfare and her reputation. He was funny, intelligent, and he could waltz. Throw in his dazzling lovemaking and he was a man worthy enough for any woman in the nation—except when you factored in the train-robbing past. That was the factor Judge Parker would be coming tomorrow to rule upon. Olivia was afraid of what the outcome might be.

Chase and the lawmen were down at Sophie's using their muscles to move chairs and tables around so that her main dining room could be transformed into a makeshift courtroom. Rumor had it that the entire town would be on hand for tomorrow's trial, and Sophie hoped to accommodate everyone who wanted to attend.

Olivia stood up, intending to walk down to the hotel to visit with her mother, but she was stopped by Horatio Butler entering the office.

"Good morning, Olivia."

"Horatio."

He scanned the small office. "You share this space with the sheriff?"

"I do."

He walked over and gave the lone cell a quick survey before turning back. "Quaint."

Olivia had no idea why he was here, but she wanted him gone. "May I help you?"

"I came to ask how much longer you are going to continue this farce."

"What farce?"

"This so-called marriage of yours."

"I don't consider it farcical, and neither does my husband."

"He's a cold-blooded killer, Olivia. He's barely housebroken."

She waited.

"I understand that you were uncomfortable with my marriage proposal, but many women are unhappy with the arrangements made by their parents. They accept it. They don't run off to Kansas to pout."

Olivia chuckled sarcastically, "You think I'm pouting?"

"Yes. Your father has indulged you all of your life. It's all that unconventional education that has you confused about your role in life."

"And that role is?"

"To turn your life over to your husband."

"You mean turn my bank accounts over to my husband, don't you?"

His mustached lips curled. "A man is better equipped mentally to handle financial issues. That's simply the way life is."

"Have you met Armstead Malloy?"

When he looked confused, she waved the question away with a dismissive hand. "Never mind. You were saying?"

He was genuinely angry now. "Were you my wife or daughter I'd take a stick to you for all this insolence."

Olivia picked up her handbag. "Well, seeing as how I'm neither, I have an appointment."

"Don't you dare walk out on me. I am not done speaking to you."

"Sure you are. Now move aside."

He was blocking the doorway. He was short but solidly built, as were most men who handled timber for a living. She didn't want to have a physical confrontation with him unless she had a Colt in her hand.

"Your father and I have decided that you're going back to Chicago. It's for your own good, and if we have to place you in an institution until you regain your senses, that is what we will do."

Olivia didn't believe her ears. "An institution." It was a statement, not a question. "Why are you so insistent upon marrying me?"

"I'm the man your father picked."

"I'm sensing there's more to it than that."

"I'll admit that certain arrangements and agreements were signed on the understanding that we would marry."

Olivia thought that over for a moment. "So you made some type of financial deal using the prospects of controlling my money as collateral?"

He stiffened, as if she'd struck him across the back with a whip. Now she understood. "You did, didn't you?"

His tight lips told all.

"Is the deal crashing around your feet, or are the other parties now demanding the money? Or are both scenarios in play?"

Silence.

Olivia shook her head with amusement, but her

eyes were hard with purpose. "Mr. Butler, you should marry a woman far less intelligent than I. And as for taking me back and placing me in an institution? Considering who my husband is, you should probably plan on heading back to Chicago without me. Neil would hunt you down like the weasel that you are, and then he and Shafts and Teresa would draw straws to see who would shoot you first. Now let me pass."

A vein stood out in his forehead. He let her see the fury in his eyes, then moved aside.

She sailed by without further word.

By the time Olivia made it to the hotel she was angry enough to shoot Butler herself. That he'd threatened her with a forced stay in an institution brought back to mind the advice she'd been given a few days ago by the spinsters. They'd been concerned about Butler wanting to harm her, and Olivia had to admit that on the surface, they'd been correct.

She heard all the hammering and activity in the dining room, but she chose not to stop in; tomorrow would be soon enough for her to view the transformed space. Right now she was intent upon seeing her mother and confronting her father about this institution nonsense.

Olivia's knock upon the door to the Presidential Suite was answered by her mother, who smiled at her daughter and said, "Come in, dear. How are you?"

Olivia entered. "I'm well, Mother."

"Your father is off seeing the sights. He's attempting to determine what it is you find so wonderful

about this town. Have a seat, dear, I've something I
need to discuss."

Olivia sat.

"I've decided to leave your father."

Olivia's eyes widened.

"When we go home to Chicago, I'll be seeking out
a good barrister to handle the papers and whatever
else is necessary."

Olivia was speechless for a moment, then asked,
"Why?"

"I'm tired of being alone, Olivia. It was bearable
when you were home, but in the last year, the house
has been like a tomb."

"But Mother—what has changed?"

"I have, dear."

The response surprised Olivia.

Eunice continued, "When you defied your father
about this marriage to Horatio—which you know I
never approved of—I went in search of my own
spine."

"I see," Olivia replied, but she didn't really. She
knew her mother had been unhappy for many years,
but it had never occurred to Olivia that Eunice
would seek such a drastic solution. "Are you sure
about this plan, Mother?"

"As sure as I've ever been of anything in my life,
and I've decided to spend what life I have left here
with you in Kansas."

Olivia stared. "Oh, really," she said, trying to
keep the horror out of her voice. "Why here?"

"You lead such an interesting life here, dear. I believe I'd like a bit of that myself."

Speechless, Olivia couldn't make a sound. "But Mother—"

"I won't have to live with you and your Neil very long. Once I get on my feet, I'll find my own place, of course."

Olivia's eyes were plate-wide now. "Of course."

Her father came into the suite then, and Olivia had never been so happy to see him in her life. She'd originally wanted to confront him about Butler's nefarious schemes, but she decided that was a minor issue compared to what her mother had just revealed.

Her father walked over to where the women were sitting and tossed a newspaper onto the settee. He growled at Olivia, "Have you seen the paper? You made the front page."

Olivia sighed and picked up the issue of the *Nicodemus Cyclone*. Sure enough, the banner headline read: "Female Mayor Weds Notorious Outlaw." She set it back down.

Her father snapped, "And his trial is tomorrow?"

"Yes."

He did not look happy. "I'm beginning to think you are not in full control of your faculties. Horatio believes you should seek medical attention, and I may have to agree. There's a doctor—"

"Oh, James, stop badgering the child," Eunice voiced impatiently. "She's a grown woman and married. She's no longer under your control. Life goes on."

Olivia couldn't decide whose jaw dropped the furthest—her father's or her own.

James studied his wife and said tightly, "Eunice,

you must still be suffering from the long trip here. Maybe you should go and lie down."

Eunice countered with, "I feel fine, and why is it that every female who defies you has to be suffering from something, James?"

He stared at his wife as if he'd never seen her before.

"I just told Olivia something that I am now going to tell you. I'm divorcing you, James. Just as soon as we get home."

"What!"

"Don't play deaf. You heard me."

James turned his eyes to Olivia, but Olivia kept her face emotionless. He asked his daughter, "What have you been filling her head with?"

Eunice shot back, "There you go badgering her again. Talk to me, James. I'm the one ending this dried-out marriage, and she has absolutely nothing to do with it."

Olivia glanced over at the door and wondered if she could slip out without them noticing.

Her father asked Eunice, "Have you lost your mind?"

She smiled serenely. "No, I have not."

"You're pulling my leg, correct?"

"Nope."

Olivia had never seen her parents argue before, and this prologue was more than enough. "I should go."

Her mother replied in an amused voice, "Coward."

The playful taunt took Olivia so much by surprise that her smile bloomed before she could suppress it. "Mother? I am not a coward."

Eunice studied her only child and said softly,

"No, you aren't. You're the strongest young woman I've ever had the pleasure to meet. You stick to your guns and continue to live life on your own terms. I am very, *very* proud of you." She turned to her husband. "And now, James. I am going to lie down."

That said, she stood, went into the bedroom, and closed the door.

Olivia and her father were left staring at her exit in the now silent room.

On the heels of that, James Sterling went over to the large windows and stood before them. He stared at the glass, his arms crossed, his face perturbed.

When he still hadn't spoken after a few moments, Olivia departed quietly.

Chase was back at the office. "Seen today's edition of the *Cyclone*?" he asked.

"Yes," she said glumly.

"So you'll know, Malloy is campaigning to have you removed as mayor at tonight's Elder Board meeting."

Olivia slumped. "It's to be expected, I suppose."

"He's saying you're not upholding your oath."

"Which says I am to uphold the law and to conduct myself in an honorable manner." And by society's standards, there was nothing honorable about marrying an outlaw for any reason. Olivia's day was getting worse and worse, and tomorrow was the trial. "I feel like stealing a horse and hightailing it to California."

"Not allowed," he said. "You've been good for this town. Because of you, Henry Adams is solvent for the first time since the founding."

"That's because of the vice taxes Malloy's been paying."

"And whose idea was it to make him pay?"

Olivia accepted the credit without comment.

Chase said, "Do you have any idea how long it's been since Cara Lee has had new books for her students?"

"No."

"Since '82, when Virginia Sutton died, but because of the vice funds there are brand-spanking-new books."

Olivia looked him in the eye.

He said, "Granted, marrying Neil might not have been the best plan, but it's all you had. I met Horatio Butler. I'd have married Neil, too."

She smiled.

"You'll weather this storm, Olivia. Just hang on."

She was so proud to call him friend. "Thanks, Chase."

"You're welcome."

The Elder Board meeting didn't take long. One half hour after it began, Olivia Jean Sterling was stripped of her duties. A new election would be called next week to find her replacement. In the interim, Chase was appointed the town's new executive. Malloy had nominated himself for the post, citing his previous run for mayor, but he lacked the backing of enough Board members to put the nomination to a vote.

As Olivia left the hall, she passed Malloy. He gave

her a nasty little smile. She ignored him and hurried
home.

Neil was on the back porch when he saw her
walking toward the house through the tall grass. Her
slow steps made him believe the Elder Board meeting had gone badly, and his heart ached. Because of
him, there was a good possibility she was no longer
mayor. His beautiful, radiant Olivia was facing
more challenges than Hercules, and it was his fault.
She was like a city under siege: from her parents, the
newspapers, the gossips, the Elder Board, all because she'd chosen him to be her husband in order
to preserve her way of life. Society didn't like independence. If it did, none of the tribes would be captives on reservations, and women like Olivia
wouldn't have to make hard choices in order to keep
themselves free of men like Horatio Butler.

Neil wanted to throw her over his horse and ride
her away to a place where there were no worries.
Places where renegade men and women of all races
lived hidden in the mountains and valleys in the
wilds of Texas, Mexico, and California; out of the
sight of soldiers and all others who enforced laws
that stole rights, land, and cultures. The two of them
could be together and never be disturbed by so-
called civilization ever again, but it wasn't a solution
based in reality. His Olivia Jean hadn't been bred for
that type of hard existence; she didn't know about
living on the run, or cooking beans over an open fire;
she couldn't hunt rabbit or elk, or slaughter a sheep
for its wool, but knowing her and her indomitable

spirit, she'd try to learn, and do them all without complaint, no matter how much she hated it.

So running away was not the answer. He didn't need to change her life; he needed to change his own.

When Olivia looked up and saw Neil walking toward her with his arms wide, her heart swelled with all the emotions she felt inside. Hiking up her skirts, the former mayor ran to him and let herself be enfolded in his strong embrace. His heart beat strong beneath her cheek, and she closed her eyes and savored the closeness. "I'm no longer mayor."

"I'm sorry," he whispered, and he truly was.

"It's okay, I'm more worried about tomorrow."

"Don't be. It'll be here soon enough."

Olivia didn't want him to go to prison or have to flee to Mexico; either way, she'd never see him again more than likely, and she didn't want that. She wanted to come home to him each day and have him hold her until the stresses and frustrations melted away. She wanted to explore the parts of him that she still didn't know, and enjoy him exploring her depths in the same way. Horatio Butler didn't understand. Why would she choose a bounder when she could have a man who made her scream and holler and could cook rabbits for her under the stars? Neil might not be socially acceptable, but in her mind, neither was Butler.

Losing her job had saddened her, though, and she was glad he'd walked out to meet her and offer her the comfort of his arms. "You're a very special man, Neil July."

Neil raised her chin so he could look into the face

that he might not ever get to see again after tomorrow's trial. "You think so."

"Very much so. My father would never have walked out into the grass for my mother."

"I'm not your father."

She smiled, "And I'm glad about that." The memory of her encounter with her parents rose in her mind, but she decided she'd tell him about their arguing later. Right now she just wanted to relish his closeness.

"You're very special, too," he told her. "So much so that back at the house, dinner is waiting for you, along with enough hot water heating for three baths."

She leaned up for a kiss. "You spoil me."

"You're easy, and besides, it's what a man is supposed to do for his woman."

She searched his eyes. "Am I your woman?"

"I think you are," he replied softly. "What do you think?"

"I think I am, too."

Neil held her against his heart again and wrapped her up tight. "Oh, Olivia. What's going to happen to us?"

"I don't know. I don't want to live without you."

"Or me, you."

She reached up and tenderly touched his cheek. "No matter what happens tomorrow, you will always, *always* have my heart."

He kissed her bent fingers. "You deserve better."

She shook her head. "For me, there is no one better."

He gave her a smile. "Let's go home."

She nodded.

They linked hands and walked back to the house.

Over dinner Olivia told Neil about the episode with her parents. "I have never heard her speak to him so forcefully before. It was the most amazing thing."

"Was she serious?"

"So much so, Papa and I were speechless."

"Will she really divorce him?"

Olivia shrugged and reached for another piece of the cornbread he'd made for their meal. "I honestly don't know. Divorce is much more acceptable these days, but will she actually go through with it? Only time will tell."

When she finished dinner, they cleaned up the dishes, then Neil said, "Come on outside on the porch with me. Got something to show you."

"What is it?"

"It's a surprise."

"What kind of surprise?"

"A *surprise* surprise."

"But—"

He grabbed her hand. "Come on. Need to rename you Woman With Many Questions."

She grinned and let him lead her out.

To her delight, she saw that he'd made her a blind of sorts for the back porch so she could bathe outside in the fresh air. Canvas had been tacked up around one corner, effectively closing the space in on two sides, and he'd added a horizontal piece of wood, which was attached to the lip of the roof at one end and the wall of the house at the other end. Across it hung another piece of fabric that screened off the third side. "This is wonderful."

"Look inside."

He pulled back the drape, and the smiling Olivia entered. Inside was a large, gleaming, claw-footed bathing tub. She turned back, confused. "Where'd you get this?"

"Had Shafts and Tee steal it out of Malloy's place last night."

Appalled, she gritted out, "Neil!"

He laughed. "I'm only kidding. *Dios*, you're easy to get. I bought it off of Handy Reed this morning. He said someone ordered it but never retrieved it. He's had it for months."

She punched him in the arm. "Don't scare me like that."

"Hey, quit beating up on an injured man."

"Only thing injured on you is your *brain*."

Olivia scanned the space again and saw the upside-down barrel that had originally served as the porch's table standing in the corner by the tub. Atop it were the lantern, a wrapped bar of scented soap, and some folded bath sheets. It was all so lovely and so thoughtful that she began to cry.

"Bought the sheets from Sophie." Neil looked at her face. "Olivia, why the hell are you crying?"

She shrugged and sniffed. "I don't know. You are so wonderful to me."

He smiled and eased her against his chest. "No crying allowed. Makes me hurt."

She smiled and wiped at the moisture in her eyes.

He told her softly, "This might be our last night together for awhile, and I wanted it to be special."

She held onto him as tightly as she could. No moment in Olivia's life had ever equaled this—not Oberlin; not owning her own shop; not coming to Kansas. She would never, ever forget him, no matter what the future held.

"Ready for your bath?"

"Yes."

"Then you go get yourself ready and I'll bring the water."

Olivia headed to the door, then stopped and turned. "Neil?"

"Yes?"

"I love you. . . ."

He nodded. "I love you, too, *querida*."

And it was a special night. He filled the large tub with buckets and buckets of hot water, then took the soap and slowly and sensually soaped her up. He paid particular attention to her breasts and the secret places within her thighs, and by the time he'd rinsed her clean, she'd already had her first orgasm. He then wrapped her pulsing and throbbing body in the bath sheet and carried her into the kitchen. He laid her tenderly on the cleaned-off table, kissed and caressed her until she parted her legs, then pulled up a chair and had her for dessert. Only after all her screaming and hollering faded away did he pick her up and carry her to the bed.

He made love to her like a warrior going off to war in the morning; completely, totally, tenderly. He whispered endearments he'd never whispered to another woman, and she did things with him she'd never do with any other man but Neil. Dawn was lightening the sky before they let each other sleep.

But Neil didn't sleep long. He watched the dawn break up the shadows and held his wife close. Eventually, he got up and left her sleeping.

When he stepped out onto the porch, Two Shafts was sitting there. "Morning, brother."

"Mornin'," Neil replied.

The hush of the dawn settled for a moment, then Shafts said, "Came to see if you'd changed your mind."

Neil's desire to ride away and leave today's court proceedings behind was strong, but his feelings for Olivia were stronger. "I haven't."

"She mean that much to you?"

"Yep."

Shafts, sitting on the lip of the porch, turned and studied his brother, then turned back and faced the prairie. "Sitting here thinking about the first time we met."

Neil smiled. Both he and Shafts had been at the Indian school. They'd known each other in passing, but that had been all. Neither had had any idea they were related until one day their father had shown up to visit; upon seeing him, both boys had run to him, crying, "Da! Da!" To this day, Neil could still see the surprise not only on their faces but also on the face of his father. He'd come to see Neil and had had no idea his Comanche son was at the school as well. The boys were ten and had been together ever since.

In fact, it was the headmaster of the school who'd christened them the Terrible Twins. "We've been together a long time."

"That we have, and had a good run, too."

"Yes, we did."

They both floated in their memories, then Neil asked, "You heading home?"

Shafts nodded. "No sense in Parker trying to put the whole family in prison."

Neil agreed. "Tee already gone?"

"Yeah. You know how she hates good-byes."

He did. "I told Olivia if I'm sentenced, I'd take off for Mexico, but I won't. I'll go ahead and serve my time, because I know she'll be waiting."

"She's a special woman."

"That she is."

Shafts stood. The brothers embraced. They held each other tight for a long, silent moment, then parted.

Neil said, "I'll have Chase wire Wildhorse with the verdict."

"Okay." Then Shafts said firmly, "If you need me, you know how to find me."

"I do." Neil felt as if his heart was breaking.

Shafts's voice was soft. "May the Spirits guard your soul, brother."

"And yours, too."

Neil stood silent as Shafts mounted his horse and rode away.

Chapter 16

⟨∽⟩⟨∽⟩

Olivia awakened at seven o'clock. After such a short sleep, her well-loved body was sated and satisfied, but overall she felt terrible, and her mind was foggy and disoriented. Noticing that she was in bed alone, she listened for sounds in the house but heard none. Throwing back the sheet, she hurried into the kitchen, hoping that Neil hadn't changed his mind and was gone.

He was in the chair on the back porch, looking out at the prairie. At the sound of her approach, he turned and smiled. "Mornin', Mrs. July."

"Morning, Neil." She walked over and put her arms around him. She kissed his cheek. She didn't tell him she thought he'd ridden out. Instead she asked, "How about some coffee?"

He covered her hand with his. "Sounds good, but

I can put it on, you go and get washed up. They'll be coming for me in an hour or so."

Olivia's lip tightened. The day was here. "Okay. Be back shortly." She went in and left him to sit alone.

Neil watched the wind play in the grasses and saw a hawk slowly circling in the sky. He studied it for a moment. The predator was looking for prey. Parker would be circling over Neil in much the same fashion in a few hours, and admittedly, he was afraid, not of imprisonment—he'd been held captive in so many forms over the course of his thirty-eight-year life that the prospect didn't worry him much—but of having to live without Olivia.

Chase and Wildhorse came for him at eight-thirty. Both men wore sober looks and met Olivia's eyes with a sadness that equaled her own.

Neil said, "Mornin'. I was hoping Parker had come down with the pox."

Chase shook his head. "No. He got in late last night."

Wildhorse said, "We have to put the bracelets on you."

Neil stood. The marshal fastened the iron restraints around Neil's extended wrists, then keyed the circlets shut.

Chase said to Olivia, "You should probably get over to Sophie's as soon as you can. People are already lining up to get in."

She nodded, but her eyes were on her husband. Not caring about propriety, she walked over to him and held him tight. "I love you," she whispered fiercely.

He smiled, kissed her, then stepped back. "Let's go," he said to the lawmen.

Olivia fought back tears as they put him in the buggy and drove away.

There were so many people on Main Street that it looked like the circus had come to town. Vendors hawking popcorn and lemonade, competed for customers with *Cyclone* reporters selling yesterday's headline edition, and with a man selling badly drawn portraits of Neil on postcards. There was also a woman touting her "authentic" Seminole turbans and ear ornaments, and an ice cream stand courtesy of Malloy Mercantile. As the former mayor, Olivia was pleased to see all the visitors—their presence would undoubtedly swell the town coffers—but as Neil's wife, she was appalled at the crass display.

As she made her way down the crowded walk, she nodded at those she knew and ignored the rubes who pointed and stared.

"That's the woman," she heard one woman whisper.

Another voice explained, "No, she's not the mayor anymore. The town fired her after the marriage."

As word spread that July's woman was heading to the hotel for the trial, a ripple of excitement moved through the crowds.

People wanted autographs. "No."

Photographers yelled for her to stop so they could take her picture for the papers back east. "No."

Dressed in her best bustled ensemble, hat, and gloves, Olivia kept her eyes and steps focused ahead.

A tired-looking White man in a travel-crumpled suit rushed up, saying, "Mrs. July. I'm from *Harper's Weekly,* would you grant us an exclusive interview?"

"No."

Another man. "Mrs. July. I'm from Bloomingdale Brothers in New York. We'd like your approval for a line of Neil July firearms we plan to sell—"

"No."

By the time she reached the door where the Blake brothers stood guarding the entrance, she felt like she'd run a Lakota gauntlet.

"Morning, Olivia," Jackson said grimly. "Quite a sight, isn't it?"

The line of people waiting to get in seemed to stretch to Topeka. "Unbelievable."

Griffin said, "You can go on in and get a seat. Doors will be opening in a few minutes. They'll bring Neil in right after."

"Thanks."

Griffin opened the glass-paneled door, and she stepped through. The quiet assaulted her. After the din outside, it was as if she'd stepped into the hush of a cathedral. Sophie was there, looking very solemn, and she gave Olivia a strong hug.

"How you doing?"

"Trying to remain hopeful."

"That and a good set of prayers will get you through."

Olivia nodded.

"Do you want to go up and see your parents first?"

"No." She had enough on her plate right now. The last thing she needed was her father glaring at her.

"Then go on in. Good luck, Olivia."

She nodded and moved on.

The room had been set up with rows upon rows of wooden chairs divided by an aisle. In front of the first row of seats were two tables, one positioned on each side of the aisle. Facing the two tables was a lone table. She figured the lone one was where Judge Parker would preside.

Because she had no idea which of the tables Neil would be sitting at, she didn't know where to sit. While contemplating that dilemma, she heard footsteps and looked up at the bald, bearded Black man entering the room. She'd never seen him before, but from his well-made suit, highly polished shoes, and air of authority, she assumed he would be playing some role in the drama to come.

"Good morning," he said to her. "Are the doors opening already?" He looked down at the watch chained to his watch pocket.

"No. The sheriffs let me in early."

"I see."

On the frontmost desk he began placing writing paper and pens, then some books—one of which was the Bible.

Olivia asked, "I don't mean to disturb you, but do you know which table Neil July will be sitting at?"

The man stopped. "Why?"

"I'm his wife, Olivia Sterling July."

He could not hide his surprise, it seemed, and for the next few, silent seconds he studied her. Then he gathered himself and said very formally, "Pleased to meet you, Mrs. July. My name is George Winston—Judge Parker's private bailiff."

It was Olivia's turn to be surprised. "Pleased to meet you as well."

"The July party will be using the table to your right."

"Thank you." She took a seat in the first row and settled in.

Winston went on with his duties. When he finished, he directed a polite nod her way and exited the room.

Olivia tried not to let her worries and fears over Neil's fate rise and torment her, but it was next to impossible. Judge Parker was by all indications a very harsh jurist, and Neil was guilty of some very serious crimes. She just wanted the whole thing over and done with so she and Neil would know the next step.

Ten minutes later, the doors were opened and the spectators surged in. Griffin came in and hollered at folks to stop pushing, but they streamed by him like locusts. The first two rows were reserved for families, dignitaries, and the press. Olivia couldn't imagine what kind of dignitaries were expected or why they would be interested. Her answer came a few moments later when a gaggle of White men in good suits began to fill the row opposite her. They were soon joined by men wearing the uniform of the United States Army. She could hear the suits introducing themselves to the uniforms. *The railroads and the army.* Olivia closed her eyes and sent up a quick plea to heaven.

Then her own crew of dignitaries arrived: Cara Lee, the Two Spinsters, the Reverend and Sybil Whitfield, Asa, Sophie, and some of her campaign supporters. They all sat in her row. When she spied the Olivia Roses pinned to their blouses and lapels, her lip trembled with emotion. Cara Lee, seated beside Olivia, gave her a hug and whispered, "It'll be all right. You'll see."

By now, the courtroom was nearly filled to capacity. There were a few seats here and there, but only a few. Olivia spotted her parents seated in chairs about halfway back. Both looked serious; both nodded. Beside her father sat Horatio Butler. The look of satisfaction glowing in his eyes made Olivia wish for Teresa and her Colts, to put the fear of God in him. Instead, Olivia looked away.

Speaking of Teresa, a dark-skinned woman dressed in one of the most stunning bustled ensembles Olivia had ever seen entered, then began looking around, as if for a place to sit. The black dress, with its cinched waist jacket and jet buttons, was as fashionable as the woman's ostrich-feather-trimmed hat. Her face was coyly hidden behind the short sweep of a frothy veil. With all the commotion, Olivia wasn't sure if anyone else noticed her, but

Olivia certainly did. The woman made her way down the aisle, and when her eye caught Olivia's, she winked.

Olivia's eyes widened. *Teresa?* Olivia surveyed the woman again. It most certainly was! Neil's sister looked nothing like herself, which was probably the reason for her transformation, but what a transformation she'd made. No one would associate this elegant and feminine lady with the two-fisted, Colt-carrying, smelly woman she'd been when Olivia had first met her. This version had polish, panache, and style. When Teresa took a seat near the back of the room, the stunned Olivia sat back down.

Cara asked, "Are you okay?"

"Yes," Olivia said. "I'm fine." And she was, knowing Teresa had risked her own freedom to come and support her brother.

Then, through the side door the bailiff had used earlier, came two more well-dressed White men. Their arrival was met with catcalls and hisses from the partisan crowd. They took seats at the table opposite Neil's designated table and set their expensive-looking black satchels on the tabletop. Olivia felt safe in assuming the new men were the railroad lawyers. The derision they received was not unexpected; folks out west hated the railroads for their perceived greed, the livestock the trains perpetually ran over and killed, and all the smoke and noise the trains brought to towns. Folks knew the trains were necessary, but they didn't have to like the entity behind them.

Next to enter was the handcuffed Neil. He was escorted in by Chase and Wildhorse, and behind them walked the Preacher. Many in the room broke out in cheers and applause. Neil smiled in response. To many people, Neil and his brother were folk heroes. They, like other outlaws on the High Plains, represented all those who wanted to thumb their noses at the civilization slowly transforming the west.

Neil threw Olivia a wink before he sat down, then he and Preacher put their heads together for a discussion. Olivia leaned over to Cara and asked quietly, "What's the Preacher doing?"

Cara whispered back, "He's Neil's lawyer."

Olivia was very surprised by the response. "*Is* he a lawyer?"

Cara shrugged.

Olivia sent up another prayer. She thought Neil looked calm, though, and she had to applaud his strength; had it been her on trial, Olivia knew she'd be as skittish as a long-tailed cat in a room full of rockers.

Bailiff George Winston entered then, and the crowd quieted. "All rise for the Honorable Judge Isaac Charles Parker."

The room filled with the sound of chair scraping and the noises of folks moving around. Then the judge walked in; an average-looking man, midforties in age, with a long, flowing chinlock and neatly cut hair. "Have a seat, everybody," he called out.

People seated themselves and waited to see what would happen next.

Parker said, "From this moment on, this is a courtroom, and anyone who disrupts these proceedings will be escorted out."

He took his seat. "Now, before me today are three cases—*The Union Pacific v. Neil July; the United States Government, specifically the Army v. Neil July,* and *the State of Kansas v. Neil July.*"

He then looked out at Neil. "Not real happy seeing you here, July. Not happy at all."

Neil didn't respond.

"Who's representing the prosecution?" Parker asked.

The two men stood and gave their names as Wendell Peck and Arthur Cambridge.

"From back east?"

Peck, who was apparently the main spokesman, said, "Yes. Our firm is based in New York City."

Parker turned his attention to Neil. "Where's your lawyer, July?"

The Preacher stood up. "Here, sir. Vance Bigelow."

"Preacher?"

"Yes, Your Honor."

"Since when did you start practicing law?"

"Since '62, sir. Got my certificate at the University of Edinburgh."

The railroad lawyers looked as stunned as the judge, who looked as stunned as Olivia and everyone else in the chairs.

"Edinburgh, *Scotland*?" Parker asked.

"Yes, sir. My mother is from there. The laws here wouldn't let me attend law school, so I studied for the bar in Scotland."

Parker asked, "Why didn't I ever know this before?"

"Never came up."

One of the lawyers stood and said, "Your Honor, we protest. First of all, how do we know he's telling the truth, and secondly, may we remind the court that a man like him is patently forbidden by law to participate in these proceedings."

The crowd hailed down catcalls like rain.

Parker banged his gavel. "Quiet! Quiet!"

The crowd complied, but a low grumble of disapproval remained.

Parker studied Peck, with his sparse hair and bulbous nose. "I'm assuming you're saying that because of his race?"

Peck nodded.

Bailiff Winston leaned down and whispered something to the judge. Parker listened, nodded, and Winston stepped back. "My bailiff reminds me of something I find quite relevant. Are you familiar with the name John S. Rock?"

Peck was not.

"Well, Mr. John S. Rock is a lawyer from Boston. He was admitted to practice before the bar of the United States Supreme Court in February of eighteen and sixty-five."

Peck asked, "And how is that relevant, Your Honor?"

"Mr. John S. Rock is a colored man, Mr. Peck. If it's good enough for the Supreme Court of these United States, it's good enough for me."

The crowd applauded. Olivia had never heard of Mr. Rock. She was glad Bailiff Winston had, though.

"Quiet!"

The crowd complied.

Parker said to Peck, "So, shall we get this show on the road, or do you have other objections you want to raise? As for Mr. Bigelow's veracity, the court will take him at his word. Present your case, Mr. Peck."

Peck didn't look pleased.

For the next two hours, Neil's crimes were put on stage. Peck brought out a large map of the United States, which he displayed on a wooden tripod. On the map he placed pins in all the places Neil had robbed trains in the past five years. There were close to fifty, and Olivia was appalled.

Peck had dates of the robberies, the times they'd been committed, and how much loot Neil and his gang had gotten away with. The total reached into the tens of thousands. He then trotted out witnesses, army payroll masters, and railroad presidents who all testified to the havoc caused by the defendant, Neil July.

Peck finished up by saying, "And we ask for the maximum sentence the court can mete out."

Then he sat.

Olivia sighed. The case against Neil was so strong she could see no way out. Cara Lee reached over and patted Olivia's hand in sympathy. Olivia gave her a small smile of thanks in reply, but inside Olivia was devastated.

After the railroad was done with their side of the story, it became Preacher's turn. His face was grim when he stood. "Your Honor, Mr. July does not dispute the facts presented by the prosecution. He admits and accepts full responsibility for his actions of the past. But they are in the past, Your Honor. Mr. July is a changed man."

Parker studied the Preacher. "How so?"

"The fact that he is *here* in this courtroom speaks to that issue."

The crowd laughed. They all knew of the many times Neil and his brother had escaped some local jail in order to avoid trial. Parker banged the gavel and said, "That is a point well taken, Mr. Bigelow."

Peck stood and said, "Surely this court is not going to be fooled by the old saw that Mr. July has found religion."

Parker said, "Sit down, Peck. Bigelow didn't interrupt the prosecution, so afford him the same courtesy, and be assured that this court will not be fooled by anyone, not even fancy lawyers from back east."

Hearing Peck being put in his place made the crowd say, "Oooo."

Their reaction caused Parker to shake his head and show a small smile. "Go on, Mr. Bigelow."

"Mr. July wants the opportunity to redeem his life, Your Honor. Before turning to crime he served this country well in the Union Army as a member of the Ninth, and with the Negro Seminole scouts. In '75, he and four other scouts were awarded the Congressional Medal of Honor for bravery."

Olivia stared and Cara stared right back.

"When the government turned its back on his people and left them to starve, the men were forced to feed their families any way they could."

Parker said, "When I was in Congress, I served on

the House Committee on Indian Affairs, and I'm very familiar with the story."

"Then you are aware of the hardships the Seminoles faced as a result of the government's betrayal."

He nodded.

Peck jumped up. "None of this is relevant, Your Honor. This country is filled with destitute, starving Indians—"

Parker cut him off. "One more peep out of you, Peck, and you and your cases will be *ir*relevant. Do you understand me?"

Tight-lipped, Peck nodded, then sat.

Parker nodded at the Preacher to continue. "Mr. July is here on good faith, Your Honor. He could have escaped after recovering from his injuries had he been of a mind to, but having given Sheriff Jefferson his word that he wouldn't, he kept it so he could participate in these proceedings today."

Parker asked, "What kind of injury?"

"He was shot in the back."

Parker stiffened. "By whom?"

"A local store owner named Armstead Malloy."

Parker looked out into the crowd. "Stand up, Mr. Malloy, if you would please."

Malloy stood and showed his self-important self to the crowd, many of whom booed. His eyes hardened.

Parker said, "Thank you, Mr. Malloy. You may sit down. I just wanted to see who I shouldn't have sitting at my back when we break for lunch."

The crowd howled.

Malloy sat down in an angry huff.

"Proceed, Mr. Bigelow. Any witnesses you'd like to call?"

"Just one. Mrs. Olivia Sterling July."

The stunned Olivia dropped her handbag. She quickly reached down to retrieve it, then stared, still stunned. No one had told her she would be testifying. She wasn't prepared to testify, but she stood and walked with all the dignity she could muster to the chair by the judge's desk.

Just as the other witnesses had done, Olivia placed her hand on the Bible and recited the oath. When she finished the words, she sat down.

The Preacher looked at her kindly. "State your name for the record, please."

"Olivia Sterling July."

"And how long have you and the defendant been married?"

"Just a few days."

The Preacher nodded, but before he could ask his next question, the judge interrupted. "Mrs. July. I'm real surprised by you being here. Why would such a fine upstanding woman as you appear to hitch your wagon to a varmint like July?"

Olivia's eyes narrowed. "My husband is not a varmint, Judge Parker."

He nodded, "My apologies, but the question still stands, why?"

"The truth?"

"Yes, ma'am."

"Initially it was to escape a forced marriage to a man I could not abide."

"I see, and July was the only man available?"

The crowd laughed. Olivia smiled too. "No, Your Honor, but he was the man I picked."

"I see. What do you do to make your living?"

"I'm a modiste and I was, until last evening, the mayor here in Henry Adams."

Parker stared. "The mayor?"

"Yes, sir."

Parker looked at Neil, then back at Olivia, as if he was confused. He then told the Preacher, "Indulge me for a moment, Mr. Bigelow."

"Sure, Judge."

"Why aren't you mayor anymore, Mrs. July? Was your elected term over?"

"No sir, I was removed because of my marriage to Neil."

"Weren't you aware that that might be one of the consequences of marrying an outlaw?"

"Of course, Your Honor."

"But you married him anyway."

Olivia nodded.

He studied her. Then he turned to the audience. "What kind of mayor is she, folks?"

Chase said, "Your Honor, under her leadership Henry Adams is solvent for the first time since its founding in '79."

Cara stood. "When that bushwhacker Malloy opened up a sin palace, the taxes she's making him pay have provided new books for the school."

The Reverend Whitfield called out, "And a new organ for the church."

"And equipment for my hospital," Delbert added.

The judge studied Olivia again. "Maybe we should run you for governor, Mrs. July. Where are you from?"

"Chicago, sir."

"And what do your parents think of your marriage?"

Eunice Sterling stood. The crowd saw her husband grab her sleeve, as if wanting her to sit, but she gave him a soft whack with her handbag. They all laughed. "My name is Eunice Sterling and I am Olivia's mother."

Parker said, "And how do you feel about this marriage, Mrs. Sterling?"

"I fainted when I first learned who she'd married."

The crowd laughed.

"And then I got to meet him. He's not a bad fellow, Judge. He made us dinner and said grace. Back east we never hear about train robbers being able to quote the Bible, you know."

The crowd was amused.

"But he's very tender and very protective of Olivia. If he weren't a robber, he'd be the perfect man for her."

And she sat down.

Then Horatio Butler stood.

Parker asked, "And you are?"

"Horatio Butler. I'm the man she was supposed to marry, and I beg to differ with Mrs. Sterling's delusions about July. The first time I met him, he pulled a gun on me."

Parker said, "Mrs. Sterling didn't sound delusional to me. Why did he pull a gun on you?"

Olivia answered. "My father had hold of my arm, and Neil thought Papa was about to hurt me."

Parker said, "We don't go in for manhandling our women here, Mr. Butler."

"I understand, Your Honor, but a man like him has no business running around loose. He should be locked up, the marriage voided, and Olivia made to return to Chicago."

The crowd booed and hissed.

Parker raised an eyebrow. "Ah. I see. Sit down, please."

Parker then turned to Olivia. "Do you think your husband is a changed man, Mrs. July?"

Olivia looked at Neil. "I know he'll never rob any more trains, if that's what you're asking."

"Why are you so sure?"

"Because Neil and I want a life together, and we can't have one if he stays on the wrong side of the law."

Judge Parker nodded. He then looked at the Preacher. "Do you have any more questions for Mrs. July?"

"Just one."

The Preacher looked at Olivia and asked earnestly, "Do you love your husband, Mrs. July."

Olivia looked over at Neil. "Yes. Very much."

"Thank you."

Olivia walked back to her seat.

The judge looked over at Neil and said, "You're a lucky man, July."

"I know, Your Honor."

"Okay. I'm ready to decide the case."

Olivia went still. The courtroom was quiet enough to hear a feather land on cotton.

"In the case of July v. all these folks, I find him guilty as charged, on all counts."

Olivia rolled back against her seat, her hand to her mouth. Tears sprang to her eyes. The crowd stared on in shocked silence. Olivia looked back at Teresa. She had her head down, as if she, too, was reeling from the judge's words.

Parker then said, "Sentencing will take place at three this afternoon." He slammed down his gavel. "This court is dismissed until then." And he walked out, escorted by Bailiff Winston.

Chapter 17

～～ひOひ～～

Olivia peered at her watch. It was almost one o'clock. She and her supporters were in one of Sophie's upstairs rooms licking their wounds and partaking of the luncheon buffet Sophie had been nice enough to provide. Olivia didn't eat much because she was too upset.

Griffin Blake walked over to where she was seated and said, "I'm real sorry, Olivia. Parker must have had his mind made up before the case started. Dix says it's not like him to rule so quickly."

Olivia took what little solace she could from his words and thanked him.

Jackson Blake walked over. "Your parents are asking to come in. Yes or no?"

"Yes, but not Butler."

He nodded.

A few moments later, her parents were by her side, and Olivia stood to let her mother hold her.

Eunice's voice was thick with emotion. "Oh, my dear sweet child, I am so sorry for you. So sorry."

Olivia knew tears wouldn't help, but she let them fill her eyes anyway. "It's okay, Mother."

"No it isn't, but you'll make it through. Just keep praying."

When Eunice released her, her father stepped up. There was pain in his eyes. He held out his arms, and Olivia went to him. "Oh, Papa."

He held her close, and Olivia cried in earnest for many things. Her father whispered, "I don't care for him at all, but I care for you, and I know how hurt you must be."

He pulled back a moment and handed her his handkerchief. She blew her nose and wiped her eyes. She could see her friends looking on with concern.

Her father said, "Can we go someplace and talk privately?"

She nodded.

Eunice had her own handkerchief out and was dabbing at her eyes.

Olivia told her, "Papa and I will be right back."

Her mother nodded and gave her a watery smile. "Go ahead. I'll be here."

So Olivia took her father into one of the adjoining bedrooms and closed the door.

He said, "Let me start by apologizing to you for being so bullheaded about this marrying you off to Horatio. He may be a good business partner, but I know now that he is not the husband for you. In my opinion July isn't either, but you made your pick. You'll have to live with him. I won't."

He smiled, and when she did too, he asked, "Now, what will you do when July goes off to prison?"

She shrugged. "Stay here and wait for him to come home."

"That may be a long time, Olivia."

"I know, Papa, but I plan to stick by him." She then asked, "What about you and Mama?"

He looked at her with confusion in his eyes. "I don't know what's come over her."

"She's lonely."

"How can she be lonely, she doesn't live alone."

"She feels as if she does."

He went silent.

"And she's felt that way for many years. Do you love her, Papa?"

"Of course."

"When was the last time you told her so?"

He didn't answer.

"When was the last time you took her to the theater, or out to dine?"

"I'm a busy man, Olivia."

"And you have always provided well for us, but Mama misses you."

He held her eyes. "Eunice and I are in our fifties. We're too old to be carrying on like moonstruck adolescents."

"Says whom?"

He sputtered for a moment.

"Papa, if you love her, you need to show her, tell her, so she doesn't go looking for those things from someone else."

"Do you really think she's serious?"

Olivia nodded. "I believe she is." Olivia wanted to ask him if he'd ever made love to Eunice on the kitchen table but decided that was probably not a subject a daughter should be asking. "So what are you going to do, Papa?"

He shrugged. "Woo back my wife, of course. I certainly don't want her to leave me, and now that you've explained it, I believe I understand her complaints."

"Good, because I don't want my parents to divorce."

"Neither do I." He held out his arms again and asked, "Pax?"

She went to him, hugged him tight, and whispered, "Pax."

Peace. It felt good. They'd been at odds for nearly a year, and she was glad things had been righted between them. "Papa, did you know that Horatio made some sort of business deal and put up the money he assumed he'd get from me when we married as collateral?"

Her father stared. "Really? No, I didn't."

"That's what he told me."

Her father stepped out of their embrace and paused for a moment, as if thinking.

"What's the matter?" Olivia asked.

"What you just told me explains a lot."

"About what?"

"Is there a telegraph office in town?"

"Yes. Down by the livery at the end of the street. Who do you need to send a wire to?"

"There's something I need to check on." He kissed her cheek. "I'll be back by three. Tell your mother to hold me a seat if I'm late."

Olivia nodded, then the very confused daughter watched her father hurry from the room.

After the verdict, Neil had been taken to a small room on the first floor and locked in with the Preacher to await the call to return to the courtroom. Sophie had provided a small buffet, but Neil hadn't felt much like eating.

He kept seeing the stricken look on Olivia's face when Parker handed down his ruling, and each time it broke off more pieces of his heart. Had he been able to peer into the future when he was younger and see the pain he would cause his beautiful and gracious lady, he might have robbed fewer trains. "Thanks for your help, Preacher."

"I didn't do much, obviously."

Neil didn't want him to feel bad. "You didn't have a whole lot to work with. I am guilty, you know."

"I do, but I wish I could have come up with an angle to at least get you some leniency in the sentencing. As it is, sounds like he's going to drop both shoes on you."

"Sounds like it to me, too." And Neil was resolved. He had nothing to be upset about. At some point everybody has to pay the piper, and his turn

had come. What he hadn't known was how many
trains he'd robbed. In the old days he would have
been impressed by the numbers of pins on the
board, but now, each pin represented a coffin nail in
his future with Olivia, and he was neither impressed
nor proud. "Will you stop in and see her now and
again, so I'll know she's not needing anything."

The Preacher nodded. "You know I will. Jefferson
will look out for her too. She'll be fine. She'll be worrying about you, though."

"I know." That was breaking his heart too.

They heard the lock turn in the door, and both
men turned to see. Chase stuck his head in. "Five
minutes."

They nodded, and the door was closed and locked
once more.

The Preacher said, "Will you pray with me?"

Neil said, "Can't hurt."

The Preacher smiled as he picked up his Bible and
leafed through to the passage he wanted. "This is
from the Forty-seventh Psalm." He composed himself, took a breath, and slowly began to recite.
"'Praise ye the Lord; for it is good to sing praises
unto our God; for it is pleasant; and praise is comely.
The Lord doth build up Jerusalem; he gathereth together the outcasts of Israel. He healeth the broken
in heart and bindeth up their wounds. He telleth the
number of the stars; he calleth them all by their
names. Great is the Lord, and of great power; his
understanding is infinite.'"

"Amen," Neil said solemnly.

"Amen," the Preacher echoed.

* * *

Neil was brought back into the courtroom, and this time no one cheered. It was as if the spectators were too intent upon hearing Judge Parker's decision to do anything but sit tensely and wait. Walking to the table, Neil visually searched for Olivia, and upon finding her in her seat, he smiled softly. He could tell by her reddened eyes that she'd been crying, but her answering smile warmed his cold soul.

Judge Parker used his gavel to reopen the proceedings, and everyone in the room looked his way. "Stand up, Mr. July."

Neil got to his feet. The Preacher stood, too.

"I'm sentencing you to seven years of hard labor at the federal prison at Ft. Smith, Arkansas."

Gasps went up. The railroad people applauded, but Olivia was left reeling. The words rendered her frozen; numb, so numb, that all she could do was close her eyes and shake her head at the horror of it all. *No! No!* she wanted to cry. She looked back at Teresa, who appeared numb as well.

Neil tightened his jaw, but it was the only emotion he let anyone see.

But Peck and his cronies were grinning and shaking hands and preening over the job they'd done. Peck stood up, "Your Honor, on behalf—"

"Sit, Peck, I'm not through. This is going to be a three-, maybe four-part equation."

Everyone stared. A surprised and wary Olivia sat up, attentive.

"Now, let me begin by saying I know Mr. July. He and his brother helped me on an investigation this past spring down in Texas, and they did a bang-up job. But Mr. July is an outlaw, and by the count of all the money he's stolen, he's very good at his profession. However, he's never shot anyone or abused a woman during a robbery. He doesn't take down a train by removing ties from the track, setting it on fire, or by using dynamite—all methods that would hurt or maim. He's also a Congressional Medal of Honor recipient."

Parker then looked out at Olivia. "I was, and am, very impressed by you, Mrs. July."

Olivia was startled by being addressed so directly.

"Being married to you may be July's last hope of keeping his soul out of hell."

Olivia could see Peck's angry, reddening face.

"So, I'm suspending the sentence. I—"

The cheering of the spectators drowned out whatever else the judge had to say, and he began to bang his gavel. All the noise filling the room covered the sound of the gavel, the judge's angry demands for order, and the furious objections being screamed out by Peck.

Olivia was so flabbergasted that she couldn't move. Everyone around her was jumping up and down, but Olivia was still trying to determine if she'd heard the judge correctly. *Was Neil really going to go free?* She wanted to take off her hat and throw it in the air, but she was still waiting for confirmation of what she thought she'd heard.

Finally, order was restored, but the buzz in the room was loud.

Peck yelled, "You can't do this!"

"I am appointed by the president and approved by the Congress to rule as I see fit, and like I said, I'm not done," Parker declared. He then looked into Peck's steaming red face and said, "Answer me this: Which safes on your trains are the easiest for thieves to crack?"

Peck looked offended. "I don't know. Ask July, he's the thief."

The judge's emotionless eyes turned to Neil. "Do you know? I don't need to know the name of the safe manufacturer because we don't want to give a leg up to somebody trying to walk in your boots."

The spectators laughed.

Neil, not certain where the judge was going, replied, "Sure, I know."

The judge then asked Peck, "Which safes are the most difficult?"

Peck shrugged.

The judge asked the suits and uniforms seated in the chairs behind Peck, "Can any of you answer the question?"

They couldn't.

"Mr. July, can you pick out a Pinkerton posing as a passenger?"

"Most times, right away."

"How, may I ask?"

"Their clothes are usually new—boots too. They stand out like a beard on a woman."

"Thank you, Mr. July."

He then proceeded to ask Peck a few more questions about how long it took to break into a safe, what kind of terrain train robbers favored, and whether or not trains were robbed when it rained. Peck and his group couldn't answer any of them.

He then asked, "Are any of you men a president with the railroads?"

One man stood and announced himself as president of the Kansas Pacific.

Parker said, "It seems to me, in light of all these unanswered questions, that you'd be a bit concerned about your lack of knowledge in the ways and means of the folks robbing your trains."

"I am."

"Good, because in exchange for his suspended sentence, Mr. July is now your employee."

Neil yelled, "What?!"

The judge said, "You love being on trains so much, Mr. July, I'm going to make you ride them for the next seven years. You are to make yourself available to the railroads and advise them on how to keep me and the rest of their passengers safe from men like you. And, if you don't like it, I can send you to jail."

Neil wanted to protest. Work for the railroads! He'd rather be boiled in oil, but then he heard himself. He thought about the future he and Olivia might really get to have, and he supposed he should shut up, so he did. "Thank you, Your Honor."

"That's better. I'm also extending this decision to include Mr. July's brother and sister."

Peck jumped up. "I object!"

The president of the Kansas Pacific placed a hand firmly on the lawyer's shoulder and ground out, "Sit down! Do you know how many people are going to pay to see the Julys on our trains, and how much money we're going to save once they make us rob-proof? Thank you, Your Honor, the Kansas Pacific accepts your decision."

One of the uniformed men stood and said, "The army signs on, too. We lose a lot of payroll gold to July's friends, and we'd love to be able to stop them."

The man representing the state of Kansas just threw up his hands and shrugged.

The judge announced, "Then if we are all agreed, this proceeding is closed."

A bang of the gavel later, it was all over.

The spectators went wild. Olivia had never been so happy in her entire life. Chase removed the bracelets from Neil's wrists and Neil ran to Olivia, grabbed her up, and held on tight. "Oh, thank you for marrying me."

She laughed and cried and held onto him like she'd never let him go. "I'm so happy."

Their supporters congratulated them with pats on the back, and everybody had tears in their eyes. Olivia's parents came up, and Olivia accepted a strong hug from them both. James Sterling stuck out his hand to Neil, who, after looking into his father-in-law's eyes, accepted the gesture. Both men knew it would be some time before all the issues between them were settled, but it was a start.

Sophie announced she would be throwing a party tomorrow for the happy couple. Olivia was glad that it wasn't going to be tonight, because she wanted to share this evening alone with her husband; they had a whole lot of screaming and hollering to do.

While they continued to accept the hugs and congratulations of the spectators in the hall, Neil placed his arm around Olivia's waist and squeezed her tenderly. In reality all he wanted to do was take his wife home. Making love wasn't even a priority at this point; he just wanted to hold her in the quiet of their bedroom and savor this new lease on life he'd been given. As it was, the well-wishers had formed a receiving line and were all waiting their turn. By the number of folks waiting, Neil figured it would be Sunday before he and Olivia were able to sneak away.

When the lady in black stepped up, Neil knew her right away. He hugged her almost as hard as he'd hugged Olivia. Teresa was his only sister, and he loved her like the desert loved rain. He stepped back and surveyed her disguise. "Look at you."

"I clean up pretty good, don't I?"

He grinned.

Teresa then hugged Olivia and whispered emotionally, "Thank you, Olivia, so very much for being you."

Olivia hugged her back. "You're welcome."

The two women faced each other, and Olivia could see the tears beneath Teresa's veil.

Teresa said, "I've never had a sister before."

"Nor I."

Teresa stuck out her hand like a man. "Welcome to the family, sister."

Olivia shook her hand. "Thank you, sister. And you look stunning, by the way."

"Thought if I dressed like you nobody would know it was me."

Olivia laughed. "You were right."

They hugged again. Teresa kissed her brother on his cheek, then stepped away to allow the folks in line behind her their opportunity to greet the happy couple.

By Olivia's estimate, she and Neil received hugs from every person in the valley. She hugged the Preacher, the Blake brothers, and Marshal Wildhorse; then the members of the Elder Board, who offered her her job back (she said yes, by the way); newspaper reporters, folks she'd never met, and giggling adolescent girls who went all cow-eyed when Neil shook their hands.

The last person in line was the president of the Kansas Pacific. He wanted to talk with Neil about coming down to Topeka for a meeting. Olivia excused herself so that they could speak privately, and she and her supporters and her parents went outside to grab a breath of fresh air.

The streets were still crowded, and the mayor was glad to see the wealth of folks going in and out of the stores and shops. She hoped they were spending lots of money, but her mind wasn't really on mayoral things. *Neil was free!*

Cara Lee asked, "How long do you think you're going to grin that way?"

Olivia looked at her friend. "Christmas, maybe."

They both laughed.

Eunice tapped her daughter on the shoulder. "Olivia, your father and I are going up to our room. It has been some day."

Olivia agreed.

James said, "And while we're up there, Eunice, how about we talk about the trip to California I'm taking you on."

Eunice stared. "California?"

"Yes. I thought maybe we'd take a second honeymoon. A little moonlight . . . candlelight."

Olivia heard a thump. She looked around and saw her mother out cold on the walk. She gave her shocked father a shake of the head, then knelt and hollered, "Sophie!!"

Eunice was revived and taken inside by her husband. Olivia watched their departure with a knowing smile.

Cara joked, "Now I see where you get all that fainting from."

Olivia laughed and elbowed her in the ribs. "Hush."

Rachel and Daisy were heading home. They passed out kisses and hugs and promised to see everyone at tomorrow's party.

Cara said, "I need to find my husband—"

"Excuse me, ladies. Either of you know Armstead Malloy?"

Both women turned and met the brown eyes of a rather large, fashionably dressed, brown-skinned woman. Beside her stood three young children.

"Yes," Olivia answered. "He owns that big mercantile across the street."

The woman eyed the place, and her jaw seemed to tighten. Olivia and Cara shared a look.

Cara said, "My name is Cara Jefferson. I'm the sheriff's wife, and this is Olivia July."

"Pleased to meet you, ladies. I'm Elvira Malloy, Armstead's wife."

Olivia and Cara Lee picked their jaws up off the walk, and Olivia said with a joyous light in her eyes, "Welcome to Henry Adams, Mrs. Malloy. Are these your children?"

"Yes." She then introduced them as Robert, William, and Annie. They were aged five, seven, and eight.

Mrs. Malloy said, "Town always this crowded?"

"No," Olivia replied, unable to take her eyes off Elvira Malloy. "Special doings today. Would you like me to take you to your husband?"

"Yes, and Mrs. Jefferson, you may want to bring your husband."

Olivia did her best to hide her exultation. "Come this way, Mrs. Malloy."

As she led the Malloys down the walk to the Lady, Olivia looked back and saw Cara Lee gleefully rubbing her palms together.

The Lady was packed. With all the visitors in town, business was booming.

Elvira asked, "What is this place?"

"It's called the Liberian Lady."

Elvira stared at Olivia. "Why on earth would he be here?"

Olivia could hear the piano player pounding on the keys. "He owns it."

"What!" Elvira screamed so loud people stopped to look.

Olivia nodded.

Elvira scanned the building's fancy façade, the men going in and out, and she said, "He was supposed to be here founding a CHURCH!"

It took all Olivia had not to roll on the ground with laughter.

Steam pouring from her ears, Elvira said, "Miss Olivia, would you mind my children for a moment?"

"I'd love to."

So while Olivia gathered the children to keep them out of the line of fire, Elvira Malloy pushed open the Lady's newly hung double doors and stormed inside. Eight-year-old Annie, the spitting image of her mother, looked up at Olivia and said to her as only a child can, "I think Papa's going to get a whipping."

Holding back her laughter, Olivia said, "I think so, too."

That evening, Neil and Olivia were on the back porch, and she had Neil in tears telling him about what happened next. "She came barreling out of the Lady and had Malloy by the ear. If she had been a cussing woman, the air would have been blue. Instead she dragged him off quoting Scripture about evildoers and harlots and being on the brink of the pit."

Neil was having trouble breathing. "What did the children do?"

"They were running behind her trying to keep up.

Oh, Neil, it was the funniest thing I've ever seen. Everyone on the street stopped and stared."

"He was sent here to found a church?"

"That's what she said. Can you imagine? He's supposed to be a deacon, for heaven's sake."

"She didn't know he was here?"

"Apparently she didn't know where he was until she saw the drawing of him that was in the *Cyclone* reproduced in a paper in St. Louis. All the money he spent building the mercantile was the life savings of the congregation."

Neil chuckled and shook his head. "It's a strange world, Olivia. A strange world."

"I know, and I can't wait to tell her about the reward money he's been so proud about. He's supposed to get the bank draft tomorrow. Looks like he won't be putting a new addition on the Lady after all."

They shared more laughter and then quieted as the memories of the day passed silently between them. Neil looked her way. "I don't think Parker would have given me that suspended sentence if it hadn't been for you."

Her heart swelled. "I just told the truth, and I think he knew what was in your heart."

Neil wasn't so sure, but he was glad to have her in his life. "Thank you, Olivia."

She touched his cheek. "You're welcome."

The kiss they shared then was filled with all the love and hope of the future. As the kiss deepened and hands began to roam and breathing began to rise, Neil picked up his wife and carried her inside.

* * *

The next morning, Olivia left Neil sleeping and went to her office. No one was on the streets, and she savored the quiet and the blessings she'd received. She and Neil were about to embark on a life free of worry but filled with love.

The office was locked as it was every morning, and as she put the key in the lock, she felt a gun in her back.

"Scream and I shoot you right here." The voice belonged to Horatio Butler. Olivia didn't move. "Let's go."

"Where are you taking me?"

"Away, and your father is going to pay me to get you back."

"You're kidnapping me?"

"Yes."

"Well, I'm not going."

He increased the pressure of the gun. "Yes, you are. The people I owe money to won't wait any longer, and neither will I. Now, move!"

But before she could do so, she heard another voice that filled her with joy.

"What the hell are you doing! Drop it, you bug!"

Teresa July.

Her voice hardened. "Drop it or I'll send you to the devil right now."

Olivia felt the pressure of the gun removed from her back. She heard the gun clatter onto the walk. Only then did she turn around.

Sure enough, there was Teresa in her dress, holding one gun in Butler's back and the other against his balding head. To her further surprise, standing beside her was Two Shafts. He nodded at Olivia and gave her a smile.

Teresa wasn't smiling; she looked angry enough to spit. "Have you lost your mind?" she asked Butler. "This is my sister! My brother's *wife!*"

Butler was visibly shaking.

"You okay, Olivia?"

"I'm fine, sis."

Teresa nodded, then lifted her skirt, showing off the leather trousers beneath so she could stick one of the guns back into her gun belt. "Get a rope, Shafts, and tie him up."

Shafts walked over to his horse and brought back a rope. Butler tried to fight, but Shafts was too big and too strong.

"Let me go!" he demanded.

Shafts chuckled. "In a while, but right now we want to play with you."

Olivia had been around the Julys long enough to know that whenever the word "play" was mentioned, some outrageous act was sure to follow.

Shafts knelt to tie Butler's feet and ankles, and the armed Teresa warned Butler, "Kick my brother and you'll walk around on stumps."

The fuming Butler didn't move while Shafts tied his ankles, but when Shafts picked him up by the back of the suit and brought him up to eye level, he shrieked.

The big Comanche said to the horrified Butler, "We are going to have so much fun."

He then carried the yelling and squirming Butler

over to one of the buckboards parked on the street, asking, "Olivia, do you know who this belongs to?"

"Handy Reed."

Shafts tossed Butler into the bed none too gently, then climbed up to the seat. Teresa hurried to join him.

Shafts said, "Tell him we'll bring it back later."

Olivia realized that as the mayor she wasn't supposed to be condoning the carting away of town visitors for humorous purposes by Neil's siblings, but she figured they wouldn't hurt him—Butler deserved it—and the Julys would bring him back when they were done.

Shafts and Teresa drove off with a wave. Olivia waved back and went into her office.

The party thrown by Sophie for Olivia and Neil was attended by everyone who could fit inside the big ballroom. Olivia had on one of her best gowns, and Neil wore the new suit he'd purchased at the small mercantile owned by Henry and Harriet Vinton.

Olivia and Neil were seated at the head table, taking a break from the dancing, when her parents waltzed by. Olivia said to her husband, "I think they're going to be all right now. Did I tell you he's taking her to California for a second honeymoon?"

"No. That's a surprise."

"So surprising, Mama fainted again."

Neil chuckled.

Chase walked up. "We finally found Butler."

Olivia tried not to smile. "Where was he?"

"He was tied to the Grandfather."

Neil looked confused, so Olivia explained, "Grandfather is a big old oak tree. Only tree around here for miles."

Neil said, "Tying him to an oak doesn't sound real playful."

Chase said, "I'm not done. Picture this: He's seated on the ground. The rope binding his wrists is connected to a long rope that is tied to one of Grandfather's low branches. Just beyond the reach of his tied hands is a knife and a full canteen of water. Now if Butler can reach the knife he can cut himself free, but—"

"But—" Olivia echoed.

He started to grin. "On the branch that the lead rope is tied to is the biggest hornet's nest in the state of Kansas. If Butler moves, he rattles the nest."

Olivia began to chuckle. She felt sorry for him. Almost. "Was he stung badly?"

"No. I guess after the first few stings he was too terrified to move. He was in tears when we found him."

Neil laughed. "Bet he wishes he'd never left Chicago."

"Well, he's going back. Seems your wife's former fiancé has been embezzling funds from her father."

Olivia was shocked. "That must have been what Papa was checking into when he went to the telegraph office yesterday."

Neil looked confused again.

She patted his hand. "I'll explain later."

Neil grinned. "So can we charge him with attempted kidnapping?"

"Only after the courts in Chicago are done with

him. Olivia's father said he wants Butler prosecuted to the teeth, so it may be a while before the Illinois penal system turns him loose so we can get a chance at him."

Olivia said, "Job well done, Sheriff."

"Thanks, Olivia. Oh, Dix and the others headed out after we found Butler. Since Jack's on his way to Chicago for business, he'll make sure Butler reaches the authorities. The others said they'd all swing back this way sometime soon and bring their wives."

Olivia thought that would be a wonderful idea.

Chase then looked out over the folks filling the ballroom. "Now I need to find my wife. She's going to have my hide if she doesn't get to dance at least once tonight. You two have a good evening."

After his departure, Neil said, "Well, guess that's everything, Madam Mayor."

"Sounds like it."

The orchestra started up another waltz and Neil asked, "Shall we dance?"

"I'd love to."

As he led her out onto the floor and took her into his arms, Olivia savored his strength and his love. In the last year, she'd run away from home, been robbed by an outlaw, become a mayor, and married said outlaw. As Neil remarked yesterday, it was a strange world, and Olivia couldn't wait to see what else it had in store. In the meantime, she looked up at the man whose life was now entwined with her own and said, "I love you, Neil July."

He held her eyes. "I love you, too, *querida*. . . ."

Author's Note

〜◦◦〜

The all-Black town of Henry Adams Kansas, is a
fictional one, but the towns upon which it is
based are not. Nicodemus, Kansas, was established
during the Great Exodus of 1879 and at one time
was the most famous Black settlement in the country. Although its population has waned in the years
since its founding, Nicodemus continues to be a
source of pride. It is also a national historic site.

I created Henry Adams for my first Avon novel,
Night Song—Chase and Cara Lee's story. In the ten
years since its publication, I've received many letters
asking about their fates. I hope their small role in
Neil's story satisfied that curiosity and made all the
Night Song lovers smile.

We first met Neil July, Two Shafts, the Preacher,
and Griffin Blake in the *Taming of Jessi Rose*. Griff's

brother Jackson played a small role in Marshal Dixon Wildhorse's story, *Topaz*, and he had his own story told in *Always and Forever*.

Writing Neil's and Olivia's story gave me the opportunity to not only give this outlaw his own book but also to revisit the fascinating history of the Black Seminoles first explored in *Topaz*. Presently, the Black Seminoles of the twenty-first century are still fighting to reclaim their heritage, but like their ancestors, they are determined to prevail. One of the most interesting and complete books I've come across on the history of Neil's people is *Africans and Seminoles* by Daniel F. Littlefield Jr, published by Banner Books, University Press of Mississippi.

Other sources that aided me in writing the history were:

William Loren Katz. *Black Indians: A Hidden Heritage* (New York: Atheneum /Macmillan Co., 1986).

William Loren Katz. *The Black West* (Garden City, N.Y.: Anchor Books, 1973).

Edwin C. McReynolds. *Seminoles* (Norman Okla. University of Oklahoma Press, 1957).

Scott Thybony. "The Black Seminole: A Tradition of Courage," *Smithsonian* 22, no. 5 (August 1991).

August Meier. *Negro Thought in America: 1880–1915* (Ann Arbor, Mich.: University of Michigan Press, 1995).

K. Porter. "The Seminole Negro-Indian Scouts, 1870–1881," *Southwestern Historical Quarterly* LV, no. 3 (1952): 359–76.

For more info on the founding of the all-Black settlements and the conditions that fueled the Great Exodus of 1879, these sources are key:

Nell Irvin Painter. *Exodusters: Black Migration to Kansas After Reconstruction* (Lawrence, Kans.: University of Kansas Press, 1986).

Eric Foner. *Reconstruction: America's Unfinished Revolution 1863–1877* (New York: Harper and Row, 1988).

Acknowledgments

When my husband, Mark, died of cancer in November 2003, his passing shattered my world. I'd like to take a few moments to thank some of the people who helped me out of the darkness and back into the light: My family, friends, and the good people at Trinity Episcopal. The Diva whose care and concern never faltered. Debra, Donna, and Mrs. Anne Denny. Alicia. Cynthia Smith and the ladies in Peoria. Sarita Brewer and the East Coast crew—the daisies were gorgeous. My L.A. crew: Shareta, Angie, Linda, and Cheryl. The Escapade Book Club in Oaktown—thanks, Christine and Fedelies. Michele from Philly and the great ladies aka the Hotties on COL. My fans in Dallas, Atlanta, Austin, and Shreveport. Carrie Miller. Shirley Bolden and the members of the African American Book Club in Ypsilanti, Michigan.

Fran in Plano. Nancy Copeland. Ava Williams and Gloria Larkins—my angels. Lareeta Robinson and the wonderful and caring ladies of Little Rock. Bette Ford, Francis Ray, Felicia Mason, Evelyn Palfrey, Bridget Anderson, and Carla Fredd took time out of their writing to send me love. Rochelle Hardy aka The First Fan, her mom, Darcy, and her sister Stacy. All the attendees of PJ 03—the prayer ring on Sunday morning strengthened me for the battle. The ladies in Beverlyland, my Yahoo Web site. Every day, no matter how bad the day had been or how heavy my burden, I knew I could log on and be soothed. They laughed with me, cried with me, and prayed with me. My agent, Nancy Yost, for her special prayers and for having my back.

Last but not least, a big thank you to my editor, Erika Tsang, and the folks at Avon for their understanding, patience, and support. Even though this book was turned in five months late, they knew what was most important.

In closing, I'm sure I left some people out, but to all of you listed above and any who were not, you are a blessing in my life. Yes, I miss Mark dearly, but as my mom's friend Edna told me, "Wipe your tears so that you can see where God is leading you next." Wise advice.